I0562944

TO SERVE
AND
DECEIVE

JOHNNY GUNN

ALL RIGHTS RESERVED

No part of this book may be reproduced or transmitted in
any form or by any means, electronic or mechanical,
including photocopying, recording, or by any information
storage and retrieval system, without permission in writing
from the author, except in the case of brief quotations
embodied in reviews.

Publisher's Note:

This is a work of fiction. All names, characters, places, and
events are the work of the author's imagination.

Any resemblance to real persons, places, or events is
coincidental.

Solstice Publishing - www.solsticepublishing.com

Copyright 2016 Johnny Gunn

To Serve and Deceive
A Novel
By Johnny Gunn

Dedication

This book is dedicated to my lovely wife Patty who, bless her soul, reads every single word I write.

Chapter One

"I saw the whole thing, Jason, start to finish." Francesca owned her little coffee house for almost 20 years, and called most of her customers by name. "Sami came in, ordered a cup of French Onion soup, you know how she loved my French Onion soup, well, I was just getting ready to take it to her when these two guys came in." Her big brown Italian eyes rolled up, displayed a genuine dislike for these two, and I could see hatred around her mouth. I have often wondered if it's a European trait to show emotion through facial features as well as body language, and Francesca was telling the world how she felt. Francesca Ripoldi had never been this open with me, but since Sami's murder, she had transferred her love for Sami to me. Not the same devotion she held for Sami, but close.

"I never saw either one before, Jason. I'd 'a remembered them. Hair slicked back, hadn't shaved for several days, dirty shirts and trousers. These aren't the kind of people who normally come into my shop, you know what I mean?

"Well, anyway, I said, 'be right with you, gents,' and they walked right to Sami's table, pulled out these big guns, and just started shooting. They must have shot that poor girl four or five times each, point blank. God, Jason, it was terrible. She never saw it coming. Never had time to be frightened, or even to show that she recognized the freaks.

"They didn't look at another person in the place, just walked up and shot poor Sami all to hell." The full emotions of the event returned and Francesca was trying her best to hold back her tears, but at the same time, wanted me to know exactly what had happened. I slipped my arm around her ample waist and held her close. Her sobs were coming right along with all the details.

"Sami's blood splattered all over the walls, the floor, on some of the customers. It was horrible, Jason, just horrible, and then they walked out the door, just cool as hell. They came in to do one thing, and they did it. Poor Sami, poor Sami." Tears rolled down her apple red cheeks, and she wiped them away with the hem of her apron. "The only gangsters I've ever seen were the ones in the movies, Jason. These men had hate written so deep in their eyes. They were evil, Jason, just evil."

Francesca was born in Switzerland, just over the border from Italy, and had come to this country as a teenager just before WWII. "I remember seeing the evil in the eyes of the German Gestapo agents, Jason, and there was this kind of hate in the killer's eyes as well." She took my hand and squeezed so gently, and slipped into a booth.

"Sami always said the first thing she fell in love with was your gentleness, and the second was your compassion for others. Don't let your hate for these men over ride those qualities. You're a fine man, Jason, and your hurt is deep, but don't let it become hate."

We sat for hours, sipping coffee, crying, and remembering so many wonderful things about Sami. I knew she was gone, mutilated by gangsters, and I'll never know why. More than once during this time with Francesca, my large body was wracked by sobs as well, and more than once I knew my eyes were red and overflowed with despair. I also knew I had to leave, get the hell away from what I thought was going to be the best days of my life. I knew I had to run, go. I couldn't wait because if I did, there would be other deaths, and I'd be responsible for them.

The swell had the feel of an early fall storm as I eased the *D-Anne* out of Noyo Harbor and into the blue water of the Pacific Ocean. Long undulating waves, one following the other for as far as the eye could see, made high and fast by the quick moving frontal system that highballed out of the Gulf of Alaska, tried to break across the bow, but my trusty steed rode them out with the sureness bred into blue water trawlers.

My emotions had been as storm tossed as the foamy white combers that smashed into the high, rocky cliffs of the Mendocino Coast, but I had to keep reminding myself; I'm not running away. I was not. It's just simply a case of I didn't want to be there if she wasn't there. Sami was tall, dark as a walnut husk, with a flashing smile, and almost iridescent green eyes.

Sami had been a journalist for ten years before returning to university and finishing her doctorate in Greek Literature and how it influenced following civilizations. She was a woman who couldn't finish the second kiss without experiencing an orgasm.

The waves were high, filled with white caps, quartering from the northwest as I left the safety of the harbor, turned to meet them bow-on, roller after roller. *D'Anne* was big and strong, 51 feet long, steel hulled, broad in the beam and deep in her keel. She was a working trawler when I got her. Had it really been twelve years? Stripped of her fishing gear, and outfitted as a home, *D'Anne* and I had been around the world. I put the finishing touches to her new look below decks, converting her to accommodate two people, not one, but again, it was just one on board. Just one for this journey. One person, thousands of memories.

As I left the safety of snug harbor, I remembered a saying, "A blue water sailor's dream is to be at sea," but this time, I wanted to stay in port, stay in Noyo. The Noyo River's headwaters were in the Cascade Range of northern California, north of a little town known for its logging history. The river made its way to the coast. The community of Noyo Harbor, unlike many of the little coves and harbors along this stretch of coastline, often called dog coves, included a fine harbor for craft of many sizes, and was home to many people.

The dog cove at Point Arena, where the Garcia River comes to the sea was another of the little coves that included a surrounding community. Most of the dog coves were as wild today as they were hundreds of years ago. I rather doubt anyone had ever counted the number of little coves between Cape Mendocino and Point Reyes, but only a few are safe for blue water boats.

I arrived at Noyo Harbor three years ago, looking forward to a summer on the California north coast. Noyo was just south of Ft. Bragg, and north of fabled Mendocino City. The way I planned it was a full summer of exploring this exciting area, from the sea, and from the land. When I used the word explore I meant to use the word fish. I would rather fish than do most anything else in life.

On my first visit to Ft. Bragg, and a stop at a little coffee bar, I was accosted by a voluptuous Italian goddess. "One doesn't put ice water in one's Latte," she indignantly informed me.

"I do," I said, "and will if I want to." But, I was smiling, despite the strong tone of my response. I always figured it was my life, and if someone didn't like it, fuck 'em.

"Hi Mr. 'I'll do as I please.' I'm Samantha Bertorelli. My friends call me Sami." The smile was devastating. This was a woman who knew exactly what and who she was, and I wanted to get to know her. I had always been fascinated by strong, beautiful women, sometimes to the point of embarrassing myself. My eyes roamed about this goddess, and she continued to respond with her delightful smile. And she returned the long looks.

"Hi Sami, I'm Jason Caldwell."

"The TV producer?"

"The retired TV producer."

I was not what one would consider the tall, dark, and handsome Hollywood type, rather the tall, slightly overweight, going bald, late fifties, but always looking type. Sami didn't seem to care about that at all, only that we got to know each other, that our intelligence levels were close, and that we could have fun. Fun whether or not we had our clothes on.

Sami moved on board *D'Anne* two weeks later, and three months after that, we were married. Sami was a tenured professor at the College of the Redwoods, and it took some long hard arguments to get her to ask for a leave. One of those arguments was making me promise to redo our home below decks.

We were scheduled to leave on or about the first week of November for a long, slow cruise down the west coast of North America, make our way through the Panama Canal, and tour the Caribbean. If we were back in a year or so, fine. If not, fine.

Other than being highly opinionated, S. Bertorelli, known as S. Bertorelli-Caldwell, didn't have a mean bone in her luscious body. So why did two small time San Francisco hoods walk into Francesca's Cafe and blow her away during an incredibly busy lunch hour?

The Ft. Bragg cops cornered the two within half an hour, and in the ensuing shoot-out, two punks, one cop, and one tourist died, and one town kid was shot through the leg. And dead thugs don't talk. The cops called it a robbery gone wrong, which was exactly the opposite of what every eye witness said.

The Ft. Bragg cops considered the case closed, and that's it, so me and *D'Anne* had pulled anchor, but I was not running away. I had to keep telling myself this or I'd go right back to Ft. Bragg and start a war with those idiot cops. Francesca was right, I knew it. Those two came to the coffee shop for just one reason, to kill my wife. And the hate was building. I could feel it surge through my system every time I thought about Sami, every time I looked at our pictures, every time I took a breath. Francesca was right, I know that, but I couldn't control this hate. I was holding a picture, a self portrait is what Sami called it, which showed us standing on the after deck of *D'Anne*, both of us holding our salt water rods, and me, I was the heavy, bald, smiling like an idiot one, and she, the beautiful one was in a bikini top and little wrap around sarong skirt, smiled up at me. I was holding a cod I'd just caught. It was time for that picture to be hung in the wheelhouse of Sami's home.

Over the years, I had written many crime movies and TV series, and I had never written a script that read like this real life piece of shit. If someone had brought me a script like this, I would have thrown 'em out of the office. The most successful series of shows I ever did was called "Code 3," and it was realistic to the core. This episode would not have made the show.

I did a motion picture that was nominated for an Academy Award about two desperadoes who killed just for the thrill of killing. They traveled coast-to-coast, robbing banks, killing cops and bystanders, kidnapping, raping, and then killing, but it was nothing like what happened to my Sami.

For the first time in my life, I was really in love. I had been in love with the thought of being in love, but this was honest. I didn't have the best reputation around the ladies in Hollywood, I mean, I loved a good romp in the hay, and I guess I hadn't always been discreet, but it was so different with Sami.

Maybe I was running away. If I stayed, I'd get into a hell of a problem with that one detective. Owen Riley, chief of detectives. That was what his card said, and he couldn't investigate his way out of a parking ticket. He looked me right in the face and said it was obvious to anyone except maybe an egotistical Hollywood type that what happened at Francesca's was a robbery gone bad.

"Mr. Caldwell," he snarled, "you made a few movies about crime, but that doesn't make you an investigator, or even someone who can carry on a conversation with a real investigator. All the information we have, and there's lots of it, indicates those two punks were looking to rob the people in the coffee shop.

"They panicked, Caldwell, and your wife paid for it. I'm sorry, but those are the facts of the case, and even a Hollywood producer can't change them. Go back to writing so-called crime movies, Caldwell, and leave the real investigations to those of us who are professionals."

I'm sure Riley will never understand just how close he was to a broken jaw at that instant. I was already in a devastated state of mind, and now, I was being ridiculed by a two-bit punk cop. Two men walked into a coffee house, walked directly to Sami's table, pulled guns and blew her away, didn't bother another soul in the joint, and he called it a robbery gone bad. It had taken so many years for me to learn to control my quick temper, and I guess that was the only reason Owen Riley didn't have a broken jaw, which of course would have then put me in jail for smashing the stupid prick.

I went to talk to the chief of police, and he backed up what Riley said. I was sure there were some in Ft. Bragg who knew the whole story. Riley was right, in one respect though. I was just a retired old movie producer, and I knew I couldn't go up against whatever led to Sami's death.

Sami was so peace loving, so dedicated to her studies and teaching. Her treatise, repeated at every opportunity, was, simply said, if people could just read and learn from the classics of ancient literature and philosophy, there wouldn't be any crime, there wouldn't be any violence in the world. Simplistic, but she believed this commentary, and seemed to live her life that way.

The most peace loving person in the universe, gunned down by two strangers, and for no reason. Did they mistake her for someone else? But how could they? Sami was a beautiful woman, the most beautiful I've ever known, and I couldn't imagine someone mistaking her for someone else. She was statuesque in every sense of the word, tall and thin, long legs with a delightful little bottom end, high pointed breasts, and shoulders that proved the fact that swimming is still the best exercise one can do alone. Her long tapered neck was a perfect platform for a head that featured a face like Athena, cascading locks that never quite seemed to be under control acted as a frame.

There was a lot more to this than I would ever know, and what was so disturbing, there was a lot more than the police in Ft. Bragg would ever know, unless of course, they were behind the whole thing. Manipulating this crime from what appeared to be a professional hit to a robbery gone bad, was a conspiracy I wouldn't be able to write about. Even more stupid, as I thought about it, why would the cops in Ft. Bragg want to kill a college professor? Unbelievable.

Yes, maybe I was running away after all. I was going to finish that cruise Sami and I planned. I was going to take my beautiful boat and cruise along the coast of California, maybe stop at Catalina, maybe not, cruise down the coast of Mexico, maybe stop and maybe not, cruise along the coast of Central America, and I know I wouldn't stop. Drug and gun runners felt they owned the ocean along that coast, and many was the sailor who had lost his boat to pirates.

I would have to fuel up when I reached Panama, and then navigate my way through the canal and into the Caribbean. *D'Anne* had a wonderful marine diesel engine that pushed me along at a whopping eleven knots on a good day, but was very efficient when it came to fuel consumption, and I would have fuel in the tanks when I topped them off.

I remembered the first time I took her out on a long cruise. I spent lots of time learning my way around my new home, put all the electronic gadgets on board to make life easier, gadgets I called them, but so important; Radar units, global positioning navigation, auto pilot. They weren't toys, by any stretch, and they did make life so much easier, but one must also remember to keep current on the old ways of navigation, just in case. It was a Coast Guard officer during a navigation class who said, "Don't throw the sextant away, people. Without those satellites, or power, it's your insurance." I spent days on end traveling up and down the coast, tested both *D'Anne* and myself in overnight excursions, and finally, filled the fuel tanks, the fresh water tanks, the freezer and the refrigerator, and I set a course for Hawaii.

It would be a ten day cruise, and I had fuel for thirty, water for thirty, and food for two years. I left nothing to chance and of course, the third day out I sailed into a tuna feeding frenzy and caught a large yellow fin. That put the freezer over the top, and for the next five days, all I ate were tuna steaks. Life could be so cruel, eh?

***

My life on that adventure was that of a blue water sailor. Days on end I would be tucked into a deck chair, I would watch tropical skies filled with billowing white clouds, feel the rhythm of Pacific Ocean swells that started five thousand miles west of where I was, squalls would open up over my head, cleaning *D'Anne* stem to stern. I would catch the rain in a water tumbler that would be filled with two ice cubes and a finger or two of Scotch, and of course, I would be serenaded by the sounds of splashing blue water across the bow. I wanted to spend the rest of my days facing that terrible life.

If the days at sea were dramatic in their spectacle, the nights were nothing short of exhibitionist. No spectral light from anywhere, and quadrillions to the tenth power of stars peered into my life. I had seen our heavens from north of the equator and south, I had followed the North Star and Southern Cross, and survived storms from the Alaskan Gulf to the Indian Ocean, and my only dread was someday I would be beached, tethered somewhere away from blue water, unable to leave the security of some snug harbor.

So now, I was headed for the Caribbean. I would lose myself in those warm seas, fishing, drinking rum, learning again how to speak Spanish. Damn it, Sami and I even enrolled in Spanish classes so we would enjoy this trip even more. Spanish was the national language on many of the islands, along with French and Dutch. One week she would do all her speaking to me in Spanish, and the next week would be my turn. We were getting very fluent, and had too much fun as well.

It took that little Italian bombshell about two weeks to convert her knowledge of Italian and Latin to Spanish, and she could cuss with the best of them. I always told her she was cheating.

Yes, I was running away, but at the same time, I was bringing all my memories along with me.

It was what I had left, just memories, a few faded photographs, and a burning desire to smash whoever was responsible. I wanted to find that person and skin him, run him through with a long thin filet knife, crush his skull and break his bones. I had never felt this kind of hate before, and I was afraid of it.

Chapter Two

"This is the most incredible piece of criminal arrogance I've seen in all my years with the bureau. Those cops in Ft. Bragg don't intend to do anything at all, do they? Are they so sure of themselves they think every investigative agency in the world is blind?" Katie Dollarhide was wearing out the carpet in her bosses' office, high atop FBI headquarters in Virginia, just outside Washington, DC, repeating her tirade over and over. "John, those goons walked into that coffee shop and blew away one of the finest agents we've ever had, and the local cops are treating it as a robbery gone bad. Holy shit, John, they can't be that dumb.

"No, I didn't mean to say that. They can't be so naive as to believe we're going to simply sit around and let them continue with their drug dealing, their distribution, their money laundering. That cop shop is the dirtiest in the country, John, and they think we don't know it."

Katie Dollarhide was more than just Special Agent, she was international lead, front person, for the FBI's division of the war on drugs, and she had lost her number one investigator. Tall, thin, blonde, and mean as cat shit is the way she was usually described, and the description fit. "I'll tell you John, if I could, I'd mobilize the damned National Guard and march into that little cop shop with tanks, artillery and helicopter gun ships. There wouldn't be a Ft. Bragg police station when I got through. Those detectives, there's a word that should never be used when discussing Ft. Bragg police, those dirty bastards are throwing shit in our faces, John, and we're supposed to just sit still and take it. They are responsible for Sami's death, and damn it, I'll prove it." All the time she was talking, she was circling, stomping her feet every few steps, slamming a fist into a desk, or into her open hand. A more formidable foe would be hard to imagine.

She had just about worn herself out, and collapsed into a big over stuffed chair in the offices of John Chandler, number two at the FBI, and the man who not only had the ear of the Attorney General, but had been a personal friend of the current president before he was elected. Fly fishing was the passion that bound he and the president, and Chandler took advantage of the situation as often as possible. He had an investigator's mind, and Dollarhide knew she could unload like this.

She looked long and hard at Chandler, arranged herself in a more lady like pose in the chair, never cracked a smile, never gave away the fact she knew she had possibly gone a little too far in her dissertation. "I can't put anything in writing about this John, but I believe those cops are as dirty as any in the country. Tons of drugs come ashore in their jurisdiction, and they haven't made a serious drug bust in years.

"Sami had her finger on the operation, but didn't have enough proof for us to do anything. She knew there were Pelligrini people, probably Lopez people, and surely cops with family connections. She knew this, John. That's why she's dead."

"Katie, do the local police know that Bertorelli was one of ours?" Nothing had been released to the news media at the time of Sami's death of her affiliation with the bureau, and Chandler asked an obvious question.

"Sami was so deep in cover, John, even her new husband doesn't know she was an agent. I mean, right to this minute, he doesn't know, so it is very doubtful that any of the local police would know. At least the cops who aren't members of the crime families she was investigating. She was working on the continuing merging of Italian, Greek, and Colombian drug cartels and families. Pelligrini and that bunch. The average beat cop probably didn't have a clue, but those higher up the command structure almost had to know, and those who control them. Somehow, they found out. There's my job, John. Find out how they knew. The average man on the street, or politician in this town only knows Alberto Pelligrini as a patron of the arts, as a philanthropist; they aren't aware of how evil this man is. He has people killed for almost no reason, John.

"And now, Pelligrini is mobbing up with the cocaine cartels in South America, with the distribution networks from the near east, and it wouldn't surprise me if he didn't already have ties to the Asian markets. The Pelligrini family is the largest drug organization in the world, John, and Sami was working to put the whole picture together for us. Because of her work, we have photographs of the top dogs with the names they're currently using, dossiers of what they've done in the past, and for whom they did it, and what their connections are on a world scale. Sami's death is devastating, not just personally, but for our investigation.

"We had met just a few weeks ago, and she was worried about her cover, worried what would happen when her husband found out about her real calling in life, and worried about the continuing spread of the Pelligrini hold on drugs and his family's merging with Colombia.

"If Pelligrini found out about Sami's investigations, and sniffed out her cover at that college, her new husband is in serious trouble as well. And, he doesn't know it." Katie's mind was going back over the last few months, trying to find out how Pelligrini found out about Sami.

She was so good, Katie remembered. "We met several times, and she was always able to feed me information about drops up and down the coast, about air transportation into the inland drug distributors, and knew the names of so many dealers. John, losing Sami is going to be a huge blow to our operations."

Exhausted, but still boiling with anger, Katie finally left the office and headed back to her hotel room at the Watergate. Staying at the Watergate was a splurge, she knew, but every once in a while, a girl needs to splurge a little. "I spend my whole life living out of suitcases, staying in horrible places, meeting with agents who often look more like criminals than investigators, surviving insect attacks in the jungle, damn it, if I want to spend just a little time and money on myself, I will." Her argument was with herself, of course, an argument she had whenever she bought an extra bottle of fine wine, a pound of special chocolate, or a little bottle of imported perfume. She bought all three on the way back to the hotel. Despite the niceties of her hotel room, her mind continued to work on what had to be done. "How the hell do I replace Sami? My God. How do I keep her new husband alive? How do I bring down this drug culture?

"One thing," she was thinking, "Sami always kept me up to date on what she was doing. I know most of the operation is centered in the Caribbean, but that's still an awfully large puddle of water. Hard drugs, opium and heroin come from sources connected to Afghanistan and Pakistan, from crime families in Italy and Greece, and end up at distribution points on various islands in the Caribbean. Pot and cocaine come from Colombia and other South American outlets to these same distribution points. There is a merging of all the operations at that point.

"That's what Sami was working on, locating those points. Getting married wasn't the smartest thing she ever did, and then doing it in such a manner that we never had a chance to tell the groom about her. Shit. The only thing I know about this dude is Sami said he was the best she had ever had in bed, that he was older than she thought the man of her dreams would be, and that he was a retired Hollywood producer.

"That's what we need, an egomaniac of a Hollywood type to really blow this investigation clear to the moon." Anger boiled to the surface, but it was a controlled anger, the kind that allowed for good old-fashioned common sense thinking, and Katie had to get some answers soon. She walked over to the phone and called a friend of hers in the identification section at the bureau.

"George, can you put together a dossier on a guy named Jason Caldwell? He's retired as a producer of films and TV shows in Hollywood. George, this is the guy who married Sami Bertorelli before she was assassinated. I need to know just about everything you can dig up." Then, Katie put in a call to another friend of hers, a Coast Guard Commander who works in the drug interdiction program.

"I don't give a damn if his boat is 10,000 miles off shore, I want to talk to Commander Petersen now." She didn't lose her temper too often, but Katie Dollarhide also didn't take any shit off anyone. "Stupid bastards, who cares if it's a boat or a ship, or where he is." She was temper driven right now. "Damn it, sailor boy, this is FBI Special Agent Dollarhide, and if you don't put me through to him, you'll wish you'd never heard my name." That brought a smile to her face, and her mind eased up a bit. "I hate to do things like that," she chuckled to herself, all the time she relished the picture of the guy on the other end of the phone shaking like a leaf.

Katie Dollarhide had been with the FBI since graduating from law school in Sacramento, California, and had worked her way up through the ranks the hard way. "It's been almost twenty years now, and I still have that rush every time I feel a case coming together. Twenty years. Amazing." She'd fallen in love a couple of times during her career, but never married, never had children. "I'm married. Damn it, I give my life to the Bureau, nurture it just as I would a child. If I ever do meet that one special guy, he'll have to measure a step above what I'm already committed to."

She liked to tell the story of meeting with one agency director who hated the concept of women as agents, and telling him to get his own coffee. "During a meeting where we were discussing criminal activity in unions, I think probably talking about Hoffa or some of his lieutenants, this pecker head says, 'Missy, would you get us some coffee?' Missy, he called me. I sat still for about three seconds, looked him right in the eye, and told him to get his own fucking coffee. He tried to have me dismissed from the agency, but obviously, I prevailed." Tough as nails on the one hand, as well put together as any movie star on the other, and willfully dedicated to the agency, she was beginning to feel better. She was coming down from her anger, remembering what a good life she's had.

"I always wanted to be an investigator, and I always wanted to work for the best, so it had to be the FBI. I've been recruited by DEA and other Justice Department divisions so many times, but I'm FBI to the bone. Maybe that's why Sami and I got along as well as we did. We were the best, and now, it's just me. God, I hope I'm tough enough to finish this off."

Her memories were cut off instantly by the voice on the phone.

"Eric. I've got a hell of a problem." Katie spent a lot of government money on the rest of that telephone call to Commander Eric Petersen, aboard his cutter as it cruised in waters off the coast of Guatemala. "His name is Jason Caldwell, Eric, and he has a fishing trawler he lives on. He and Sami were going to head for the Caribbean, ostensibly for a combination honeymoon and vacation.

"No, he doesn't even know yet that Sami was an agent. She was going to do some snooping down there, but Pelligrini must have gotten word of it. Eric, I'm worried that we have a leak in the bureau. Caldwell is not any kind of a suspect yet, but I've got George doing a background work up for me.

"I need you to let me know what you can find out from your end about him, and about those two guns that blew Sami away. They came to Ft. Bragg from San Francisco, we know that. Probably Colombian money, or maybe even straight from Pelligrini."

Katie knew that in the last couple of weeks, distribution of drugs to the north coast of California had been increased considerably, and Petersen backed it up. "I'm betting that someone in that Ft. Bragg police department is working for either one of the cartels, or for Pelligrini. They come whipping into those little dog coves in extremely fast boats, and they're gone before I can do anything." Dollarhide could almost hear the commander shaking his head. "It's as if they know where I am, and they are so versatile they can make a drop hours away from me. You know, I say me, but I mean all of us involved. I have the *Roosevelt* and the *Simpson* in my command, and they know where we are every second of the day.

I agree with your thought. There's someone feeding this information to them, and that someone has knowledge that could only come from the agency.

"We'll never get it, but I'd sure like at least two more cutters out here. Or a half dozen old PT boats. Or those fast little boats they had in Vietnam. We might be able to catch some of them then." Commander Eric Petersen had written so many reports detailing how the gangsters were getting the drugs onto the coast, he was all but a walking billboard of coastal history.

"That coast is among the roughest areas in the country, pocked with hundreds of little coves, they're called dog coves, and large boats and ships simply can't maneuver in the tidal water. The currents can be fierce. During California's early history, loggers would sled giant redwood trees into the coves, raft them, and barge them to the big mills. In many of the cliffs and beaches around the dog coves, even today, you can see evidence of the logging operations. Great slides where trees were put in.

"Of course, none of that was criminal. It was during prohibition that criminal elements discovered just how useful a dog cove could be. Boatloads of Canadian and illegal booze came ashore all along the California and Oregon coastlines. How many thousands of gallons of whiskey? Probably less than the total tonnage of drugs now coming ashore in the same places." Katie could hear the irony of his words, could almost feel his helplessness.

He was never sure but suspected the drug dealers on the boats had some aerial surveillance as well. "They know where I am, and I have the most sophisticated radar available. I never see them, but they know where I am." He had asked several times to be able to use some of the submarine tracking satellites to find the drug boats but had been turned down repeatedly.

"The northern California coastline is a delivery haven." Many of Petersen's reports and pleas for help were filled with data provided by Sami Bertorelli and those who worked with her. "She had a handle on something, and it led to her assassination. I bet she was about to let you in on what she knew, someone high up in the organization, or high up in the agency, found out.

"Keep me informed Katie. These people have to be stopped. The whole damn coast is littered with criminal activity. Along with all the European and South American drugs flowing on shore in these dog coves, now there are illegal aliens adding to the problem. Asian freighters come up the coast, drop off boat loads of illegals, never slowing down, more or less stopping, adding to the burden of Coast Guard activities.

"They put those poor people in cargo containers, Katie, and slip close enough to a cove to simply drop the damn container in the water. Sometimes there's a boat to tow it to shore, sometimes, it just sinks. We don't have the foggiest idea how many illegal aliens have been put on shore, or how many have simply drowned and disappeared."

It was a long conversation, and Katie felt slightly better when it was over. "I don't know if we can ever stop any of this Eric, but damn it, these people are slowly destroying our way of life. This isn't what millions of Americans have died to protect." She was preaching, she knew, and Eric knew it also, but ... "damn it Eric, there are times one simply has to preach."

Their friendship had survived much more than a simple sermon on the phone, and they wished each other the best as they hung up.

***

Katie stretched her long limbs and felt the deliciously warm water surge around her, felt the oils and perfumes working their way into her taut muscles and joints, let the effects of a glass of Cabernet slow her mind down. She knew she wouldn't be able to indulge like this again for a long time, knew what a terrible task was spread out for her.

Samantha Bertorelli had been an agent for a few less years than Katie, had come to the bureau from a different angle. First as a journalist, then law school, then straight into the field. She actually picked up a law degree and her doctorate in Greek philosophy at the same time. The two were a match, and smart heads in the department recognized it, put the two together with Katie acting as the boss, but giving Sami unrestricted space in which to work.

At first, it was small potatoes, gun runners in the middle east, drug dealers along the coast, illegal aliens shipped from the far east, terrorists from everywhere. The FBI was continually searching for those who want our way of life to change, to be altered to fit some other agenda. National Security has no borders, and as the two became a strong team, the work branched into an operation with worldwide scope. With tears streaming down her face, Katie Dollarhide was sitting in a bath in the Watergate Hotel in Washington, DC, alone. No longer would she have backup of Sami's quality.

She spent a restless night, tossing and turning, waking often, trying to put together ideas that made sense, trying to ferret out clues from dark recesses of the mind, numbed by what had happened. "To hell with it. I can't sleep, I might as well do something useful." Her wardrobe in her traveling suite, as she called it, consisted of a couple of business suits, a couple of shirts and pairs of jeans, a couple of pairs of low slung pumps, color coordinated with the suits, a pair of sneakers, and a pair of hiking boots. Of course, underwear, "...when I feel like wearing it," jackets and scarves. Home for the past 20 years seemed to be wherever she and her traveling suite landed.

"Some day maybe, it might be fun to have a home, but I wouldn't know what to do around it. I'm certainly not the homebody type. Now there's a thought. I don't even know how to turn on a vacuum cleaner." Laughter rolled around the big hotel room as she dressed in a charcoal suit. The other was navy, and she would have had to look to tell you which one she picked that morning. She simply could not linger over bacon and eggs and coffee, hailed a cab, and headed for Chandler's office, arriving before the number two man.

She walked into his office by way of the coffee area, a steaming cup in hand, laced with sugar and powdered creamer, to find Sarah Costello at Chandler's desk, a file folder opened in front of her. "Bertorelli's husband was some looker. This came in for you this morning."

"I hope you don't make a habit of going through Mr. Chandler's desk, Costello. You've broken a pretty big rule here, and I don't want to find out this happens a lot." She was about to continue when John Chandler came in. Sarah Costello got the hell out.

"Is that what you were looking for about Sami's husband? Do you think he's involved in this?"

She shook her head no as she took the report, just a few pages long and with some pictures, and went over it carefully, still shaking her head. "He's just a normal, everyday guy. Damn good looking, but no criminal background at all John. I don't think he's even had a speeding ticket. He's going to be dead soon, and he won't know why. He won't know his brand new wife was murdered because she was one of the best undercover agents in the bureau, and the bastards that did her in have to believe he too is an agent.

"What if we try to turn him, John? What if we just lay our cards and chips out in a row and ask for his help? We might save his life if nothing else, and if he gets angry enough, he might be of some help to us."

It took Chandler three days to convince the current director and attorney general that Katie's plan was a good one. Katie headed to the California coast for a meeting with Eric Petersen at the Coast Guard station in Alameda, inside San Francisco Bay. Petersen didn't have any better information on Caldwell than she was able to get from headquarters.

Petersen was a big man, Nordic in every respect, with flowing red hair and beard, and a roll to his gait that told anyone interested that he'd spent most of his life at sea. There was a set to his broad shoulders and thick neck that also gave clues, information that said, 'don't mess with me.' "Deacon did most of the workup on this, Katie. He's an old CG hand now at bureau headquarters, and he can't find anything the least bit out of line with the guy. What's your plan?"

"Deacon knows his stuff, Eric. Let's just ride with this when we meet Jason Caldwell. I can't believe he's involved, but if he is, let's let him spring the trap. All of this of course hinges on whether Chandler can get permission for us to talk to the guy.

"How do we get together with the guy? Can we just show up at his berth in Noyo Harbor? God, Eric. FBI agents and Coast Guard officers at his boat will sound alarms around the world. What's your opinion?"

"The power of the Coast Guard is amazing, Katie. When we know he's going to sea, I'll simply contact him by radio and tell him we need to talk to him. That sort of thing happens regularly, and this guy is a blue water sailor, he knows the rules of the sea. He may be an ex-Hollywood type, Katie, but first, he's a blue water sailor."

"I'll be honest, Eric, everything I've ever read about Hollywood types makes me wary. If he's just some damn fool blow-hard, filled to the brim with self importance, I'll toss him off the fan tail of that boat of yours."

"It's a ship, Katie."

Chapter Three

"Motor Vessel *D'Anne. D'Anne.* This is Bodega Coast Guard, do you read? Over."

"This is *D'Anne.* I read you five-by. What can I do for you?"

"Captain Caldwell, this is Commander Eric Petersen. When you clear Noyo Harbor, please turn to a heading of two-four-oh degrees and remain on that heading until you rendezvous with my Cutter. Do you copy?"

"Roger Commander, I copy. Two-four-oh degrees. Is there a problem?"

"We'll talk when we meet. Petersen clear."

Brief and to the point, I thought. If I was paranoid, I'd wonder what I'd done to warrant this. Two hundred forty degrees would be West-South-West, Two hundred seventy would be due west, that is, straight out to sea. If he was that far out to sea, how the hell would he know I'm leaving Noyo Harbor? Or could this be a scam? More than one drug runner has become a pirate, stealing fine sea-worthy boats and killing all on board. It was time for me to go into protect mode.

Anytime you venture into international waters, you're fair game to the pirates, most of whom simply want a boat that isn't mixed up in any criminal activity. That you own the boat is of no significance, that you might want to continue living means nothing. Throughout waters from Canada south to Ecuador, and all around the Caribbean, there were horror stories about pirates stealing boats and killing everyone on board. The activity in Asian waters was just as bad, and throughout the South Pacific as well. Most of it was connected in some way to the flow of illegal drugs. I'm not sure a study has been done, but it wouldn't surprise me to find out there was more piracy on the high seas today than during the 1600s and 1700s.

I established my heading and activated the auto pilot, turned on the 360 degree radar, and set its sensitivity at three miles. Any blip within three miles of *D'Anne* would kick off an alarm that would raise me from a dead sleep below decks. The autopilot was tied directly to global positioning satellites, and *D'Anne* would steer a true course, would even make corrections for winds and water current. What a change from when all a sailor had was a sextant, some outdated charts, and personal knowledge. Hell, just about anyone could be a blue water sailor today. Until they got in trouble, that is.

After cruising in waters infested with drug runners, and scum like them, I have prepared myself. I broke out a pair of M-16s, each with ten clips of 30 rounds, and my kicker, a Garrand M-1 with a grenade launcher and five pineapples. What was crazy, I was illegal as hell owning these things, and yet, without them I was vulnerable to those who have no use for any law. When I was in international waters, I was no longer a potential criminal for owning some self protection. I was the captain of this boat, and this was my territory; damn those torpedoes, I was the captain, I made the rules.

OK, Commander Petersen, if you're not who you say you are, we would have us a war. Sami used to try to make me get rid of my armament, but after reading some horror stories out of the Caribbean, and South East Asian waters, even that anti-gun zealot decided we should have them on board. I always found her stories of being a journalist so interesting, and marveled at the fact she traveled to all these exotic places, but never gave a second thought to personal safety. I mean, Greece and Sicily, the Caribbean, South and Central America, and she never carried a weapon of any kind. Hated them.

D'Anne cruises at a comfortable eleven knots and it was about nine hours before a blip on the radar kicked off the alarm. Coffee went everywhere when I hit the wheel house at a dead run, shut off the alarm, checked the radar scope and saw my target dead ahead. And dead in the water. At three miles, as I looked through my binoculars, there was no doubt I was looking at a Coast Guard Cutter. Bright white with those distinct diagonal slashes; this was the U.S. Coast Guard, and fitted out in a frigate class ship. She was long, thin, and fast, and well armed as well. This class ship served well during WWII, and were known primarily as destroyer escorts, DEs.

I eased the *D'Anne* to within about 100 yards and went to all stop. A skiff from the cutter was already on its way over with three Coast Guardsmen on board, a Chief and two others, but no Commander. I went aft and dropped the boarding platform and opened the gate.

"Hello *D'Anne*. Chief Daniel Curtis, U.S. Coast Guard. Permission to board, Sir."

"Hello Chief, permission granted. Welcome aboard."

I took an offered line and made fast their skiff while the chief and one sailor stepped onto the platform and up onto the after deck.

"Commander Petersen requests you join him aboard the Cutter *Roosevelt*, Sir. He also requests I leave Seaman Alexander here aboard *D'Anne* while you talk. For safety purposes, Sir."

"Of course, Chief. Do I need to bring anything with me?"

"Not a thing, Sir."

"Alexander, there's coffee in the galley, and don't be worried about the armament in the wheel house.

I wanted to be sure you folks were really the Coast Guard."

Chief Curtis chuckled at that as we scrambled into his skiff. My mind was burning with questions. Questions I knew the chief either couldn't or wouldn't answer. Why would the Coast Guard want to talk to me? And why all the cloak and dagger stuff, 100 miles off the coast, extremely brief radio messages, apparently a specific location, and out of territorial water to boot? Would this have something to do with Sami's death? Too many questions and no obvious answers.

The closest I've been to anything dealing with crooks was when I was producing that TV series, "Code 3," and of course they weren't real. I always insisted that some really competent law enforcement guy be available to check the scripts for accuracy. That one ass-hole from DEA was a real pain, but even he was sourly pleased by our attempt at accuracy. By the time he got through with our actors, they thought they were DEA agents. They could have used him to train the cops in Fort Bragg. They'd have been the better for it.

***

The skiff came alongside the cutter, on the lee side to prevailing waves and wind, and we scrambled onto a boarding platform. The skiff actually rode on top of the waves, while the larger cutter burrowed deep into them. Getting from a skiff to a larger vessel was a matter of timing. At the height of the wave, if your timing was correct, you simply stepped onto the boarding platform. A little too early, or for that matter, too late, and you crashed. Injury and death was not out of the question. I waited for the third wave, just to make sure of my timing, before I stepped on board the cutter. I did remember protocol, even though as a civilian, I didn't have to.

"Permission to come aboard, Sir," I said to the Officer of the Deck as I stepped nimbly aboard. There was a genuine smile on the face of the young Lieutenant, and he promptly saluted and gave his approval.

"The Captain's looking forward to meeting with you. Follow me please." We went through passageways, up gangways and stairs, and onto the bridge of the cutter. "Commander Petersen," the Lt. said, "may I present Captain Caldwell. Mr. Caldwell, Captain Petersen."

There was another civilian on the bridge besides myself, but I didn't recognize her. The bridge was enormous compared to the wheelhouse of the *D'Anne,* with every electronic gizmo ever invented. Standing this far off shore, we were out of the ground swell, and gently rocking and swaying to the open sea. While the cutter moved up and down, rhythmically, just a couple of feet at a time, that little skiff was rising and falling four feet at a time, like a cork in a raging, trout infested river.

The Commander and I shook hands. "Please, unless you are planning to shoot me or something, let's drop the captain stuff. Just call me Jason."

"I'm a Commander in the Coast Guard, and Captain of this ship, but I don't have any problem with the Eric stuff at all," Petersen said. "I'd like you to meet FBI Special Agent Katie Dollarhide. Katie, this is Jason Caldwell. Let's retire to the Officer's Mess and talk."

Special Agent Katie Dollarhide shook my hand, and I gave her one long going over with my eyes. I've always been that kind of asshole. If they were gorgeous, I just can't help but look. And Katie Dollarhide was nothing if not gorgeous. Long flowing blond hair, bright green eyes, and a deep honey complexion. Was it tan or natural? I wanted to find out.

I remember when we were shooting "Code 3," there was some talk that I shouldn't always use the most beautiful actresses and actors, that I should use people who would be more along the lines of John or Ann Citizen. If Katie Dollarhide was what FBI agents looked like, my actresses weren't anywhere near attractive enough.

Her body was nicely proportioned with long legs starting from enchantingly developed hips. Yeah, I looked, but I have to say, though, she returned the favor as we descended two decks to officer country. Was it in the genes that allows a man to mourn his wife on the one hand and ogle a beautiful woman on the other?

The Mess was large and comfortable, and we went to one of the tables and made ourselves at home. Naugahyde, not leather, but nicely appointed, with hidden lighting, a set of coffee pots, all fresh and full along one bulkhead, condiments along another, and everything was very clean and shiny. Some swabbie could be proud, but probably wasn't. There were curtains covering the portholes, and the deck was covered in an indoor/outdoor type carpet. This floor could get wet and survive. A steward appeared out of nowhere and offered coffee all the way around. I of course said yes, as did Petersen. Dollarhide said no, but asked for a soda.

Petersen was the picture of a Norseman at sea. Deep red hair, he sported a full beard, slightly curled moustache, and less than military, his head was covered in a tangle of curls and waves. A thousand years or so ago, and Eric Petersen would probably have been known as Eric the Red, and would have commanded a fleet of Viking war and exploration boats.

I've never been known to enjoy nicknames, but Eric had to have been called either Red or Viking as he was growing up. There was little doubt that he was in charge and as soon as everything was served he told the steward we were not to be bothered under any conditions. That sounded ominous to me, and for the first time in a long while, I actually had feelings of anxiety. Petersen added to that anxiety immediately by outlining what our little meeting in the middle of the Pacific Ocean was all about, and I was right, it was about Sami.

It was interesting, watching as Petersen made himself comfortable, swishing a hand across his moustache, first one side, then the other, twirling the ends just slightly. He had set his own stage. The FBI agent seemed to be lost in her own thoughts.

That was a pretty head, I wonder what's inside it? I hope this trip out here, a hundred miles at sea, wasn't just some kind of fluff piece to keep me quiet. That was what happened in Fort Bragg.

Chapter Four

"So, this is the man who stole Sami's heart away. I've wondered what kind of person he would be, and if I'd drawn a picture, this wouldn't be the scene. He's sure of himself, and big, but certainly not in fine physical shape. Thirty years at sea, and I can spot a real sailor from yards away. Jason Caldwell is a real sailor. I hope he's man enough to take on what we're going to steer him into." Eric Petersen was trying to size up the man he was going to try to turn into an undercover agent in the drug interdiction program. He liked what he saw, so far. "Character, that's what I need to find out now. Can he be trusted, counted on if it becomes necessary?

"This is such an evil business. People die in many jobs, some jobs and professions are just inherently dangerous, but in this job, we send people to their death. Those who do the killing don't even know who it is they are killing, and what's more, don't care." He had watched as the skiff tied up to the *D'Anne*, watched as Jason Caldwell climbed aboard for the short ride to the *Roosevelt*, tried to learn something from what he was seeing.

"I envy this Caldwell. I could spend the rest of my days on that little trawler of his, cruising the oceans and seas of the world. I do that now, but doing it, I send people out to die. I want to do it his way."

Petersen's mind was flooded with memories of voyages to save those in shipwrecks or storms, but also, of agents dropped off somewhere, never to be heard from again. "There's irony in that. Most people think of the

Coast Guard as that branch of the service that saves lives, protects those at sea, and for so many years, I've been required to send people off to certain death.

"Will I see Jason Caldwell again after these meetings? In my own way, I hope he tells us to go to hell, gets back on his little boat, and sails into the sunset. But I already know better. I can see the eyes of a man who wants to do the right thing, even if it kills him."

Petersen was looking intently at Jason Caldwell, almost staring. "Look at his eyes, and the jut of the jaw line. He's out of shape, physically, but I wouldn't want to go up against him intellectually. The sea. That's the answer; the sea. When a man takes a small boat like the *D'Anne* to sea, alone, his true character is worn on his sleeve. Caldwell is very sure of himself, and would be a fierce adversary in any conflict.

"And I'm in awe of him. If he tells us to go to hell, I'll salute him for that."

***

"Jason, I asked you to join us here, first because of the high security, and secondly, because of the high security." There was just a hint of a smile, and I was very glad to see that at least a touch of levity could exist in our meeting. "The two men who killed your wife are well known to agent Dollarhide and the FBI, to the Coast Guard, and the DEA. They worked for Manuel Lopez who in turn worked for the Calle Cartel in Colombia."
I was stunned at this, and I couldn't understand how this fit in with Sami. "What the hell is the connection here?" I stammered, and it was Dollarhide who put the picture together.

"Mr. Caldwell, you knew your wife as a university teacher, a professor in literature, arts, ancient philosophy, and you also know that she was a working journalist for many years before that.

"There are aspects of her life you are not aware of. While she was enjoying her career as an international journalist, she was approached by the DEA and the FBI, not in concert I must admit, to work clandestinely as a procurer of information."

"My wife was an undercover agent?" I was stunned. She withheld that from me? This woman I would have laid down my life for lied and cheated to me? "This can't be true. Sami was the most gentle, loving person I've ever known. She taught how civilization has progressed through great writing and philosophy. She simply could not be involved in killings and criminal activities.

"You'll have to do more than just bring me a hundred miles out to sea where I'm trapped and tell me this. Many things I could accept, but a government agent? No, this isn't true."

Dollarhide spoke up immediately. "Jason, I'm aware this has come as a shock, but I do have the proof you need, and you'll have plenty of time to see it. Sami was one of our best, and that's why we have brought you here. Not to demean her memory or make her less in your eyes.

"To be very honest with you, we are breaking every code there is for undercover work in telling you these things, and Sami would not have told you even if she was being tortured. The bureau tried all of the tricks in the book to keep her from marrying you. We were afraid we would lose her services, and as I said, she is, was, among the very best.

"We believe there is a connection between the Colombian drug cartels and the drug families in the Mediterranean. Her background, her knowledge of the languages and lifestyles, and most of all, her many years as an active news gathering person in the area, made her a natural for gathering information for us. The two men who killed Sami were from that area. One was from Greece, the other was Italian.

"They were sent to San Francisco by Alberto Pelligrini who lives in Sicily, and is head of a big crime family there, and there are branches of the family here in the states, connections to Hong Kong and Malaysia, and partnerships in Afghanistan and Pakistan. Mr. Pelligrini runs a world-wide gang. The two hit men were turned over to work for Lopez. Both of these men, Pelligrini and Lopez, are at or near the top in their families, and are known to be responsible for the deaths of other agents. I know I'm going awfully fast here, Jason, but it's important that you understand all the connections. We know these things because Sami had put the pieces together for us. She also had informed us of your plans to travel through the Caribbean, and we were in turn asking that she keep an eye out for certain people and events.

"It appears as though Pelligrini or Lopez, or someone in Colombia also got wind of this. Your wife was very high on many hit lists, Jason, and one of the angles we're working on right now is how the police department or at least some of the cops in high places, in Ft. Bragg got bought off. There was no investigation as you well know, despite the fact that five people, including two underworld hit men and a cop were killed. And of course, we haven't been able to say a word about Sami's involvement. Our investigation is proceeding, and heads will roll, Mr. Caldwell. Heads will roll.

"I worked on two different cases with Sami, and I can tell you her loss is tremendous within the bureau."

"You don't know what loss is, Agent Dollarhide. Sami, my sweet, loving, Sami was an undercover FBI agent? Sami wanted me to get rid of the armament I keep on the boat. Sami detested guns and violence.

"You're going to have to give me some time here. Everything you've told me is the opposite of the Sami I love. The violence, the guns, the subterfuge.

"You said your investigation is continuing. What exactly does that mean?"

"Jason," Dollarhide was looking right into my eyes, "there is a big contract on you at this moment, signed, sealed, and delivered. Lopez knows we know who he is, and so does Pelligrini, and they both want you out of the picture. You are a catalyst here, Jason.

"These crime families and cartels don't know what you know or don't know, and they are going to be looking to get you out of the picture."

"And now," I pipe in, "you have made me aware, and that has increased the stakes. Thanks a fucking bunch."

For all these years I wrote novels and screen plays, produced some really big movies and TV shows, won Emmy's and other awards, and most of the stories dealt with crime and violence and dead people and drugs and booze and whores and shit, and now, as the old joke goes, I are one.

"You dirty bastards. I was right, you got me out here in the middle of the ocean, trapped, can't get away from you, and that means you want something from me." Was I set-up? By professionals! "You welcome me on your cutter, Captain Eric, The Viking, all smiles, knowing I am a simple little fly who flew into your web, and you are ready to pounce and kill. And you, pretty little agent of death, FBI Special Agent, purveyor of evil, you tell me my wife was a liar and cheat, and then say I'm next to die because of some perverted war on drugs.

"All these people are dead, five in pretty little Ft. Bragg, because somebody wants to smoke a joint? Give 'em all the nose candy they can stand. Let them kill themselves with needles and crack and coke and pot.

"You dirty bastards." It was all I could say, and Petersen and Dollarhide sat very still and quiet. The silence probably only lasted a few seconds, but during that time my mind was doing wind sprints, remembering all the things Sami and I had done, had talked about, had planned. How many times did we take the *D'Anne* out to the kelp beds, supposedly to fish for cod and snapper, but never being able to because of natural urges? We rode at anchor off the kelp beds near Davenport, California for two complete tide cycles and never caught a fish. Never wet a line, even. Almost forgot to eat.

One time in particular, will always stand out in my memory. Petersen, you bastard, you can't take my memories. We were off the coast of Davenport, just north of Santa Cruz, drifting near a large raft of kelp, naked to the world, having a wonderful little private party. Sami could do things no other woman I've ever known could do, and she was doing a few that day. All at once, we heard whoops of joy, cheering, and a long blast of a boat's horn.

A party boat with at least forty drunken assholes had quietly come alongside, and had been watching the festivities. Bless her soul, Sami simply waved, took my hand, and we went below decks. I found some pants, climbed to the wheel house, and we headed out to sea. We laughed about that for months, but at the moment, I would gladly have shot the skipper of that party boat.

How many times did we drive to San Francisco to spend a weekend of being tourists, do some shopping, only to spend two days and nights in our hotel room, making whoopee? We would actually make lists of places to go, things to do, put the list on the hotel room table, and not leave the room. Ten thousand fresh crabs and iced cod within blocks, and we'd eat room service, if we could remember to order. This sweet, gentle soul is gone. I'll never taste her mouth, smell her distinctiveness, be in ecstasy with her again.

And then, my mind did exactly what these two evil people had planned all along. I started wanting to get revenge, to pursue and gouge out the lives of those responsible for Sami's death. To rip and sunder the very souls of those who made the contract. My muscles tightened, and I guess that was what gave me away, because it was Petersen who started talking.

"Even if you run away, Jason, even if you tell us to go to hell, it won't change the reality of Pelligrini and Lopez. They plan to kill you exactly the same as they killed Sami. And we won't be able to offer any protection."

Well, there was a statement I agreed with. "It seems you didn't offer much protection to my wife either." The anger surged through me, and I planned to use every drop of it. "If she was such a fine agent, why did you let her get gunned down in a little fucking coffee shop in Ft. Bragg?" I found myself able to ask these people serious questions, and I couldn't get the time of day from the Ft. Bragg Police Department. Again, my mind was tracking. Maybe they really were telling the truth.

Dollarhide was looking down at the beige top of the table, fiddling with her glass of soda. "Sami hadn't looked at her E-Mail for three days, Jason. A coded message was sent to her, warning of a possible hit."

I was frozen. She was right. Sami hadn't gone to her office at the college for three days because of a combination of a weekend and a holiday. "Is that the only way you got messages to her?" Impossible. This is the 21st century. This is November, 2010.

"When someone is deep underground, Jason, the less contact the better. In Sami's case, because of the school and her marriage to you, our contact had to be extremely clandestine, and this was in her best interest."

"As well as yours," I snorted.

Petersen jumped in before I could reach across the table and smack Miss FBI Agent Dollarhide. "Anger is natural at this point Jason. But aim your anger at those who are truly responsible, not at the agency your wife worked for. Katie and I have something to offer you that might help ease your anger and pain."

Now it was 'Katie and I,' just us three, good old Eric the Viking and lovely Katie the Agent, across the table from Jason the Dip Shit. Their proposal would direct my anger, my resentment, my loss toward the criminals, and I would now replace Sami Bertorelli-Caldwell as an undercover FBI operative. My mind was again in high-overdrive, trying to remember everything that had been said. I could not be more positive that I have been set-up by absolute experts.

"Are you really a Coast Guard Commander?" It just dawned on me. This whole damn thing was a set-up by the FBI and the DEA.

"Yes, I am, but I'm assigned to the drug intervention section. I work closely with the FBI and DEA, at times with the BATF, and even other branches of the service, in particular with the Navy and Air Force.

"The reasons for this meeting Jason, are to make you aware of the danger you currently face, and to bring you into our service. Sami was an extraordinary operative, and her loss to our service is tremendous. It is unfortunate that you have been drawn into, as you succinctly put it, our web, but you have."

Petersen took a deep breath, looked at Dollarhide who was still averting her eyes from both of us, and continued. "You can get up and walk out of here, go back to the *D'Anne*, and spend the rest of your life watching your back. Or," and there was that long pause again, "you can listen to our proposal. You will still spend a great deal of time protecting your back, but there will be others helping."

I could almost feel a curtain forming around the three of us, as if nothing else in the world existed. I could feel my loss coupled with hatred of those responsible, and that loss had been ever so slightly tinged with a form of deceit I've never encountered. Sami didn't really lie to me, but she certainly wasn't forthcoming with honesty either, and I was being told that my life was in the same kind of danger Sami faced daily. Was her deceit a form of protection for me? Was this her way of keeping me out of danger? Petersen broke into my thoughts, but that curtain stayed in place.

"I'm not going to give you some kind of pep talk about the war on drugs or any of that shit. Sometimes I don't believe in the scope of this war either, but you have a personal stake in this operation now. Katie called you a catalyst, and that's what we need, someone who will draw these bastards out into the open. A target might be a better word for it, Jason."

At last some honesty. A target. "Petersen, Dollarhide, I'm going to be sixty years old soon. I'm retired. My old movies and TV shows bring me lots of residuals. I'm not cut out to be an undercover drug agent. I don't believe in violence, I'm not against someone smoking a joint once in a while, I drink gin martinis, I like red meat.

"How in the hell could I possibly be any kind of service to you? Yes, I'm angry and I have a great feeling of loss and pain over Sami's death, and I would like to see justice, but I'm not a revengeful person. Retribution? Yes, but in the name of justice. Jousting with windmills is not in my character."

"That's exactly the point Mr. Caldwell." Dollarhide rejoined the conversation. "We are not asking you to get on a white horse and follow the sunset into a thief's lair. What we would like you to consider is to continue with your plans to explore the Caribbean, to visit many ports, and to allow us to every once in a while aim you somewhere. You won't be shadowed. You won't be asked to make reports. But you will be contacted, secretively to be sure, for your observations. There will be money deposited in your bank accounts, probably from one of our covert publishing companies, probably more money than you currently receive from your royalties, but you will be mostly on your own.

"You will have contacts that we will establish, and you will find that you won't trust anyone but them. You were right in keeping an arsenal on your boat, and yes, we know all about it. You are right in not trusting us, but regardless of what you decide, your life is at risk, with or without us. Sami was right in her own mind asking you to get rid of your protection, but I'm very glad you didn't. She was probably the only operative, investigator, in the bureau who never carried a weapon of any kind. She always said that if they came after her, she wouldn't be able to do anything about it anyway. And, I guess, she was right."

Dollarhide seemed to drift off again, looking down at the table top, eyes almost glazed. My mind wouldn't stop spinning, completely out of control. What an amazing turn of events this had been. My sweet, delicious Sami, who read to me from Greek classics, in Greek, who left clothes scattered from one end of *D'Anne* to the other the minute we cleared the harbor, who wouldn't even take her own fish off the hook, more or less allow them to be killed. This magnificent intellectual, an FBI agent.

"Jason, every person has only one person he must be true to; himself. Your memories will never be taken away, your soul will not be stolen, and possibly you will be able to help solve what has to be a personal and very devastating loss." The Viking was also a philosopher. "There are times, particularly when I'm on the high sea, far from land, I have trouble connecting this war on drugs to some kind of reality, but then something devastating, like the loss of Sami Bertorelli, brings me back.

"This war has become personal to all three of us, and each of us must find a way to answer. Each to himself. I would be pleased if you were on our team."

This was the kind of honesty I was looking for in Fort Bragg, and all I found was a chief of detectives who couldn't investigate where he pissed that morning, and a police chief who seemed to be the detective's parrot. It would be very important for these two to keep talking, but they certainly were on the right track.

I think I understood Petersen. He was very deep, heavy in his thinking, sprightly in his observations, and someone a man could trust. FBI special agent Katie Dollarhide bothered the hell out of me. I didn't know if I could trust her at all. I'm not sure she wasn't lying to me.

Chapter Five

Katie's mind was alive with thoughts of Sami, drug kings, violent death, and the possibility of even more death. "God I hate this job sometimes." She was listening to Petersen and Caldwell, but only with half her mind. The other half was on her own thoughts.

"In our last meeting, she told me what Jason was like, but I didn't pay that much attention. He's just as strong and beautiful as she said. I can see why she fell in love with the jerk, but I can't help but remember that last job we did. That job had given her the idea her cover was in jeopardy, and then she makes the situation that much more difficult by getting married. Everything else being the same, this jerk is still in big trouble. The bad guys think he's an agent, or working for an agent.

"Sami had put together a large dossier on two drug runners from Greece and had forwarded it to me. We then got together at a little B&B in Inverness, just north of San Francisco, to go over all the details. Sami left very little out of her reports, and generally we could get through them quickly. It was pretty safe at Inverness since the proprietor was a retired agent whom I've known for the last ten years.

"She had been working in Europe for several months, trailing leads that went nowhere, as she put it, but kept running into a lot of the same people." Her mind rolled the entire conversation out for her, and her gaze remained on the table in officer country.

"I think that's important to remember, Katie. Even though I never have been able to put Pelligrini physically into this picture, all the people he works with are painted in with vivid colors.

"What I'm saying is, all of the people are Pelligrini people which means, we're dealing with his mob, and now, ties to South America." There was just the gentle movement of the big ship, riding in the swell a hundred miles off the California coast, and the rocking lulled Katie's thoughts, but focused them as well.

She remembered it was when she came back, and then did a couple of turns into the Caribbean that the picture started to get really ugly. She could see Sami, sitting across from her, could almost hear her words.

"Here are all these same people again, all of Pelligrini's people, but no Pelligrini. Keep this in mind, Katie. He wasn't there, but his name and those who work for him were. This is a Pelligrini operation."

***

Alberto Pelligrini is a name to be reckoned with in many different circles. In Europe, he is known as a patron of the arts, offering money and help to varied artists and artistic endeavors. He has sponsored opera, ballet, galleries, and theater, even spent lavishly to create a symphony orchestra for an Italian town that couldn't afford one.

Conversely, he's known to be responsible for the deaths of hundreds of people, not just members of other crime syndicates, but even of his own, and of police agencies investigating his activities. The FBI has him at the top of the list of major criminals on a world scale, and holds him personally responsible for Sami's death. Pelligrini has attained a dual status: That of international terrorist and international drug kingpin.

In Washington, D.C., Alberto Pelligrini is known by politicians of every ilk and persuasion, and his passion for liberal projects is vast. The more the government spends on the people, he says, the more the people are free. That can also translate, if the people don't have to spend money on necessities, they can spend it on his drugs. There are many politicians whose personal bank accounts hold Pelligrini money, and there are an equal number of politicians who are unwilling to accept the possibility that Alberto Pelligrini is a drug lord, murderer, crime boss. Sami knew him as criminal, murderer, drug king.

"This big guy, the one we call Wiley, is really dangerous, Katie. He's high in the organization, maybe even a trusted number two or something close to that. He's a sneaky bastard who uses people and things to get his way. I met him the first time at a press conference in Milan, and the bastard tried to rape me in the middle of the patio at the reception afterward. Here are all these people, dressed immaculately, and this pig is trying to get into my panties right in the middle of the patio. I should have shot him. Maybe that's why I don't ever carry. I might just decide to use a pistol or Uzi at some point.

"But this last time I ran into the bastard, at that convention in San Juan, he told me, right to my face and in front of all kinds of people that instead of fucking my brains out he should have just shoved a knife in my gut. In other words, Katie, he may have already made me for some kind of agent. I think if he thought I was a U.S. agent, he probably would have killed me right there. I'm not sure what he may think he knows, but it bothers the hell out of me. He's called Wiley for a reason, and even though his real name is Carpenter, Wiley is his character.

"Anyone who seriously did their homework would know I haven't had a story published for several years, why am I still saying I'm with the press. I need another cover, dear heart. I need to get off this case." Sami's cover was blown. Any other agent would have run for shelter, headed for DC headquarters, or at least gone underground for a long period. Not Sami. Her work wasn't done, and she was depending on us to get her a new set of identification tags. She knew she had to get off this investigation, but she also knew she couldn't just walk away from it. "Katie, I know so much about these people and their organization, they have to get rid of me.

"I've put it all in my report, every name and place, just in case. Find someone to replace me, Katie. In the meantime, though, I'm certainly not quitting. This is the time to bring these bastards down. Read what I've written about the coastal operations, and the people, and pass it on to whoever replaces me."

***

Those thoughts continued to rumble around in FBI Agent Katie Dollarhide's head as the conversation between Petersen and Caldwell continued as well. "Under normal circumstances, I would have put her into an office situation, assigned new agents to the case, and let Sami see to it they were brought up to speed. She knew I couldn't do that, and she knew this would be the most dangerous time of her career. Now, in an irony no one could predict, her widower is about to be her replacement.

"When an agent gets known, it's time to get her off the job, and we were trying to do that with Sami. Just too damn late. We didn't see the red flare soon enough, and Sami paid the price.

"She was so good at getting people to talk about things, I don't know if this jerk she married can match up. A damned egotistical Hollywood type? One thing to remember, Sami said he was the best lay she'd ever had. And he does have tight buns. Damn it, girl, get your mind back on the job. There's time for him later." She looked up from her position at the table in time to see Jason Caldwell looking right straight at her.

"It's hard to think with those beautiful eyes staring at me. I understand more and more how Sami was feeling."

***

She looked hard at the two men who were looking equally hard at her, and she let her mind speak out. "We have pictures of all the people Sami fingered to be working for either Pelligrini or the Colombian cartels, but somewhere, there's a picture that's missing. I know there is an agent in the bureau who is feeding all this shit to these bastards, but how the hell do we find him?

"Mr. Caldwell, we can't guarantee your safety no matter what you choose, but regardless of how you decide to live your life, our little mole in the bureau is going to know you are one of ours, and that will put you at the top of the bad guy's hit list. As an operative you will at least have the knowledge we have, will have the opportunity to help bring down the people responsible for Sami's death, and have whatever back up we can provide.

"I'm going to call John and see if anyone has volunteered to take over Sami's investigation. That might be a lead. If someone is anxious to be a part of this job, it could be because he already knows too much about it."

Both men saw doubt in Dollarhide's face, could almost hear doubt in her voice as she spoke. That worry came to the surface immediately. "Eric, I'm worried that we might be throwing Jason to the wolves. We told him his life is in danger, and if he works with us, we can protect him some. But if my suspicions are right, and we have a mole in our operation, we might not be protecting him at all.

"Jason, as you already know, these guys don't play by rules. If someone gets in their way, they blow him away. No questions asked. We're asking an awful lot here." She let her gaze drop back to the table top, and all she could see was that terrible picture of Sami, sprawled on the floor, bullet holes everywhere, blood on the table, the wall, the carpet, and soaked into her clothing. She clenched her fists, opened, clenched again, a trademark everyone in the bureau respected, and she cried, softly, mostly to herself. It was the first time in years that she had cried where someone might see.

"I'm not weak, but I miss that woman, and I mourn her loss. I hope somehow I can help bring an end to what she was trying to do. Jason, Mr. Caldwell, I hope someday you'll understand how close we are in this agency. I hope you'll be one of us."

It was very quiet for several minutes, each of the three with active minds assessing what has been said, what is known, and most importantly, what isn't known. As Sami might have reflected from her journalism background, "we need the who, what, when, where, and why. I think we only know the what right now and that isn't enough."

Chapter Six

"I understand what you're saying, and I want you to know just how much we appreciate what you're doing for us. If there is any way you can get one of ours assigned to either the drug interdiction ships, or to a land based operation that works out of California, we can put a lid on this. I'm going to do everything I can from this end to help you, and remember, don't try to contact either Mr. Pelligrini or the gentleman from Colombia.

"Goodbye, Corazone, and keep in touch." The man called Wiley hung up the phone, smiled at his boss, Alberto Pelligrini, and lit a large cigar. "She is going to have a former Coast Guard officer, now an FBI agent, and one of ours, assigned to the California division. It appears that we were right, Don Alberto. That Bertorelli woman married another agent. He's one we didn't know about, but we do now."

Alberto Pelligrini was not what one might think of as a typical gangster. He had received a classical education in Italy and France, and attended economics and business schools at Harvard and Stanford, before assuming leadership of his criminal family. Tall and wiry, aristocratic in many ways, Pelligrini would stand for nothing less than perfection from those who worked for him. His public persona was that of a man of the world, wise and intelligent, looking always for another way to bring the good life to those less fortunate than himself. Personally, and within his own business, the real Pelligrini was far different.

He was vicious in every way, and thought nothing of having people who get in his way exterminated. Gracious in public, he was cruel to those who crossed him. There were some who say he takes great pride in publicly condemning those who failed him or who got in his way. He was known to advocate torture, not just to get answers, but as a means of keeping others at bay. Fear was a close and dear friend, and Alberto Pelligrini used it regularly. He was known to keep photographs of those he killed by torture, and was also known to show those photographs to associates at inappropriate times; to frighten, to intimidate. "If you can humiliate a minion, preferably in front of his peers, you can own his soul. He will bend his knee at every opportunity." At the same time, he moved with elegance and grace through the halls of politics and art, education and science, dressed as one might expect from an aristocrat, not a common drug dealer and murderer.

He was smiling at what Wiley told him. "Good Wiley. Stop him the same way you stopped that little bitch of an agent. This operation in California is too lucrative to lose now. Have we got everyone in position to continue bringing as much stuff as we want onto the coast? I'm worried about not having our own people running the entire operation. I don't like having to share any of this with those Colombian pigs.

"If you can get rid of them, it would be a great day, Wiley. A great day." Alberto Pelligrini had been approached by one of the Colombian Cartels about a reciprocal deal, and it had sounded good. Funnel Italian, Greek, Middle East drugs through the Caribbean, across to the Pacific, and up the coast to California, and by way of Miami, up the eastern seaboard as well. A network already existed, just join in, and co-mingle the profits.

That was the part that grated on Pelligrini. "More than five years now, and I have taken over the whole operation. My boats. My people. My risk. Why the fuck am I giving those bastards money? I own the cops. I own the shit.

"I want you to start making some plans, Wiley. It's time we moved those fuckers aside and did things our way. Use some muscle, some tough guy stuff, but remember, you're where you are because you're smart. Don't just be a tough guy, Wiley, be a smart bastard when you're tough.

"I want the whole damned operation. Got it?"

Wiley had already been planning for this. After all these years, he knew his boss pretty well. Only half Sicilian, he was a big man from a rough background. Wiley Carpenter had knuckles chewed up by brawls, had knife scars across a mean face, made meaner by a permanent scowl. But Wiley was smart in the ways of Alberto Pelligrini.

It wasn't that long ago he set up the Afghanistan program and forced Pelligrini into the operation, and now, the family owns it all. They work for him, but they think they're independent. "That's the answer," Wiley said often. "Make them think they're the winners, and all the time you're ripping off their ass."

Wiley smiled at his boss and said, "That fucker Lopez won't know what hit him, Mr. Pelligrini. You can trust me on that."

Wiley's education had stopped shy of high school, and he had learned nothing since except that which Alberto Pelligrini wished him to learn. What Mr. Pelligrini wanted, Wiley saw to it that Mr. Pelligrini got. There was no such thing as conceptual thought in Wiley's brain waves, unless placed there by Alberto Pelligrini.

The Sicilian Don smiled and walked from the great hall in his palacio, just west of Palermo. Dating back almost a thousand years, the massive structure was built of the finest Italian granite and marble, filled with authentic classical furniture and original fine art from many periods. The Palacio was spared severe damage during WW II, and the gardens and outbuildings were magnificent, standing on a prominent cliff and seen from the sea and the land. A rumor had it that George Patton used the palacio for a time as his headquarters.

Pelligrini lived in the manner of ancient royalty, demanded fealty from those around him, and was murderous in his heart. "So, that bitch had a husband who was an agent. I will see to it he suffers a long and difficult death. Maybe it's time for me to take another little trip to Washington and put some pressure on those sniveling senators who so graciously accept my money. It's time to put the brakes on the FBI and DEA."

***

Pelligrini had learned years before, the best way to a politician's vote was through his wallet, and sometimes the money went for actual good things, not just evil. He had funded many art and historical projects in various regions of the U.S., and there were politicians by the legion who owed him. He had spent so much money in California, there were some who thought of him as a native son. There were politicians who knew his criminal side, but preferred to ignore it as long as funds for reelection were made available, or funds for some specific cultural endeavor appeared. In this case, the pork barrel was filled with product from Italy, and that was one of the circumstances that brought Pelligrini to the attention of the FBI in the first place.

It was illegal for a foreigner to contribute to persons or causes in U.S. elections at the federal and state levels. There were continuing investigations involving Pelligrini's political donations. According to John Chandler, the assistant to FBI Director Harold

Collins, "This Pelligrini is just half a step from becoming a terrorist in our eyes. Harold, he has funneled money through projects that are funded by him, but that are U.S. in origin. He is a national security risk in my opinion. How far are we willing to let him go in order to continue our investigation?"

"How close is your investigation of drug smuggling to issuing charges, John?"

"It is our belief that it was a Pelligrini ordered hit on agent Bertorelli, and we are not ready to file charges. This is the biggest operation in the world, Harold, taking in at least four continents, possibly five if we can tie him into the Asian problems.

"We're looking at some time down the road to bring any charges in this operation, and that's why we need a little help on other fronts. Something to slow the bastard down."

"The prick is smooth, John. I'll see what we can do on the political front, but he has so much money spread around, it will be difficult."

***

After dressing in riding habit, Pelligrini stepped into his elegant courtyard, filled with olive trees and grape arbors, flowers and vegetation from around the world; the area adorned with Italian sculpture, some dated from the renaissance. Grooms brought a magnificent Arabian stallion for him, and Don Alberto mounted for a ride through spacious gardens and forests. On some of the hill tops of his vast acreage, he could look over the azure reaches of the Tyrrhenian Sea, while from other hillsides, the achingly white buildings of ancient Palermo spread below him, glistened under a Sicilian sun.

"This life is good," he murmured as he cantered across a large highland plain, dotted with ancient olive trees. "I won't let those little pests from FBI and DEA take it from me. No. I won't."

***

Carlos Lopez was sitting at a bar near the center of Old San Juan in Puerto Rico, sipping a rum over ice. He had squeezed a section of lime into the amber liquid and was enjoying the two distinct tastes, a bite from rum and a touch of mellow from the lime. Lopez was a wiry man, about five feet six inches tall, who over dressed for every occasion, and today was no exception. His Italian silk suit contrasted with the tropical attire of the rest of the customers in the dirty little bar. His imported Italian shoes cost more than the entire wardrobe of most of the customers in Maria's, and the cigar he had lit moments before came straight from Cuba.

Being in Old San Juan was so much like taking a trip back in time, back to when colonialism was the order of the day, when Spanish Conquistadors, royalty, and Catholic Padres ruled. Old San Juan, heart of Puerto Rico, was as much European as it was Caribbean. Spanish explorers founded the city, and it reeked of Old Spain. The streets were narrow, some were paved with cobblestone, and street vendors and musicians were on every sidewalk, in every doorway, along every artery. Architecture dated from those heady days of Spanish rule, and the evil days of slave trading. There were great buildings with tropical alcoves, little alleys that seemingly went nowhere but ended at massive wooden gates, behind which the elite of the Island lived.

If one were to be put down in Palermo, Sicily, Cadiz, Spain, or in San Juan, Puerto Rico, one would have a difficult time telling one from the other. The architecture was ancient and lovely. European and Moorish on the one hand, slightly modern on another, strikingly beautiful on both. There was a constant feeling of romance, of sensuousness, a feeling that at any moment a charming young lady or dazzlingly handsome young man would appear with an offering of wine or flowers or passion.

The city is built at the end of a peninsula, the tip of which is home to the famous El Morro, a colonial fort built by Spanish conquerors designed to protect the entrance to San Juan harbor. Rusting away in the tropical gauze of humidity and salt spray, were huge cannon faced to the sea to protect that harbor entrance. This was a place for tourism on the one hand, and for a more gentle life in the tropics.

Romance flourishes in Old San Juan. Beautiful Puerto Rican women, blazing in their tropical dress, street musicians playing island music, groups of steel drum bands setting up on corners, serenading themselves as much as those around them. It isn't the least bit unusual to find a single trumpet player, sitting in a second story balcony, playing for the pure joy of the music.

The streets of Old San Juan reverberate with life, some of it from locals, some of it from tourists. Maria's Cantina is not tourist oriented, but a few come in from time to time. For the real taste of Puerto Rico, they will say. Lopez was hoping he would stand out some, and he did. Even if those present didn't know who he was, simply by the way he was dressed they would cater to his every need, and Carlo, as some of his friends called him, liked that.

He started out in life as a simple farm boy in the mountains of Calle Province of Colombia, but his mind was quick. He saw his father wear himself out trying to make a decent living growing coffee. "Coca is the answer," he knew, even as a youngster, and when his father died, Carlo contacted the right people, and started growing gold. By knowing who to kill and when, by knowing who to kiss and when, brought him even more riches, and today, he runs one of the major divisions of the Calle Cartel.

The days of Spanish noblemen have been replaced by the days of the drug lords. Where the Spanish killed every native person in the entire Caribbean area, and all the European nations used the various Islands as breeding grounds for slavery, today, the drug infrastructure is killing equal millions throughout the world, and using the islands of the Caribbean as transportation portals.

Drugs coming from Europe, North Africa, and the Indian subcontinent are routed through the islands, eventually making their way to distributors in Mexico and the U.S. Some of course find their way to various countries in South America as well, while product from South America comes to the distribution points and then on to either European and North African, or to Mexican and stateside distribution. Drug dealers and suppliers are truly kings on many of the Caribbean islands.

There are hundreds of islands in what's known as the Greater and Lesser Antilles, and drugs from Europe and the Middle and Near East are vectored through them to be mixed with South American drugs, usually in one of the Central American nations, before being shipped up North America's west coast. The drugs bonded in the Caribbean also make their way to Florida and other east coast areas.

Tito Vasquez, owner and manager of Maria's, was hovering around the table, and finally spoke to the drug master. A visit by Carlos Lopez could be good for his pocket book.

"Senor Lopez, it's so good of you to stop in here. If there is anything you need, I'll get it for you. Anything, Jefe." Lopez smiled at the bar owner, indulgently perhaps, and waved him off. He was waiting for two of Pelligrini's men, and didn't want any small talk from a bar keep. His mind was very keen, and he knew one thing; he hated having to do business with these arrogant Europeans.

"The Italians are the worst," he was thinking. "They feel they own the world, and the rest of us are here to do their bidding. Someday, I think, I'll pull the plug on these bastards and see what happens." Lopez had made a deal with Pelligrini to distribute Pelligrini's heroin and opium along with his own cocaine and marijuana, and in turn, Pelligrini would do the same for Lopez's drugs in Europe. It should have been a sweet deal for both, but Lopez learned early on, Pelligrini intended to be boss, and Lopez was expected to jump whenever he was told.

"Hey, Tito. I was wrong. Hey, a day like today, I'm meeting two business associates, but I'm horny, you know what I mean? Get me a woman, Tito, and I'll take that room upstairs." He got up, grabbed his bottle of rum, glass and lime in hand, and headed up the stairs. "Bring a woman to me, Tito, and when my associates arrive, bring them upstairs too."

Vasquez had several women working for him, and he knew he would make some good money from Carlos Lopez. There wasn't much work in Old San Juan for some of the young people, and prostitution wasn't such a bad way for a pretty girl to get enough money to get out. New York. That's where most of them wanted to be. "That's where the money is. New York." Some just wasted away, to become old and worn out before they were 40, and others were able to make the jump to New York, only to learn things weren't any better for them there.

Many of the little bars in Old San Juan had a few hotel rooms overhead, and bartenders and cocktail waitresses could make a few extra bucks turning a trick or two rather than becoming full blown prostitutes. Vasquez hired some very attractive cocktail waitresses.

He sent young Nadia upstairs and told her she had to split with him, 75-25, with her getting the 25. She frowned, but knew she couldn't say no, and started upstairs. She had never been with Carlos Lopez before, but knew from some of the other girls he liked to be rough on his women. This scared her, but she continued up the stairs, and knocked ever so lightly at his door.

Lopez was working out the new drop schedules for northern California and that made him nervous. "All these changes aren't good. We got rid of that FBI agent, the Ft. Bragg people are doing their part, we know there is going to be a new agent, even who he is, and now they want to make changes to what we are doing. It's not good." Lopez was uptight, and a good release was a woman, pretty, but not so pretty that a little lump on the jaw wouldn't matter, or a black eye.

"They like it too," he always told himself. "Just being with me, makes them special with the other girls, so a little love tap on the kisser makes them famous." More than one of the girls that Vasquez kept around wanted to show Lopez just how special they were.

"If I could, I'd put a knife right through his skinny little pecker," Amanda told her friends. "Bastard broke my nose, gave me a black eye, and then knocked out a tooth. He thought it was pretty funny, me on my hands and knees, naked as the day I was born, trying to find that tooth.

"I found out later, that puta was standing on it. Someday, I'll put a knife in his pecker, then his heart."

Sami had been working to turn one of the girls working for Vasquez when her cover was blown, and it was Lopez who ordered the hit. Rosa Garcia was only 17-years-old, but she had been working for Vasquez for two years. She hated Lopez more than any of the girls, and had told Sami about it.

"I was only 15-years-old when I went to work for Tito Vasquez, and I was pretty, Sami, really pretty. Look at my nose now. I look like a prize fighter, and it's all because of that pig Lopez.

"I know now that some men have a hard time reaching climax, but I was so young, I didn't know. I giggled a little bit because he was working so hard, and he lost his temper and hit me three or four times. That's when he had his climax. My nose was broken in two places, I had to have stitches over my eye, and you can still see the scar on my cheek here where his ring cut me.

"He ruined me, Sami. I will never be able to be anything else in my life now because of him. Everyone can see I'm just a prostitute, a whore, because of these scars."

Sami had Rosa ready to turn evidence over to her on her next trip to Puerto Rico, and was going to help her start a new life in Miami. "You don't need to put your life in jeopardy, Rosa, just gently question where he's been, who he's seen, where he's going. The more I can find out about him, the faster we can take him out. Rosa, I'll get you set up comfortably in Miami, and all this will be behind you." Whether Lopez actually knew about this, or just had a hunch, we'll never know. He had Sami killed, and when Rosa heard, she disappeared.

Right now though, Carlo was covered in sweat as he finally got his rocks off, and the knock at the door came at about the same time, the only thing that kept Nadia from a beating. The two men who came in were not Hispanic, but rather European, Nadia noticed. One of the men grabbed her clothes while the other shoved her out the door. She not only didn't get the shit beat out of her, she didn't get paid either. Tito would not like that.

"All right, Carlo, what's the big problem?" The larger of the two, swarthy in some respects, but at least dressed for the Puerto Rican climate, was smiling as Lopez got dressed. "The schedule changes came right from the top. Right from Mr. Pelligrini himself. If this meeting is just for you to complain some more, then we're wasting our time. Some day, beaner, you'll push Mr. Pelligrini too far." Lopez tensed up like a cobra at the taunt from the Italian.

"Don't call me that, Carpenter. Some day you'll push me too far, and remember, you're on my turf. I'm an equal partner with Pelligrini, so treat me with dignity and respect, or else." Carpenter just smiled at the little Colombian drug lord, and continued talking. His nick name was Wiley for a reason.

"I do have some bad shit to tell you though. That other FBI bitch, Dollarhide, has a new agent working, and we need to bust him dead now. He's the one who married that Bertorelli broad, and he's working his way down the coast now in his boat. Set it up, Carlos, to meet him in Costa Rican waters, and blow him away."

Carlos Lopez was finally smiling. "So that Hollywood producer is now an FBI agent. Tell me, Mr. Carpenter, is he a new agent, or has he always been one?

"While we're on the subject of FBI, what did Pelligrini do to get the FBI involved in this. Drugs and shit are the jurisdiction of DEA, so why the FBI?" Lopez was pressing, he knew, but if he could get Carpenter pissed off enough, maybe that new knife would get its first taste of blood. Italian blood.

Carpenter just shrugged, but was smiling all the while. "Our information is from Mr. Pelligrini, Carlos, so I don't know." Carpenter/Wiley didn't actually know the difference between FBI and DEA, and couldn't care. If Pelligrini had simply stayed in the drug trade, the FBI probably wouldn't be involved, but too much of that drug money was making its way into American politics, at the national level, and at state houses around the country. There was lots of talk about national security in and about Justice Department, White House, even CIA headquarters.

There was too much talk of drug cartels, of crime bosses and families, of U.S. police agencies run by criminals simply to ignore, and the FBI was not ignoring any of it. Carpenter didn't have the brains to understand this, and Alberto Pelligrini was too arrogant to care.

"The guy's name is Jason Caldwell, and he has a 50 foot trawler converted to his living quarters. The word from Washington is, he will sail down the coast, through the canal, and tour the Caribbean. Mr. Pelligrini figures it would be good to knock him off in Costa Rican waters. It would throw the FBI off track. They wouldn't expect a hit in friendly waters. He calls his boat *D'Anne* some of the time, and *Molokai II* at other times. Some kind of FBI code."

Carlos got pensive for a few minutes, remembering how Carpenter wanted to put a knife in Sami Bertorelli right here in San Juan. "Are you sure this hit is from Mr. Pelligrini, and not from you, Carpenter? I remember you telling me you tried to get in Bertorelli's pants once, and then later told her you should have knifed her. This isn't just a jealous thing with her husband is it?

"My people wouldn't like that. I have a couple of very fast boats near San Jose, Costa Rica, and either one of them would be good for a hit like this. Make me positive this came from Mr. Pelligrini, Carpenter."

Carpenter never did like the Colombian cartel boss in the first place, never did like to have to work with someone other than his own family, his own people, and now to be questioned like this was almost more than he could take. Carpenter was a very big man, not very smart, but very big.

"I have to work with you, Lopez, because Mr. Pelligrini says so, but I don't have to take your shit. If I told you the word came from my boss, that's where it came from, and I plan to tell him what you've said. Now, you move that shit across Guatemala and get it on the boats for California, and in the meantime, make that hit on this new agent.

"If you ever cross me, you little beaner, I'll smash you."

And that was the end of the meeting. "Someday," Lopez was saying to himself as the two Pelligrini men left the room, "I'm going to use his own knife on him, just as that Bertorelli agent should have done."

Lopez contacted his people in Costa Rica and the hit was set. "It won't be hard to find him in that big trawler, Eduardo, just make sure it's clean and he's dead. For political reasons, it's important to make the hit inside Costa Rican waters if at all possible, not international. If you can, try to get him while he's close to shore, but no matter what, kill that bastard. Check with our man in Washington on dates and times." The Cartel had people in high places in Washington, the same as the Pelligrini family, but it was the Italians who were able to infiltrate the police departments, not the South Americans. Seeing a Hispanic in a Washington, D.C. office was not unusual. Seeing a Hispanic in a high position in a northern California police department was.

Back at his own little plantation, Lopez put in motion, at least in his head, what he would do if he could get out of his deal with Pelligrini. "I need to know more about these people. It was so simple in the beginning. Just help distribute their stuff, let them help distribute ours, and share the profits. Now they want to own the whole damn world. I hate those fucking Europeans." He called Eduardo back and pressed him for information.

"While we're talking, tell me what you know about this bastard Carpenter. I'm going to get him alone with that knife of mine if he keeps it up." Lopez knew that Carpenter was number two to Pelligrini in the family, and was personally responsible for most of the opium that came through from the Mediterranean.

"So, this Italian with the English name is so close to Pelligrini that he's treated like a son. That will be the way I end our partnership. Killing Carpenter will be a huge pleasure, and I'll do it so everyone knows it was a Colombian who did it." His anger sated, he thought again of a woman. A peacock in Italian silk.

Eduardo had most of his operation in Guatemala, tied very close to more than one rebel group, and had pipelines going into Mexico, up the Pacific Coast, and south into Costa Rica. He had operatives throughout Latin America, and was instrumental in setting up the Lopez operation. He made the calls to get his boats ready, and alerted his people in San Jose, Costa Rica.

Chapter Seven

Pelligrini and Lopez had eyes and ears in high places, in Washington and other countries where their operations could be compromised. If the Soviet Union could put moles in the CIA, certainly crime syndicates could do the same to investigative organizations. Of course, the opposite is a given as well, with undercover agents working in both Pelligrini's and Lopez's operations. It was just a chance meeting between Lopez's Eduardo and the FBI's Carmen Santiago, but the results brought several forces into play.

"The way I understand it Eric, Lopez is going to send out some kind of fast speedboat or something to intercept Caldwell when he enters Costa Rican waters. It looks like our idea of creating a target may have been already set in motion.

"What do you know about this Eduardo? My reports here are from a field plant, and she is vague on who he is or how high he is in the Lopez group. All I have is a comment by Eduardo that well armed speedboats are going to intercept an FBI agent in Costa Rican waters. Caldwell is the only one he can be talking about."

There was a slight pause before Eric Petersen came onto the scrambled radio phone from his cutter. "Katie, I'm going to turn your questions over to Deacon. He's been putting together a dossier on everybody we know who is connected to Lopez. He has copies of the files from Washington, most put together by Sami, that he brought with him when he joined me here. He'll get back to you later today with some answers."

Katie Dollarhide was at her desk in the Federal Building in Sacramento, California, pouring over her own files from Sami, and from other agents in Latin America, including notes from Santiago. "I hope that big dumb bastard is going to be OK. Shit, I like that guy, Eric. What's his timetable?"

"He's leaving territorial waters today, Katie, so it's just a few days he'll be in Costa Rican territory. Deacon is his contact, and according to him, they arranged for no contact between them unless originated by Caldwell. In other words, he's alone out there. We can't get a message to him because he won't have a radio on."

"Deacon allowed that? OK, well, I wouldn't have given permission if someone had asked. Begin a surveillance Eric, and lets see if we can find him. Or one of those boats Eduardo was talking about. Damn. You tell Deacon that's not procedure, and from now on, either side can originate contact.

"I'll wait for his call, but tell him to get on his horse. I don't want that man dead."

Katie Dollarhide put the phone back in its cradle and put her head down on the desk. "Well, isn't this just a great puddle of bullshit. I really do like Caldwell, wouldn't mind seeing more of him. I can't let my mind work this way, can't think of him as a man, he's an agent, and he's heading for big time trouble. What the hell was Deacon thinking about, not allowing for contact?" She stood up from her desk and paced around the office, muttering, shaking her fist at the air, scowling, and muttering some more, often using those famous four letter words she's known for within the agency."I've got to get down to San Jose right away."

San Jose is the capital of Costa Rica, a big sprawling city in a very small country, but like so many cities around the world, one in which one could hide for years. "When I get there I'm going to have to depend on Eric and Deacon to keep me advised on where Jason is. I won't be able to contact Carmen Santiago or anyone else down there. What's worse, I'm going to have to work out of the embassy." Her mind was filled with thoughts of how to save Jason Caldwell first, and then how to bring down Eduardo and his speedboats.

"Jeremy, I need you in here now." Jeremy acted as secretary, confidant, and sometimes agent in the Sacramento office, and attended law classes in the evenings. He had been assigned to Katie Dollarhide for the duration of the current investigation and relished the opportunity to be in on some heavy bureau work.

"I need a diplomatic passport and identity, Jeremy. I'll be leaving for San Jose, Costa Rica tomorrow morning, so don't waste any time. You need to contact John Chandler in headquarters and tell him what I just said. No one else, just Chandler. Tell him I also need an office at the embassy, and no one is to know my real identity, and I mean no one. I will also need as secure a phone line as is possible when I get there.

"I don't have time to be nice about any of this. Tell John Chandler our new duck is becoming a pigeon and I'm on the trail. He'll know what that means. Remember, don't talk to anyone but John Chandler. When they ask who's calling before they connect you, tell them Katie Dollarhide. Anything you hear during the next 24 hours is as high a security matter as there is possible, and you are now part of this. We have an agent sailing into a trap, and I'm going to save him. Jeremy, I know you're still learning the ropes around here, but right now, I need absolute security and integrity. Don't let me down."

It was another hour before Deacon called, and Katie reamed him in every language she spoke. He apologized and said he was afraid that there might be too many ears listening to radio messages. He said he would never do it again, and if Caldwell did get hold of him, he would change the protocol.

"By the way, Katie, we gave him a name to use. Just like you joked, we call him Butterball."

She roared with laughter, the first time she'd been able to laugh in a long time. "That's perfect, Deacon. Butterball. Oh, God, how will I be able to call him that with a straight face." They laughed for a while longer and then got to the business at hand.

"Who the hell is Eduardo, what the hell is this about ocean going speedboats, and how the hell does Lopez know about Caldwell or about his plans to sail down the coast? Deacon, we have some serious problems with our security on this investigation. Tell me what you know, and then tell me about how a mole would get so well placed in the bureau."

"Eduardo Rios is Colombian, Katie, and helped Lopez build his Coca business. He's actually number two in the Lopez cartel, and is a procurer. Anything Carlo Lopez wants, Eduardo Rios gets. Sami actually had dinner with him once, went dancing afterward, and had him believing she was going to write a fine article about him for some obscure Latin American magazine. He provided her with quite a bit of information, as you can imagine.

"As for those boats, I don't have any information at all. There are ocean going speedboats of course, they have races all the time, but I couldn't tell you if that's what Eduardo was telling Carmen or not."

"OK, what about this security breach? Everything we do is known to Lopez and Pelligrini. That means there is at least one person, maybe more, very high in the bureau, who's a mole. My God, Deacon, Caldwell hasn't been at sea for a week, and they already have him made. Where he's going, what he's driving, who the hell he's screwing, for all I know.

"Think about this problem real hard, Deac. Somebody needs to be found out. If I need anything else, I'll get back with either you or Eric."

Her mind was on this possibility of a mole, and continued talking out loud, mainly to Jeremy. "The Deacon has been with us a long time, Jeremy, and if anybody can find the bastard, I think it would be him. You know, he's been with us for so long, and used his code Deacon for so long, I'm not sure I can even remember his real name.

"He's a good man, Jeremy."

"What would give away a spy in the agency?"

"I guess being in the wrong places often, making unauthorized decisions, getting other agents to talk too much. We're a pretty tight ship, Jeremy, and it's hard to accept that someone I may have worked very close with is trying to scuttle the operation."

***

By noon the next day, Katie Dollarhide was at her desk in the American Embassy in San Jose, Costa Rica. By 2:00 p.m., local time, she was informed by John Chandler from Washington that Carmen Santiago had disappeared. "I fear the worst, Katie. Somebody somewhere knows what we're doing and when we're doing it. Watch your ass, beautiful."

She went to a restaurant in the heart of the capital, one that catered to Americans, and there're plenty of them in Costa Rica, and ordered a hamburger and fries, with a chocolate milk shake. "That's plenty American. I wonder sometimes if some of our so-called secret codes are just too damned trumped up?" But the code works.

"Hi. What part of the states are you from? Didn't sound like Kentucky or Tennessee to me." The man sidled onto a stool next to Katie, and brushed his hand across her thigh. No one saw the crumpled piece of paper that was left there.

"Actually, it's Virginia. How about you? I hear a way down south accent there, somewhere." Her hand covered the note, and when he offered to shake hands, she tucked it into a pants pocket. "This is my first time here. Where would a girl get a good ol' American dinner around here?"

"Best place is Enrico's. Maybe we'll meet again."

Back at the embassy, Katie contacted Petersen, steaming south from Northern California waters. "Carmen Santiago has probably been eliminated, Eric. Another agent filled me in. Where's Jason? How much time do we have left, and where the hell are you?"

"A freighter with a Zodiac dropped off a big load of shit just south of Mendocino and we tried to catch him. Got into some coastal traffic and we couldn't tell one freighter from another. This really sucks, Katie. They know where I am and how to evade me every time."

"Our man is now entering Costa Rican waters, and I'm heading south as fast as this old frigate will go. Doing 30 knots right now. I'm still days out."

"Is there any chance we can get some air surveillance, Eric? That guy is going to get attacked and he won't know it's coming."

"I already checked, and he's too far out of our territorial waters. We couldn't send an aircraft out unless there was already a declared emergency, and we sure as hell don't want to do that."

The talk was short and brief, and Katie returned to the coffee shop, hoping for another meeting with her contact. He must have been following, expecting such an encounter.

"So, one hamburger isn't enough?"

"Show me some of the sights." They left and walked down a crowded street, and she outlined the problem. "We have an agent coming down the coast in a converted fishing trawler. He's just entered Costa Rican waters if our information is correct, and to make it worse, we're unable to contact him. This is what Carmen was working on.

"I need some eyes out there to find him, and to let me know exactly where he is. Find him and report to me immediately. Call this number at the embassy, it's as secure as we can make it. I won't leave until I hear from you. Good hunting."

It was five hours before she got the word that Jason was berthed at Puntarena, and possibly headed to San Jose, five hours that she sat at her desk thinking about him. "Why can't I get this man out of my mind? He's become so much more than an operative. I want to see more of him, but this isn't natural. I'm not like this.

"Butterball. What a great name. I would definitely enjoy feeling my hands grab those love handles, feel his weight on me. Damn, girl, he's the widower of a friend of yours, what the hell are you thinking?"

She spent lots of time picturing the two of them in erotic positions, and had worked herself into a fit by the time the phone call came in.

"I really didn't think he would come ashore. This will make it a little easier for me to warn him off. Keep a close eye on him, for me, and let me know where he goes." Her mind was back on the case at hand, but the pictures continued to linger, and she found herself not wanting to let them go.

Chapter Eight

It had been a year since I lost Sami. I acquiesced to the FBI and the Coast Guard, and at least in their eyes, I was now a retired Coast Guard Captain, with all the proper phony paperwork. I had met my contacts, I knew all the secret words and phrases, the money was being deposited in my accounts, and I was on my way to the Caribbean and what? That's a huge 'what.'

The FBI assigned one person to an agent who was working under cover, and that was for his safety only. Of course, I knew Katie Dollarhide, I knew Commander Eric Petersen, and I actually got to meet John Chandler, briefly, but the only person I was supposed to deal with was my direct contact. He worked under the name The Deacon, and if not in person, say by way of radio or something, we had a less than elaborate code to use to verify each other's legitimacy. However, on this mission, Deacon was not to contact me. I could attempt contact, but only in dire emergency. I had to admit I was not comfortable with the plan.

I didn't know Deacon's real name, and supposedly, he didn't know mine. All he knew, I was assigned to undercover work along the Pacific Coast of California, and Central America, and some surveillance work in the Caribbean. He let his guard down one day, though, and told me how much he loved my Sami. I felt good knowing that.

"Tell me again, Deacon, why this code sounds so phony to me." It really did, and we had talked about it before.

"If we're on the radio, and I'm calling you on your boat, there will be a delay before you answer. You must remember that delay. It's designed to make this sound like a less than clandestine conversation. Simply come on the radio and say you're still trying to get your pants on, or something like that. The more simple we keep this, the less someone listening might think there is something going on."

"It just sounds so phony, Deacon, but, I'll do it." Deacon smiled and thanked me in his normal slightly formal manner. He always gave the impression he was trying to impress someone. Me? I doubt it, I think it was just his manner, the same as he was always dressed precisely, never a crease out of place, a button missing, a stain of breakfast egg on his lapel. Being pretty much a slob myself, I noticed these things.

Somewhere in Deacon's past, he was trained into this behavior, military school or active service maybe, a formal education abroad in a classical country like Italy or Greece? The Deacon was tall and thin, always wore black suits with classic white shirts and striped ties. Probably where he got his code name. The Deacon. It fit, and we got along well.

One other time, he gave himself away when he started talking about one of my films from a few years ago. He wasn't supposed to know who I was, but knew just about every film I had ever produced. I was worried about this and approached Dollarhide with what had happened.

"It's a breach of protocol, Jason, but not something we have to worry about. Remember, Sami was one of the best agents this bureau has ever had, and you're her husband. Just about everybody in the agency knows who you are. Only a few however, know you're an agent. The Deacon obviously knows, but he's also your contact, so it's OK.

"I really don't think it will mean anything, Jason. If he does try to find out too much about you, make sure you tell me. The Deacon has been with us a long time and is a fine agent. He'll make you a good contact."

***

There was so much interplay between the foreign drug sources and dealers, and the distributors and dealers in this country, the FBI had become increasingly a part of the war on drugs. Dollarhide and Petersen both told me Washington looked on the drug problem almost as a national security risk. The only way the FBI can get in on the action was by way of an internal security risk.

"The way we see it," Dollarhide told me one day, "is that drug money has become political money, and by way of politics, is having an effect on American government. Therefore, a security risk. We have politicians from every level of government involved in the drug economy, we have police agencies with more dealers than the local street action.

"People talk about a drug culture without knowing just how deep it is. Meth is becoming as much a problem as crack, and like crack, can be made in the damn kitchen. There is more death from the combined illegal drug trade than from any other cause."

I was always under the impression that a snort or two of cocaine or smoking a joint or two was just a casual thing. I mean, what the hell, I drank a martini or two a couple of nights a week, but of course, the gin makers were licensed by the government, and the distribution was controlled and taxed. Marijuana was slowly fitting in that category, but I doubt that heroin or cocaine ever will.

Some of the heroine that was distributed was more poison than narcotic. And right now, underworld gang wars over control of those two brought death and destruction worldwide, and coupled with the death and destruction brought by the users trying to get enough money to buy the shit, we had lots of blood flowing.

I found it interesting when one of my trainers said more food stamps used today go toward buying meth or speed than go for food. They were a hell of a commodity, he said, and brought almost face value, the same as real money.

Eric Petersen and I had a conversation about pot one day, and he went about five steps up the ladder as far as I'm concerned. "I've heard you say you expect pot to be legalized and taxed someday. Have you really given that any thought, Jason?"

"Unlike so much of the illicit drug trade, pot almost stands in a corner by itself," I said. "It isn't the big bad bogey man like heroin. It has medicinal qualities, and obviously is easily distributed."

"That's just my point. How would you go about making a truckload of gin, or a boatload of beer? It would be quite a complex operation. Because of that, legal distribution and taxing is relatively easy. Making the breweries and distilleries legal, and taxing their product gives them a hell of an advantage. It would be impossible to threaten their operations.

"But with pot, remember it's a weed, Jason. Just drop a few seeds. Anyone almost anywhere can grow it. To claim a market would be impossible. That's also why crank is so hard to control. Virtually any bathroom will do.

"No, my friend, I don't see the day that pot is taxed. Laws may be made more lax, but I don't see a day when the stuff will be totally legal. Some pot farms are being created and regulated, and illegal farms flourish. Some distributors are being licensed and illegal distributors are increasing in number. To reach the beer and wine stage is a long way down the line and the criminal element will fight it all the way."

The man had an argument that was hard to refute, and I didn't even try.

***

So far anyway, none of the blood that flowed was mine. There hadn't been any attempts on my life that I know of. I didn't carry any kind of weapon or anything that would give me away as an operative of the FBI. One thing, though, I had stayed away from the Ft. Bragg police department. They too had never contacted me, which I found very strange. They had just washed their hands of the 'Sami Affair.' This might be what Petersen and Dollarhide meant when they said the drug scene was almost a national security concern.

It seemed obvious to me, officers inside the Ft. Bragg Police Department were connected somehow with the death of Sami. There was no other valid reason I could think of to let a murder investigation end, particularly after losing one of their own cops. The entire scene was incredible. Look at how the FBI had responded to losing Sami, and the Ft. Bragg department didn't seem to give a damn that one of their own went down.

***

The sea had been lovely and my trip from Noyo Harbor to San Jose, Costa Rica had been nice and quiet. As soon as I slipped south of Morro Bay on the central California coast I could feel the air warm up. I put myself about 150 miles off the coast coming down, and started peeling off my clothes on the second day out. Whales, dolphins, and schools of tuna were my companions, and I hadn't seen any other boats or airplanes. Those airplanes were what bothered me most. A quick strafing run or a drop of some grenades or a bomb or two, and it would be all over before I could even respond.

I don't move about the boat that there wasn't an M-16 close-by, but after two weeks, my level of suspense had dropped considerably. Warm tropical air, the delightful sound of blue water, as it split *D'Anne's* bow, a fresh tuna steak from time to time, and I was relatively calm. It was just two days ago I caught that Yellow Tail, and there was nothing left. This was the trip Sami and I planned, and as delightful as the cruise was, it was wrong. I was having a difficult time controlling my anger, and I knew if someone crossed me, I would really explode. That made for a dangerous situation. I had never been good at anger management in the first place, and coupled with this overwhelming loss, my anger created a volatile situation.

My armament was well hidden as I pulled up to the docks in Puntarena, and my papers were in order. Passport, visa, shot record, boat's papers, everything just so perfect and entirely fake. Not my name, not my boat's name, proper shot record, but not for Jason Caldwell. One thing, the FBI knew how to make up identification papers. I was cleared quickly and made the short run to the fuel dock. It took a lot of number two diesel to keep *D'Anne* humming along, and I topped the tanks to the tune of six hundred gallons on my Visa card. I also put another fifty gallons of fresh water in the holding tanks and made the long taxi ride to downtown San Jose. There were still some high browed sailors who didn't think refitted trawlers should be docked with their fancy yachts, but I remembered a bumper sticker I saw on a big rig once. "Owner operator. I drive it my way." I liked that. Fuck 'em.

Costa Rica was a beautiful little country, just north of Panama, and didn't face the terrible political problems some of its neighbors had to live with. My plan, listen to me, I sounded like I knew what I was doing, my plan was to spend a day or two, possibly meet some locals, and just be around. I knew already I would eat too much.

San Jose was the capital of Costa Rica and could be dangerous. Petit theft was rampant with tourists the number one target. One had to be on alert. I kept my pockets closed with strips of Velcro, and if quick and light fingers were to try and get into one of them, I would hear and feel it right away. At least, I hoped I would. *D'Anne*, sported the name *Molokai II*, was locked up tight, and I could use something in the tum-tum other than my own cooking. I was a great cook, I mean that, I really was, but even great cooks need a night out once in a while.

Sometimes we Americans kid about the number of Mexicans in Southern California, but the reverse of that joke was the number of Americans in Costa Rica. It seemed that Americans outnumbered Costa Ricans two to one, and particularly in San Jose. Restaurants and nightspots flourished, and I found one that wasn't too gaudy, settled in at the bar with a martini on the rocks, and watched the local action.

Big steaks were grilling over open coals in the kitchen, fresh tropical breezes were wafting the aroma around the joint, and my eyes were very absorbed in the moves of a cocktail waitress when my field of view was obscured by a gorgeous blond named Katie. I was not prepared for this. In fact, during briefing I had been told repeatedly that if I ran into someone from the agency other than my own contact, I was to ignore them completely, and if possible, get the hell out of there.

I downed the martini in one gulp, got up from the stool and started to leave. Katie cut me off. "It's all right Jason. We're breaking another protocol. Get on your boat and get the hell back to U.S. waters as soon as you can. Don't ask questions, just get the fuck out of here. Put your radio on one-two-two point seven."

I had never taken orders kindly. Never had, really, but this time I just nodded curtly, walked out of the bar and headed for the *D'Anne*. I walked fast, but tried not to look as terrified as I felt. This was really stupid. I hadn't done one single thing since Sami was killed, for these agencies or against these bad guys, and now somebody wanted to off me. It was miles back to the docks, and I urged the taxi driver on. I would gladly have paid any speeding ticket he might have got.

When you know your boat as well as I know *D'Anne*, I felt sure no one had been aboard during my time ashore, but I still checked her over carefully as soon as I had cleared the harbor. If you took a look at a map, you would see it's a long way, though from the docks to blue water, through the Pacific Ocean end of Golfo de Nicoya, finally clearing land at Cabo Blanco, and I didn't want any surprises inside this huge bay, or for that matter in Costa Rican territorial waters, and those extended out some 200 miles. Those first many hours were tense indeed, and as soon as I hit open-ocean, I set my radar for maximum distance, and went about preparing my defenses.

Rifles, grenade launchers, flare guns, and I even brought out my ten pound bag of frozen meat loaf sandwiches, just in case I didn't feel comfortable leaving the wheel house. This was not the tropical cruise I had been looking forward to. Not, indeed. Wasn't I complaining just a short time ago about not having been involved in a single agency situation? Well, It looked like I was about to be in one.

On a northwest heading, I cleared Costa Rican territorial waters on the second day, and fell into the rhythm of a long ocean cruise. I slept in two or three hour shifts, ate a bite, inspected the boat for engine or other mechanical problems, checked my position on the satellite navigation system, made log entry, and scanned the horizon and sky. I had a small open deck built just behind the wheelhouse, and I brought a deck chair up, along with a cooler, some books, my lap-top computer, and settled into my nest.

No surprises was the order of the day, and the radar alarm was set, the radio was turned to loud, and I had a Corona Beer, a meat loaf sandwich, and a copy of Homer's Iliad. And enough butterflies and tremors to keep me awake for days. It, of course, was the radio that woke me up.

"Butterball, Butterball, this is The Deacon, you got your ears on?"

I fought as hard as I could not to have to use that code, but I lost. Butterball, my ass. It took two steps and I was in the wheel house. "Hello Deacon, I'm still putting my pants on. Over." They really went all out with their codes and responses at the FBI. This was strange, though. Right from the beginning, Deacon said he would not be contacting me, that only I would be doing the contact. All that must have changed, including the new radio frequency setting that Dollarhide gave me.

"Lobster dinner with the Viking, Butterball. Probably Sunday. More later."

And that was the end of the transmission. That meant I would be making a rendezvous with the Coast Guard Cutter *Roosevelt* sometime on Sunday, which was still a few days from now. It also meant that we would not be in U.S. waters when we met. I was still a long way from that kind of safety. At eleven knots, we just didn't go fast, and this could also mean that there was stepped up activity as far as I was concerned. This was not good news, I kept telling myself. I wasn't with Katie long enough for her to tell me what was going on, what to watch for, and now The Deacon simply said to prepare for a lobster dinner on Sunday. Secrecy was really the shits.

I had to stay busy or I'd go nuts, and a full inspection of my boat was in order. My engine room was large since the hold for trawl nets and other fishing gear had been removed. I had plenty of room for a workbench, cupboards for extra parts, filters, tools and my own fishing equipment, which was plenty. I had even installed a large chest type freezer, and could keep about a year's supply of meat, fish, fowl, veggies, and fruit. Even ice for cocktails, thank you.

This was my home after all, and despite my current problems, I loved my home. No badass druggies were going to sink the *D'Anne*, not if I was alive, anyway. Chores done, I went topside, got a pail and rope and took a saltwater bath on the afterdeck, and had evil thoughts of Katie Dollarhide. I hadn't yet figured out whether I liked that woman. She was not exactly honest with me in the beginning, and she did have a way of ordering me around that grated.

But damn as I'm alive, I would love to get her in that bunk in the forward compartment. I called it a bunk, but it was almost as wide as the bow of the boat, which made it about queen size. I had to have the mattress special ordered, along with bedding. She would fit nicely.

***

It was about five in the morning, all my morning shipboard tasks were done and I was enjoying a third cup of coffee waiting for the sunrise. Tropical sunrises at sea were usually spectacular, and I tried not to miss too many of them. Just being in tropical waters was a calming experience, warm breezes wafted across the bow, long gentle swells came in endless waves of green and blue, maybe a white cap or two from time to time, big soft puffy clouds, so white you were forced to wear dark glasses, and every so often, just when you needed it, a squall full of fresh tropical water splashed from the warm sky. I always tried to save some of that water. It made the best coffee and ice, but ideally, just a splash in a glass of twelve-year-old Scotch was the answer. My little home usually had an escort of dolphins and flying fish, and as most boats, was shadowed from aft by sharks waiting for the garbage detail.

My tropical sunrise reverie didn't last long that morning. When the radar alarm went off, so did the coffee cup. All over me, again.

The blip was about five miles off the starboard bow, and wasn't moving. I was on a collision course, and adjusted my direction to stay at least a mile or more away from the vessel. It was just getting light enough for me to see it was a fishing boat, about thirty feet or so, and it stood dead in the water. It was too far away to tell if there were any people on deck, but as the *D'Anne* came around a point or two to port, the boat fired a flare to catch my attention.

"Hell, baby," I thought, "you already had my attention." What a spot. If this boat was in trouble, I couldn't just ignore their problem. We were several hundred miles at sea, but if this was a trap, I didn't dare move too close. I throttled back just a bit and tuned the radio to one-twenty-five point six, a well used frequency in these waters, and listened for a distress call. There wasn't one.

This could be a trap, or it could mean these guys had lost battery power as well as engine power, and couldn't use their radio. I made a call, but used the code name of my boat, not *D'Anne*.

"Fishing boat dead in the water, this is US registered Molokai Two, do you need assistance?"

This time I got an answer, but not on the radio. The engines on the fishing boat came to life, and it turned out I was looking right down the fuel injectors of a seagoing hot rod with two powerful racing engines that churned the water into froth. I couldn't outrun her, I knew that for a dead-on fact. I guess it was time for that old phrase, 'hull down for action'. "Come on you pricks, I've been nursing some hate, and you're in for it. Come on, bring your shit over here and wear mine."

I brought *D'Anne* head on toward the other craft, put her back in auto pilot, grabbed the two rifles, grenade launcher and bags of ammunition clips and grenades and moved as stealthily as I could to the bow sprit. I sure as hell hoped I could still judge distance.

When they got close enough for me to pick out people on the deck, all with rifles, I emptied a clip in their direction and loaded the grenade launcher. The return fire was short, and I readied the two M-16s for maximum firepower. They were really coming on fast, and I watched as they maneuvered into a position to make a run along my starboard flank. "Good boys, that will make it easy for me to put a grenade right into your wheel house." I wanted to scream my vengeance.

Their bullets were starting to punch holes in my *D'Anne*, and I started punching holes in their puny little boat back. "Shoot my boat, you fuckers, and I'll blow your asses clear back to Sicily. Come on, you bastards, let me show you what this fine little trawler can do to you." I took long slow aim, and managed to hit one of the guys shooting, and watched him fall back onto the deck.

Full automatic fire from two M-16s did keep their heads down. "Just like in training, you bastards. Bursts of two or three, and you're my meat today. Come on, fuck heads, let me show you my ass, boys." I was hot now, screaming at the top of my lungs, even though I knew they couldn't hear me. I pulled the grenade launcher up to my shoulder, and watched as some heavy fire started raking the wheelhouse of the *D'Anne*. They had an M-60 or something equally as nasty on board, but they didn't know where I was. They were still shooting for the wheelhouse and tried to rake the deck. I had the advantage here because they were not trying to keep their heads down, and they couldn't tell where the return fire was coming from, and I had a plan.

This shot wasn't going to be an arch onto the deck, I was going to fire point-blank, straight and level, straight into their command center. I wanted to yell 'pull', but kept control as I fired, and that shot pushed me back onto my haunches. I counted it out loud, "one, two, three, four, fi..." boom. Holy shit, what an explosion. Pieces of that boat went everywhere, along with pieces of some really nasty-ass killers.

The engines of the fishing boat were still churning full throttle, but those guys on board who were still alive had no way to steer the run-away, or kill the power to the engines. The wheelhouse simply didn't exist. I moved along the deck, very carefully, and continued to fire the rifles at the quickly receding fishing boat. It was on fire, and I could see three men trying to get a skiff overboard. They didn't make it before several hundred gallons of fuel exploded in a giant fireball. Those big powerful engines were gasoline powered, and burning gasoline spread across the water. I sprinted to my own wheelhouse and steered my beloved *D'Anne* away from the maelstrom.

God what a mess that wheel house was. Bullets had ripped through everything, took out some of my prized electronics, broke glass, wrecked bulkheads. My work was cut out for me now, but at least I had won the first battle.

It was then I heard the wop-wop-wop of a helicopter, and went back into battle mode. Jesus, these guys had armament. I had fresh clips in both M-16s but really didn't think I would be a match for a chopper gunship. I switched the radio back to my agency frequency, one-two-two point seven and was about to holler a mayday when a cool and professional voice came on.

"Nice shooting Butterball. This is Deacon. Got your pants on yet? By the way, big guy, don't shoot the helicopter down, I don't like to swim."

The big Coast Guard helicopter with pontoons landed in my lee when I brought *D'Anne* to a full stop. I got the skiff out and went over to the chopper. It was Katie's face I saw first, then my agency contact, and a couple of CG seamen.

"That was a hell of a show, Jason. What did you use, a cannon?" Katie was all smiles when I helped her and Deacon into the skiff for the ride back to my boat. Even the Deacon had a grin on his face.

"Do you think it's over?" I asked. I didn't but I wanted to hear what these two so-called specialists were thinking. One boat with a few guys on it with rifles? Not the big hit I was expecting, and there could still be an airplane showing up. I was pretty wired from the short battle, and didn't want to be caught with my pants really down. There was something about that kind of danger that was thrilling. My system was on fire, and I felt I could have gone on fighting for days. "Bring on the whole fucking Mafia." I shook my fist at the sky as I screamed the words, and it did help a little. How much adrenaline does one pump when danger of that magnitude was faced square on? I felt like I had at least a gallon surging through my system.

I eased the skiff up to the boarding platform at the stern, jumped aboard and tied off. When I opened the gate, I helped Katie and Deacon on board. Deacon gave me a hell of a surprise when he jumped to attention, threw one smart salute and asked permission to board.

So, Mr. Deacon, FBI agent, you were also an active duty CG or Navy?

"As I recall there is a tradition in the old navies about a shot of grog each day. From now on, there is a tradition on board the *D'Anne*, that following battle, there will be rum and brandy passed among the crew. Come below fellow warriors and scare the shit out of me some more."

So far, I had done almost all the talking, and they had let me. When I looked back, they wouldn't have been able to stop me anyway. The danger was mostly passed, in essence I had won this part of the battle, and the best way to come back down to a normal level was to talk your head off. That was what I had always done. It was while I was pouring the shots that we heard the helicopter take off. Once again, shit went everywhere, and I hit the wheelhouse at a dead run, through that narrow door and up that stairway. I knew there would be more trouble, I knew it.

Katie and Deacon were behind me, but not in a rush, and they brought the bottles and the glasses, new ones since I broke the others. "Just keep adding to the mess already created by bullets and debris." I eased up a bit.

"I'm on patrol Butterball. Remember, lobster dinner on the *Roosevelt*, Sunday for sure." And the radio went quiet. It only took a couple of minutes to get *D'Anne* back underway and on course. I hadn't lost any of the major electronics in the battle, so autopilot and radar were on and operating. I grabbed a couple more deck chairs, and we went out onto the little deck behind the wheelhouse and toasted the adventure.

"Tell me the story, Katie."

She was in the bright green deck chair, hair streamed in the breeze, long legs crossed, one ankle kept time to a nonexistent melody. Maybe the song of the sea.

"Was it D.H. Lawrence who wrote, 'the sea is cold, but contains the warmest blood of all'? I think so." Katie was wearing a pair of jeans and a sea blue tank top with only Katie underneath. I had a hard time understanding this, but she was even wearing makeup, lipstick, eye stuff, and a very exotic, erotic perfume. Was this how Katie went into combat? At this moment she looked more like a Guess? model.

"Actually, Jason, all hell has broken loose in the last couple of days, more so than anyone expected.

"We got wind of the planned hit on you just the day before I found you in San Jose," she said. "As soon as you left the harbor, we picked up Manuel Carlos Lopez, but he had already dispatched that fishing boat to hunt you down. Alberto Pelligrini would not surrender when our agents met up with him in Puerto Rico, and he is now dead. Lopez uses the name Carlos, sometimes Carlo, and is being charged with Sami's murder in federal proceedings, but we'll have to do that extradition stuff. We may have put a lid on some of his people in Colombia."

Katie was biting her lip, staring at Jason. "We didn't intend for you to be this kind of target, Jason. They knew who you were, what kind of boat you had, where you were going. Jason, they knew as much about your mission as you did. Carlos has another boat like the one you just blew up, and we don't know where it is, so we are going to have to be at the ready."

She told me about the meeting in San Juan the agency found out about, and figured Lopez got his information from Pelligrini's men. "This Pelligrini is the answer to most of our current confidentiality problems, Jason. He knew what we were going to do at the same time we did. Now, the bastard's dead. Lopez is like most of the other Colombian drug distributors I've met. Arrogant as the day is long. He offered our intelligence officer a Cuban cigar. A Cuban cigar!" We couldn't help laughing at the irony and less than subtle belligerence.

"Katie," I said, "how did they get onto me that fast. I never did one single thing for or with the agency except learn some dumb pass words, and meet The Deacon here."

"There's one big leak somewhere, Jason. Actually, two big leaks, one in my own agency, and one in the police department at Ft. Bragg. We were hoping that your actions would flush out our leak, but we never got a chance to work on it. As for those traitors in Ft. Bragg, I think we'll get them." Katie's face didn't have that glow of the winner. We had just sunk an enemy boat, killed the crew, and didn't lose a soldier. She should be cheering, and she looked like she was going to cry. Me too.

Ft. Bragg. Every time I heard the name, I saw pictures of Sami. It had been more than a year, these thoughts should have slowed down, but they hadn't. I vowed that I would put an end to this story. "Sami," I murmured, "I will. You will not have died in vain."

Deacon was looking at all the electronics in the wheelhouse as we talked, and I moved inside to answer any questions, if he had them. "Nice stuff, huh Deac?"

He picked up an M-16, aimed it right at me and said, "sure is, ass-hole." I dove through the open door, over the rail and crashed to the deck below as the rifle fired. I heard two more shots and one loud scream, before I hit the deck below and knocked myself out.

I came to, my head throbbed from the thump it took, and was bleeding like crazy. I was looking straight into those blazing eyes of Katie Dollarhide. "Damn shit that hurt. What the hell happened?"

"We know where the agency leak was, Jason. You OK?" Katie looked over the rail at me as I tried to get up. She had a nice little 9mm automatic in her hand,

and now carried that wonderful smile. She was definitely gaining points with me every time we met. She came down to the main deck with a wet towel and tended to my head. Heads bleed a lot, and mine was making nasty puddles on the decking.

"Just hold still, Butterball. I know it hurts, but this cold water will stop the bleeding."

"You're using sea water, sweetheart, and the friggin' salt hurts."

She thought that was pretty funny, wrapped my head in the towel, gently, and gave me a little nudge in the ribs. "Come on, you big baby, you'll live."

"That was too close for me. I think I heard that bullet fly past my head. Holy shit, Katie. Did you have any ideas about Deacon? Was this another one of your set ups?"

Katie screwed up her face, and answered very slowly. "This was not a set up, Butterball. I had no idea Deacon was a mole, none. Please believe me, this is a complete surprise. I know that when we first got started, I sort of held things back from you, but this situation is all yours, and I'm not holding anything back.

"I'm so glad you're OK. That was as close as it's going to get, I hope. Shit, Jason, he had you in his sights, all I did was react." She took me into her arms, and any thoughts that she was not acting in my best interests went away. Her body melded to mine, and we just stood there, swaying gently in rhythm to the waves and wind. The tropics, and combat, had a wonderful affect on the libido, not to mention nursing from an angel.

Training pays off I guess. She saw the gun aimed at me, saw me dive over the railing, heard the shot, and blew Special Agent/ Dirty Bastard Deacon into that other place. "I owe you my life, blondie."

"I didn't put two and two together, Jason, but I can now. Deacon asked for this assignment, not because he loved Sami, or wanted to get in on the drug interdiction thing, but he told me and John Chandler, he wanted to get back to sea. He said he could be an agent, and work on a Coast Guard cutter.

"We bought it, Butterball. We bought it, and you almost did." And there was that look again. "I should be dancing, Jason, but now it's time to be just a little bit terrified. If Deacon sold us out, and Lopez and Pelligrini both know where you are, and their own man is going to finish up, if they don't hear from him, they'll come calling again. I know, Pelligrini's dead and Lopez is in custody, but the organization still exists. There are still people running things." She got pensive again. "There has to be another person undercover in our bureau, Jason. Deacon has been on the *Roosevelt*, but all our orders are coming straight from John Chandler's office. Somebody in his office is also a mole.

"It's interesting, but my intern, Jeremy, asked how one would be able to discover a mole, and I outlined what I would be looking for. And then didn't look for what I had outlined. I think The Deacon fit most of what I'd said, but it didn't register with me."

I spent the next few minutes putting stuff on a couple of cuts, and Katie hovered around like a mama bear would. She is the most beautiful woman I've ever met, I think, and no doubt the most beautiful woman who ever saved my ass.

"Tell me about Alberto Pelligrini. How would a man like that get trapped and killed, actually on his own turf?"

"He did love Puerto Rico, and came often. Members of his council, I guess would be the best way to describe them, met with him at a large sugar cane plantation he owns, and we knew of his plans to be there. He was going to meet with various distributors and dealers. Big boys in the organization.

"A couple of agents found him off his own grounds and called for help. He was with four bodyguards, and the agents got help from Puerto Rican police and a couple of undercover DEA agents who were in the vicinity.

"When the bodyguards opened fire on the police, all hell broke loose. We would have preferred capturing him alive, after all, he carried the keys to the vault, Jason. We would have known a lot about the worldwide system he operates. The bodyguards killed one cop, and in turn, after hundreds of rounds fired, the other three bodyguards were dead, and so was Alberto Pelligrini.

"The sad thing, Jason is that politicians all over our own country are demanding an explanation. They are questioning whether Pelligrini should have even been under surveillance, more or less, gunned down. They still think of him as this art-loving philanthropist, not a purveyor of death. I will bet you right now, Butterball, there will be a call for congressional hearings on his death. Bet?"

"A year ago, I would have taken that bet, Blondie. Not now."

She contacted the *Roosevelt* and let them know the situation. "Eric, call John in Washington and tell him what I've said. He has to protect himself also. This is getting completely out of hand. How can these bastards have these kinds of contacts?" The helicopter returned and picked up Deacon's body, but interestingly, left Katie on board with me. We were still two days from Sunday dinner, but the appetizer was being served.

Chapter Nine

Owen Riley of course wasn't his real name, and over the years he had used so many, he often had a hard time even remembering what his real name was. It didn't matter, though. "I'm so rich right now, I could use any name I wanted, and who the hell could tell me no. What a laugh." Riley was one of the main drug dealers in northern California, and was also relatively high up on the chain of command in the Ft. Bragg police department. He worked directly for Alberto Pelligrini, and had for years.

Even though he was always happy when he thought of his money, right now, he wasn't. He just learned of the death of Alberto Pelligrini. "We've spent years setting this operation up, and now, the boss is dead." He picked up the phone and called a local number, waited for an answer, and told whoever answered, "Pelligrini's dead, Lopez is in custody. It's time to protect, and maybe fly away."

He got the call about his boss and the cartel operative from Washington. "Owen, this is Sarah. Alberto just got killed in San Juan. I think they're moving on Lopez too. Carpenter is looking for those agents Dollarhide and Caldwell. Protect yourself, Owen." He knew they would start moving in on Fort Bragg, and it was time for him to start making plans to fight them off. There was too much money involved just to run away, on the one hand, but on the other, he knew how the feds operated, and he wasn't going to be part of their plans.

He didn't wait for any kind of response, just hung up the phone, and started thinking about what to do.

"This was such a sweet deal, but the best thing to do now is close it down. It all goes back to that little Bertorelli bitch. Lopez should never have had her killed, and particularly not here. Hot headed damned Latin bastard. Pelligrini's men hated working for him, and now I know why. If this whole thing goes down, it's because he got pissed at an agent and blew her away in our own fucking front room.

"Shit. One thing though, I never suspected she was a federal agent. A friggin' school teacher for Christ sake. Funny though, nobody from any of the federal agencies has been snooping around. We must have convinced them about that robbery thing. Just the same, I'm making arrangements to get the hell out of here."

He was right, with Pelligrini dead and Lopez in custody, a net has been thrown toward the little fishies. He called Anthony Colletti at the police station and filled him in on what had happened. "Listen, Tony, get the Hummer out, mount those damn machine guns, and be ready to move when I give the word. Get rid of as much paperwork around the station as you can.

"With Pelligrini dead and Lopez in jail, we have to believe there will be federal agents knocking our doors down soon. I don't trust that little Colombian jerk at all." He figured a couple of well-aimed punches or a strong kick to the balls, and Lopez would tell the whole world about the operation.

Colletti was the muscle in the organization, wasn't afraid of using his guns or his fists at any time, and told Riley he'd take care of things. "One thing, Owen, there's a load coming in tomorrow night. Should we call it off?"

Riley loved his money more than he feared danger. "Hell no, we won't call it off. Fuck, Tony, that's a couple of million bucks coming in. Shit no we won't call it off. Handle it just as any other drop."

His mind continued turning over. "How many years have we been organizing this company? I came up from Puerto Rico with Pelligrini and it didn't take hardly any money at all to get these local jerks involved. If there's one thing I've learned over the years, flash a few dozen hundred dollar bills at a cop, and you own him.

"Colletti was the first to nibble, and he still thinks he's making the big bucks. Fucker worked for some of the big boys in New York, but they don't pay shit for his kind of work. He gets $25 or $30 thousand on a drop and he's happy as shit. I bitch about only getting a million. The others just get paid for what they do, and they think they're big time. I got smarter high school kids working for me."

Riley shredded then burned every scrap of paper in his apartment, destroyed his answer machine tape, and went through his two cars meticulously. "I won't let those bastards find anything to nail me on." His mind went back to the one time he had been picked up. It was in Texas when he was 18, and the fear is still part of him. When he closed his eyes he could see the scene, could feel the pain.

***

"Out of the car, prick. Come on, you know the routine. Up against the wall and spread 'em. Spread 'em, asshole." The Texas Ranger was huge compared to Riley's 150 pounds, and the push to the wall was like being hit by a truck. It was the DEA agent that did the most damage.

"When 'The Man' tells you something, fucker, do it." A round house right to the ribs sent Riley flying, and the pain almost caused him to pass out. "You trying to run, prick?" Then it was a boot in the back, in the kidney, and Riley lost consciousness. He woke up in the back of a Suburban, his hands cuffed behind him.

"Where'd you get the shit, prick?" The Ranger didn't wait for an answer and blasted him in the face with a fist, breaking Riley's nose, blacking an eye. "Answer me, asshole." The Ranger got a smile on his face and pulled his revolver out and pointed it right at Riley's nose. The barrel of the revolver was touching the end of his nose, and Riley was crying like the baby he was.

"What do you think, puke? You think I won't pull the trigger?" He cocked the hammer back, and the DEA agent jumped in.

"Don't do it in the car, Jack." He pulled the car over and the Ranger, Jack, jerked Riley out of the car, slamming his head against the top of the doorway, and kicked him into a drainage ditch alongside the road way.

Jack pulled Riley to his feet, smashed him in the mouth with a fist, and put the gun to Riley's nose again. Riley was crying, screaming, and Jack pulled the trigger, the hammer falling on an empty chamber. The two men almost fell down, they were laughing so hard.

"That little prick wet his pants, Jack. Look at that, he pissed all over himself." They threw Riley back in the Suburban and took him to the hospital, telling the nurses they had to physically subdue him when he tried to escape.

He was questioned while still in the hospital, and it was the Ranger, Jack, who asked the questions. "Come on, asshole, tell me about all this shit you had with you. Tell me before I get angry, little puke," and he slammed a fist into Riley's broken ribs. Riley passed out, and when he came to, both agents were in his room, one on each side of his bed.

He told them everything he knew, even things he didn't know, just to keep them from hurting him more. He talked for several days, and these memories have come back every time there had been even an outside chance he might get caught again.

"They won't ever have that chance again. I'll take on the world with my AK, but I won't be caught. I won't." Riley wasn't tough or brave when he was up against real people, but in his thoughts, he could take care of himself. One good shot to the kisser with four big hard knuckles, and Owen Riley would spill his guts.

But, he could talk tough to himself. He could talk tough to those who worked for him, and he believed in management by intimidation. "Scare those bastards enough, they'll do anything. I've never hit anyone of them, but they think I have, and that's all that counts.

"They think I've killed cops, they think I've killed dealers who turned on me, they think I'd kill them in a fucking second. I know how to run my organization, but that little Colombian fucker scares me. Fuck, he scares me."

***

Lopez was nursing some very sore and broken ribs, unable to eat because of the way they had to wire his jaw, and his right leg was in a cast extending from his pelvis to his ankle. He had talked more than any Colombian in history; talked, cried, begged, whimpered, and screamed. Carlos was finished, and more to the point, so were most of the people who worked for him. He gave out names, addresses, phone numbers of everyone he'd ever known, told agents the complete who, what, where, when, and why of the organization he controlled. He didn't know the names of Pelligrini's people except for a few, and wasn't able to rat on Pelligrini's Washington spies.

Agents were spreading out across North America, Central America, South America, and through Europe and the Middle East. Outside U.S. territory, all the agents in the world were useless unless the local government decided to work with them, and in too many cases, it was the government itself that was involved. Pelligrini money bought more than art and symphony orchestras, and DEA agents along with other federal officers continued to run up against concrete political barriers.

There were some who believed the new world order would be small governments funded in large part by illegal or criminal organizations, which would have enough money to influence larger, stronger nations. Drug money should be measured in metric tons not dollars, and governments near and around Afghanistan, parts of the old Soviet Union, parts of Africa, Asia, and South America were already under that influence. FBI, CIA, DEA, and other U.S. agencies didn't get very much cooperation when they tried to bring down international drug organizations when the governments involved were funded by those same operations.

Even when some of the agencies turned to Washington for help, they discovered far too many politicians who believed, or at least gave the impression they believed that the whole Pelligrini affair was a hoax. More than one senator had been quoted as saying something to the effect of, "Alberto Pelligrini was a fine gentleman, one who cherished the arts, one who would not dirty himself in drug trafficking." Money did wonders for a politician's point of view.

***

Wiley was in New York, pulling every string he knew, getting every member of the extended family in line. He knew just how close the feds were to finding out way too much about all the operations, worldwide. The California coastal portion of the family's influence was big, but certainly not big enough to be the driving force of the international gang. Wiley had to make sure that whatever happened in Fort Bragg didn't spill over into New York, Miami, Italy, Greece, North Africa, South America, or Asia.

"Listen, 'Tonio, I'm trying to tell you. This little fucker Lopez is still alive, and he knows as much as I do about Mr. Pelligrini's business. Mr. Pelligrini made him a distribution partner, and we have got to kill him now. Him and every beaner son of a bitch who works for him.

"We've never been this close to getting closed down. Now, here's what I want you to do. Get with that broad in Washington, the one Mr. Pelligrini brought on board, and make sure she keeps you completely aware of what's going on. Our plant in California got blown away by FBI agents before he could kill Caldwell or Dollarhide.

"I'll see to it those two die, you see to it that all our pipelines are secure. I don't want to lose what we've worked so fucking hard to build. Mr. Pelligrini wouldn't want us to do any less. 'Tonio, listen now. Keep us in business, and don't do anything stupid. Kill that fucking Lopez, and get a line on what the feds are doing.

"I'm gonna go back to Sicily, then down to San Juan, and I'll probably end up in California. I'll keep in touch."

Anthony Torricelli, 'Tonio, was far brighter than Wiley, but he also understood that Wiley was the boss, at least for a while. "Yeah, Wiley. I already got a couple guys lookin' for where they got Lopez. I met that little creep once. Didn't like him then. He's dead, Wiley, he just don't know it, yet."

Lopez was being held in Costa Rica, and that government prides itself on its close contacts with the U.S. government. The local head of the DEA, Fernando Salinas, had jurisdiction in the case, and was working with full cooperation of the local drug investigators.

"We can expect an attempt to silence Mr. Lopez, ladies and gentlemen, so prepare for that. Security alert at the highest level is the order, and Washington wants to know everything this scumbag knows. He's provided us with many names so far, and I think we are all aware that he knows more than he's told us so far. During your interrogation, don't kill him. We must keep him alive.

"We lost a tremendous opportunity when Pelligrini was killed, but this little prick can bring us good information. We must keep him alive at all costs and learn as much as possible from him.

"There is one other thing, and I have to emphasize this. An FBI agent has been found to be a mole, and has been eliminated. He tried to kill another agent involved in this investigation, and was blown away. According to our information, there is probably another turncoat working in the Virginia headquarters.

"Right now, we don't have a line on who this might be, so from today forward, you are to have no contact with FBI headquarters at all. Any information you learn from Lopez is to be given to me only, and I will forward it to those who need to know. The FBI has been compromised, and until they are able to clear the problem, we must protect our information."

Salinas had been in conference calls with his Washington bosses who had been alerted by John Chandler. It was Chandler's idea to keep the FBI out of the Lopez interrogation, and to have the information gleaned from it brought to him personally by the number two at Justice.

"Eric, I want you to pass this to Dollarhide and Caldwell. All contact on this investigation is to go through me only. We have a serious security problem here in Washington and until I can clean up the problem, I don't want our agents doing business with any other agency, or with anyone at FBI except me.

"While I'm on the subject, did you have any idea at all that The Deacon was anything but a dedicated agent? This is so troubling to me, and it means that many of our investigations dealing with Pelligrini may have been compromised."

"John, The Deacon was a former Coast Guard officer. He has shamed himself in two highly respected agencies and brought discredit to both as well. I never had a thought he might be something other than an agent, but it does indicate that we must be rigorous in our continuing efforts to end this current investigation.

"Too many people have died, good people, John. Bertorelli, our agent in Costa Rica, innocent people in Ft. Bragg. We'll end it, but we will have to maintain a strong vigilance."

Chapter Ten

"Just another tropical sunrise, Katie. This is why I get up so early. Colors like this are only talked about. You truly have to be there, cliché that it is." We were having our coffee on the little deck behind the wheel house, just as the sun blasted the tropical clouds into myriad colors and shapes, made the ocean change from its deep late night cobalt, churned its way to a lighter azure, bumped shades of orange and fiery red aside, and saw tiny rainbows in the sea mist and foam thrown about by *D'Anne*, and by the natural waves.

"This is the most exciting time I've ever had, Jason. Full war on the high seas, and then watching you make a pot of coffee. From John Wayne to the Three Stooges, Butterball."

"That's the way you have to do it, Blondie. If you don't anchor that coffee pot, a big ol' wave'll come along and you'll have a hell of a mess, not to mention multi degree burns. We're just a bobbing cork out here." There had been grand laughter earlier as she watched me tie down the coffee pot and measure less than a pot full of water. "It slops all over hell, Blondie. Wait till you watch me cook a pot of rice."

Tables and stoves and other major appliances were bolted to the deck and then small items inside the cabin were gimbaled, and I had that system devised for my coffee making. It looked like the coffee pot was just swaying about, but in reality, it was the boat riding the waves and the pot hanging over the moving flames from the stove.

Dolphins were dancing, and flying fish were flying, and I was having delectable thoughts about

Special Agent Katie Dollarhide. Her thoughts matched mine, and for an extended period I'm very glad there were no party boats to come alongside and ruin our fun. In the tropics, it takes little physical exertion to raise a sweat, and we were both covered in perspiration within a short time. The fun of that though, is washing off with buckets of cool Pacific Ocean water, and then drying each other.

"You splashed that salt water on my open wounds on purpose, didn't you."

The tinkly little snicker answered the question without the use of words. "You're such a baby, Jason. A little scratch on the head. You must be more careful when you're around the railings, captain. You shouldn't fall off high places." Naked as the day we entered this life, we spent some time chasing each other with full buckets of water. And watching the surrounding horizon for possible enemy shipping. The irony of the situation did not escape us, and it was just as hard to remember to look to the horizon from time to time as it was to keep one's footing.

Early in the morning or late in the evening, that little deck is an ideal place to be, but during the rest of the day, one has to be under the upper deck, in the shade, or below decks where a swamp cooler keeps things somewhat under control. Swamp coolers don't work that well in high humidity, but the breeze it kicks up sure feels good. Even at sunrise, the temperature was well over 80 degrees and the humidity was always close to 100 percent in the tropics. There was little reason for clothing.

There was something sensuous about being on the high seas, something maybe a bit esoteric, that allowed one's mind to explore depths it might not if land bound. My vision was unhindered all the way to the horizon in a complete circle, the sky dimpled by tropical clouds, low in the air, heavy with water, naturally colorized, thank you, and the only sound was that of water breaking on the boat's bow, and a thrumming vibration from a powerful diesel engine. It was rare, but from time to time the *D'Anne* was visited by sea birds, as well. It was at times like that that I felt so small, so insignificant. Often I was aware that I was the only human being on the entire planet who knew where I was. That could be frightening on one hand, and empowering on another. Those billions of stars late at night were a blinking, pulsating blanket of infinity. How far out could I see? Or was I only seeing deep inside myself?

I have friends who say they had these same feelings of awe, and unworthiness, when they were alone on a mountain top or in the desert. Since I retired from active motion picture and television producing, I had written three stories that were made into movies by other producers, and all three, deeply intellectual and romantic, were written while on an extended ocean voyage. The sea could make one feel so small, so alone. This adventure I was living meant nothing when matched against things like quasars and comets, compared to the birth of a star, or the raging, frenzied end to a star.

The sea did that to a person, made one understand just how insignificant a puny little human being was when put alongside the immensity of the universe. All these thoughts were flooding my mind while I was standing naked on the afterdeck of my boat, a couple of hundred miles off shore.

A hundred years from now, no, even ten years from now, would the death of those men on that little sea going racer mean anything? Would my involvement in something I don't have serious feelings about mean anything? Sami's death was different, but the war on drugs? Was there a grand meaning to what we were attempting, to what we might accomplish?

Sami and I never got a chance to take a long cruise together, so I simply can't relate what my feelings would have been, but I was well over 150 miles from shore, alone in tropical waters with Katie Dollarhide, fresh from a glorious battle that was part of a war being fought because of Sami's death. I had a deep yearning simply to turn to a heading of South by West, away from the Coast Guard, away from FBI and DEA agents, away from drugs and mafia dons and crooked cops, away to a South Seas paradise that might only exist in my mind. I can't turn away, I was very aware, but I wanted to. If I could, *D'Anne* would become home to an exploration expedition that would extend, not to just our seven seas, but to those very same stars that had enchanted me on every night I had spent at sea.

I also was very aware that during the next few weeks everything I had ever done in my life would mean nothing, and I would probably die. I didn't know why I felt that, but I had this inner dread that I would die trying to avenge Sami's death. I wanted to tell Katie about that, but I couldn't. Instead, I hugged this magnificent specimen, and talked shop. One more way I could keep my mind from exploding with fear, fear of dying, fear of failing, and still, I was filled with a desire for revenge, a way to atone for something I was not responsible for. My rage and hatred spilled to the surface, exploded to the surface during my battle with those on that boat, but all that hatred could not hide my fear.

"Tell me about those cops who were on the take in Ft. Bragg. How do we bring them down?" I was actually saying this. We. Us. Me and Katie. Just a year ago it wouldn't have mattered if I never saw her again, and now we had bedded each other, splendidly I might add, and I was talking as if we could walk into a cop shop that had been infiltrated by the highest levels of criminality, and take it down.

Her green eyes sparkled, her blond hair, matted from tropical exertion, was a mess as it blew about gently. There was a fresh glow in her complexion, and a smile bright enough to challenge the sun greeted my glance at her. "There'll be time enough for that, Butterball. Let's welcome a new day." And she spread a large beach towel on the deck. I didn't argue. The way she moped about yesterday, after killing Deacon, this was heaven.

"It's not easy pulling a gun and shooting someone you have called a friend point blank, Jason. I've known Deacon for several years, and seen him around many times. He was in the DC bureau headquarters for ages. But when he fired that rifle at you, I just instinctively pulled my pistol and shot him. Twice." It was my turn to take her in my arms, and protect her.

We spent most of yesterday just being close and talking. It took a long time, but her natural personality finally started returning. "You blew that fucking boat completely out of the water, Jason. You must have been terrified." She poked me in the ribs, and I grabbed her and we fell onto the deck, and hell, it was fun. That was yesterday.

In the afternoon, I spotted a big commotion on the water, about a mile from our position. "Tuna, Katie. Look at them. They've got a school of baitfish near the surface, and they are chowing down. Ever caught a tuna? Watch the action, Blondie. The tuna have the baitfish near the surface, and they have the school surrounded. Now, they simply dart in, snatch a fish or two and dart back out on patrol. They're the cowboys, keeping the cows herded up. Whales do the same thing in northern waters. We'll put our own bait right in with bait fish, and hang on tight, Nellie."

I brought *D'Anne* close to the melee and killed the engines, rigged a boat rod with a big flasher type lure, and cast it into the swarm of baitfish. If that lure had been in the water for more than five seconds, I'd be surprised.

"Get in the fighting chair there, Katie and buckle up." The fish was about the same size as Dollarhide, and when it hit, I thought she might lose the rod. She whooped, hung on tight, and set the hooks. There was a hell of a fight, at least twenty minutes worth, but she finally brought the blue monster alongside. I had seen Katie Dollarhide when she was in an exuberant mood, but the smile that came from her face was magnificent. She and that tuna were face to face when it came aboard. The *D'Anne* was originally set up as a trawler, and that meant the stern sat low in the water so the big trawl nets could be heaved aboard, full of fish.

"I've never caught a fish this big, Jason. What a fight." She kept a tight line and I gaffed it and brought it up on deck. We spent the next hour or more filleting it out, then cut those big filets into steaks. Katie watched as I tossed the remains overboard and then got out the hose. "Look at those sharks, Jason. Jesus, they're huge."

"Along with the tuna working that raft of bait, there are always sharks. The mean ones are the hammerheads. If you look close, Blondie, you'll also see some dolphins working that bait raft. In our world, this would be the equivalent of a farmer's market, a buffet."

The sharks that generally trail a boat had moved in, and there were other sharks that had joined the tuna in their feeding spree as well, and all of them had converged on the mess that I'd thrown overboard. "Just one more good reason we don't stop and swim from time to time, Blondie."

A water pump gave me the pressure I needed to clean the deck. I accidentally sprayed the hell out of my little blonde friend, and she shrieked in pleasure. This was going to be a fine friendship, I think.

Cleaning the decks was a job done after every fishing session. Scales, pieces of fish from filleting, pieces of bait sometimes, and general clutter could make the deck of a boat pretty damn dangerous. In the case of *D'Anne*, since she was built for fishing, the cleaning process was quick and easy. The rail along the gunwales drained into the sea, as does the stern rail.

The wheelhouse sat close to the bow, up a bit high, and this gave a large deck area in the stern. I built a small deck out behind the wheel house, and this also allowed for plenty of shade in the forward part of the stern where I installed a redwood picnic table, securely bolted to the deck. To the starboard side under that covering was a built in grill and smoker, and nothing tasted better than sitting at that table, sipping some wine or a martini, and eating a fresh caught tuna steak.

"*Roosevelt* can keep the damn lobster, dear heart, we're having fresh tuna on the grill tonight, and I just happen to have a bottle of Napa Sonoma's finest California cabernet blanc." I think we needed that little break, but stopping dead in the water to fish, knowing there may be a fast speedboat armed to the bridge looking for us, probably wasn't too smart.

We had fresh grilled tuna steaks, frozen peaches, and the finest wine I had on board. I wish we were on another heading right now. Someplace else, far away from drugs and murder and traitors. And then, we had each other again.

"How the hell old are you, Butterball?"

"I'm a few years past puberty, Blondie, how about you?" Actually she knew damn well I'm over sixty. I had told her so, but I really didn't know how old she was. Did age matter if the feelings were real? Sami was much younger than me, but we had such a real relationship. That was a strange word wasn't it? Real. True. Valid. Yes, our love was proved valid, genuine. Thoughts of Sami come through at some of the worst times. I was on a bed of beach towels, rolling on the deck of my wonderful *D'Anne*, waiting for a sunset, and I was with a goddess. I was married to a goddess. I couldn't separate them.

Katie Dollarhide was so sensuous, in her personal mannerisms, in eye contact, in reaction to stimulation. Long slow body moves with slightly lowered eye-lids told me it was time to tease, time to stimulate and have fun. Katie could smile and say yes just by the way she looked at me.

"How have you managed to stay single, young lady? I find it hard to believe there aren't half a dozen young, virile special agents hiding in your closet, just waiting for you to beckon them with your delightfully sinful smile."

She nestled into my arms, let her fingers mark time to some jazz piece only she could hear. "When a girl reaches a certain age, Jason, men stop coming around. I went past the forty year mark a couple of seasons ago, and besides, until you came along, I was far more interested in being an investigator than I was in being courted by some bumbling jerk. You don't bumble, Butterball."

As her fingers danced about on my nakedness, and I did like the tune she was keeping time to, I brushed my own fingertips along her thigh, could feel the fine, almost invisible hairs along the well defined muscle, could feel her immediate response. Katie was a tall woman, in excellent condition, could outrun a pony I think, I knew she can outswim me, and she had the most delightful legs. Strong little butt, long muscled thigh, and sinuous calf that led to thin ankle and long foot. Aphrodite in flesh, not marble.

My fingers were greeted by little spasms as she responded to my touch, and as I kissed her shoulder, I could see a slight halo around the skin as the sun outlined her dark body. God I wanted this goddess to be with me forever, to watch those large evocative eyes play about my own body, to feel her fingers probe and stroke, watch as she stretched herself to full length, welcomed me to our bliss. "We do know how to make waves, don't we, Special Agent Katie, love." Just the slightest gasp, the response was purely physical.

***

On Sunday morning, in our own way, we again welcomed the sunrise, but this time there was a hell of a racket that started at the most inopportune time. "Fucking radar alarm," I yelled, and jumped for the wheel house. There was a blip out about five miles, and I grabbed the binoculars.

"It's hard to make out at this distance, Katie, but I think it's the cutter. It's steaming right at us, and making good time. Be prepared, just in case it isn't." We got the arms ready, but it only took a couple of minutes to determine what we were looking at really was the Coast Guard. "Here, look at that picture, Katie. That's something you don't see every day. He must be making close to thirty knots and coming straight for us. Look at that."

"Hello, *D'Anne*, this is Commander Petersen, and the lobster will be served on time."

"And hello to you *Roosevelt*, this is Caldwell. Chill the wine, please, and maybe we could have a tuna steak along with that." The silence that followed took away the fun of the comment.

I could slow and stop *D'Anne* quickly since she was rather small in comparison with what Petersen was sailing. It took him a bit of time to get that big war ship slowed and then come to all stop. He sent a skiff from the cutter after we got both craft sitting dead in the water, and Katie and I headed for the *Roosevelt* while a CG seaman enjoyed the comforts of *D'Anne*. "Deja Vu, Blondie. This is how we met."

"It feels better this time, Jason. I don't know whether to call you Jason, or stick with Butterball."

"Jason is just fine," I said, scowling as hard as I could, and got a nice giggle back. "Are we on any kind of schedule, or would you tell me even if we were?"

"No time schedule, but we do have something to accomplish. This is serious shit I'm about to say, hot shot, so listen carefully. You are a widower because some ass-hole who was supposed to be a cop sold out to gangsters, and I'm in love because of that same prick. He or she goes down, Jason. Down hard.

"Only you know this right now. When we put the final period to the Sami Bertorelli murder case, I'm retired. There are some things I want to talk to you about as far as making a few changes to the *D'Anne*."

It would have been the right time for a radar alarm to go off. I know I had egg on my face, the only thing missing was the cup of coffee all over me. I just sat there in that skiff, riding full and rhythmic ocean swells, my mouth agape, and eyes wide, while this long legged vixen ate me for lunch. "Anything you want, Blondie."

***

Here we were again; Eric (The Viking) Petersen at the head of the table, Katie Dollarhide sat across from me, and all of us in the Officer's Mess on a Coast Guard Cutter, talking about murder, death, gangsters, drugs, and more death.

"It's been a hell of a year, Eric. I just killed several people. I watched them die in a gasoline fuel fire and explosion that I caused, and I don't feel bad about it.

That's wrong. I worry about pennies on my income tax, about parking tickets, and I just killed several people, and I don't have one damn regret. No remorse."

Nobody said a word for a couple of minutes, and then Katie spoke up. "If you hadn't, you wouldn't be here, Jason. I killed The Deacon, point blank. Two shots, one to the chest, one to the head. If I hadn't, neither one of us would be here.

"This is one half of our job. Ft. Bragg is the second half, and when we finish that one, Jason Caldwell, sir, I hope you will feel vindicated. You will have found the justice you talked about during our first meeting.

"Right now, at least I hope, we have a retired agent working at the police station as a janitor. No one knows he's a retired agent except us, and we can't take the chance of making his acquaintance when we get there. We won't be surprised with this guy. Chandler put him in, and only Chandler and I know about it. The Deacon couldn't give this one away.

"What I plan is a full face, wide open investigation, using as many of the Justice Department investigators as we can pull into the case. We'll need to bring the press in, make known to all that Sami was an agent, that she was murdered by agents of the criminal families and drug running cartels, and they had help inside the Ft. Bragg Police Department.

"There will be hell to pay, but if we're right, who ever that bastard is on the inside will make himself known, and flytrap will alert us. It's going to be dangerous as hell, because we won't know who to watch for. Our cover will be blown the minute we arrive in town, if it's not already blown."

This was a bold plan, indeed. Just march right in, no preliminaries, announce to the world that the police department that was supposed to be protecting you had been infiltrated by the mob, was responsible for the death of an FBI agent, two other cops, and a citizen. This could back fire, because there would be all kinds of calls for proof, and angry cries of feds trying to take over, but there was considerable evidence, and if it was offered in the press and public functions, our local asshole could show his colors and try to do something even more stupid.

"Jason," I could tell Katie really didn't want to bring this up, "I don't think the *D'Anne* is the best place for us to work from, and that little B&B in Inverness is too far away. We'll need a safe place, someplace right in Fort Bragg. Someplace we can protect, and use to protect us. Got any ideas? You lived there."

I was not sure that *D'Anne* wasn't the best, but it could be vulnerable, so I decided that I would go along with this. "The first name that comes to mind is Francesca Ripoldi. She owns the coffee house where Sami was killed, but she also has a place on the eastern outskirts of Ft. Bragg, in the hills. We might be able to talk her out of it. She never stays there, and she has never rented it that I am aware. Her feelings about the way the cops handled the murder could put her in our camp. She loved Sami, and tolerated me because I also loved Sami." The memories of the first visit to that little cabin came flooding back. Sami and I drove out there for a weekend. It was practically right in town, but in the oaks and redwoods, and it seemed as if we were miles from anywhere.

I brought enough food for an army and Sami had driven over to Marysville and picked up some really fine wine. One thing about the valleys north of San Francisco, they do provide some of the best wine in the world, and we had several bottles. The old cabin had a massive fireplace, and we set up our nest right in front of it, and only got out of bed to cook something or stoke the fire. This was the weekend I asked Sami to marry me, and it was the weekend we discovered more about each other than any two people should know.

Amazing when I look back that all the time Sami and I were together, she never once indicated she might have a clandestine life away from university, away from me. Was this lying, or was it personal protection? I would never know of course, but I would feel better if I knew. Maybe. I had been telling myself that she would have told me. Our love was so deep, she would have told me. But then, I also told myself I wasn't running away. And, I was arrogant at the wrong times, not really ego driven, but damned arrogant. Would I have been willing to accept the truth? Would I have blown up at her, maybe said and done all the wrong things? I know me, and sometimes, I didn't like me.

"The cabin holds some terribly strong memories for me, but it's the safest place I can think of. We're close to town, but it is defendable, with a gulch running along one property line, a roadway along another, and heavy forest. A full frontal attack would be the only way they could seriously press an assault."

Eric spoke up for the first time. "I can have one of my people contact her right away. If she agrees, we will also have to protect her and her shop. Jason, we need to find a berth for *D'Anne*, where she'll be safe. I have new papers here, officially naming her the *Molokai II*, and owned by Roger Funk. We can change the name on the stern right away, and I can have one of my people arrange a berth, either in Oakland across the estuary from the Coast Guard Station at Alameda, or maybe in Sausalito." The paint on *D'Anne's* stern is going to get pretty thick. One week *Molokai II*, the next week back to *D'Anne*, and again, back to *Molokai II*.

"Let's put her in Oakland." I said. "That way I can hike right up to Jack London Square, take the ferry across the bay and disappear before anyone knows I'm around. Then we can meet somewhere and head for Ft. Bragg." I liked the idea of using the Oakland Marina for another reason. Like Petersen said, it was directly across from the Coast Guard station at Alameda. The *D'Anne* would be protected. For just a minute, there was a fear in my soul. An icy hand reached out and touched me, sent a chill of cold depression through my bones. All I have left in the world right now was *D'Anne*.

Yes, Katie Dollarhide and I were close, very close, and she said she wants to spend the rest of her life with me, but really, right this minute, all I had was *D'Anne*. Katie would be with me, and I could work to protect her, but my boat would be left behind. I had that dreadful feeling I might not be around to enjoy either *D'Anne* or Katie.

"I'll make the arrangements. I think I'll steam on into Bodega Bay and Katie and I will meet you in Fort Bragg. Rent a car in San Francisco, and drive up. More than likely, we'll be there well ahead of you." I had the feeling Petersen had this all figured out before he said it, that this was a plan for some time. I didn't know if Katie was aware of it or not. She was an enigma at every turn. I wanted to trust her, put my life in her care, but there was always those questions. She hadn't always been truthful with me, even since we had become more than just FBI agents and operatives, and I wanted to trust her so much. We were about to increase the dangers of our mission, and I wanted, I needed to trust this woman. I already loved her.

Following our meeting, I took Katie to the fan tail of the big cutter, a place we would be absolutely alone. "I've gone over the top, dear lady. You mean so very much to me, and I've already lost one precious love. We have to make a pact, you and me, Blondie, that if only one of us is alive when this is over, that *D'Anne* is going to be well taken care of. I can feel chills of death all through my body when we talk about taking down this drug mob. I'm not a fearful man, I think you know that, but I have a deep dread of losing this battle. If I die in this operation, promise me you'll take care of what is now our boat. Make me that promise, Katie, please."

We were holding on to each other, rocking with the sway of the large Coast Guard ship as it stood dead in the water, almost two hundred miles off the coast of southern Mexico. "This will be extremely dangerous for everyone concerned, Butterball, and it is possible many people will die. I know you'll be protecting me, I know I'll be protecting you. And, you fucker, I've gone over the top, too."

There were hours spent, holding, talking, promising, and my mind was far more at ease than on our last visit to this ship. How far I had come, from grieving for Sami and wanting to smack this FBI agent, to having warm thoughts of my past life with Sami, and wanting to spend what time I had left with Blondie. The human mind was resilient to say the least.

Chapter Eleven

Fort Bragg was a delightful little town, tourist oriented, but not that many years ago, it was one of the centers of logging, milling, and distribution. The great forests of redwood and fir along the coastal ranges of northern California fell before the woodcutter's axes, and much of the product made its way to Fort Bragg. Operations of what was left of the logging industry had offices in the town, and one of the railroads created because of logging was a tourist line. It was called the Skunk Train, and thousands of tourists traveled to Ft. Bragg for a ride. At least one of the old lumber mills was still operating.

During the timber cutting boom times in California's early years, the mills worked constantly. Great rafts of redwood logs would be floated in, brought by barges from all the many dog coves up and down the coast. Steam engines on the barges made the job easier, and from more inland timber stands, railroads were the answer. But, it was the dog coves that made the timber industry profitable, what with hundreds of huge redwood trees rafted together in a cove, and then barged to a central mill.

The one hindrance to transportation was coastal fog, the single most important factor that made the coastal mountains home to the beautiful redwoods. Some of these trees had enjoyed their foggy ablutions for more than 2,000 years. There were magnificent wrecks up and down the coast, virtually from the time Europeans discovered the coast. According to most history buffs, Sir Francis Drake went aground just north of San Francisco Bay. There were many rafts of redwoods turned to splinters, driftwood, when barges went into the rocks.

Dog coves played a big part in the life of Fort Bragg, because of the drug runners, but most of the population wasn't aware of that. Culture and tourism defined the town, with art galleries and musical groups calling the town their own. The College of the Redwoods was nearby, the city of Mendocino was just down the coast, and the state of California maintained numerous state parks with plenty of camping and outdoor activities. In fact, most of the coastline of California was considered a state park, and that guaranteed access to the surf and sand. It also guaranteed access to the dog coves for the drug runners. Just one more piece of irony for our lives.

Fort Bragg was not a place one would think of as the center of an international narcotics ring. It had been known for years, of course, that the near-by mountains hosted a considerable number of marijuana farms, some of which had been licensed and operated legally. But these were basically local operations, small and illegal that don't have ties to international narcotics syndicates.

The marijuana industry was still a minor portion of the illegal narcotics picture, with opium, cocaine, meth, and date-rape drugs the big money makers. The international criminal organizations concentrated on the big money drugs.

When Sami told her bureau bosses she felt that Ft. Bragg might be a headquarters for some of the operations they had been investigating, she had to do some strong convincing. Ft. Bragg just didn't have that aura. In her opinion, that was why it worked so well for the dealers.

"During her presentations to John Chandler and some of us other agents, Sami ran up against lots of opposition. As I look back on it, Jason, most of that opposition came from The Deacon. His arguments were strong and well thought out, but looking back now, he was obviously trying to direct us away from here. What a bastard."

***

The Ft. Bragg Police Department was run by a well respected lawman with years of service. Randall Richardson was born and raised on the north coast of California and knew the people, knew the customs, knew what might be tolerated, and what wouldn't be. He wasn't a brazen man, rather laid back at times, but he had two big problems that no one in Ft. Bragg was aware of. He never told anyone, not even his family, but Chief Richardson loved to gamble, and loved to visit whorehouses. His marriage to a radiantly beautiful girl from Eureka, California, further north on the coast, only lasted a couple of years, and was over well before he arrived in Ft. Bragg. There weren't any children from the coupling, and Richardson never remarried.

He didn't tolerate any open gambling in the town, even gave bar owners hell when they ran football pools, and prostitution just didn't exist. But it was also a very quick drive to Reno, Nevada, and open gambling and houses of prostitution. There were of course several Indian gaming resorts between Ft. Bragg and Reno, but they were in California. Richardson knew he could be seen in those places, and opted for the longer jaunt into Reno. Richardson was well known as a high roller at several casinos, and a whorehouse just a few miles from downtown Reno welcomed him often.

Around town, he never talked about his trips to Reno. Many knew he was gone most weekends, but he allowed as how he spent those times on a small boat off the coast of Half Moon Bay fishing for rock cod, halibut and snapper. In fact, Richardson hadn't been on a boat since he was fifteen-years-old. But he was able to pick up a few pounds of cod filets on the road back.

At the casinos in Reno, a place called Lucky's in particular, Richardson was known as Randy Richards, and his checks were always accepted. His bank account under that name listed his old address in Crescent City on the very north coast of the Golden State. To drop a couple of hundred thousand over a weekend wasn't out of line, and for the casino bosses, his visits were anticipated with relish. If anyone had known he was a small town police chief, those kinds of losses would have drawn instant attention. His gambling didn't start out smoothly, however.

Because he was a small town police chief, Richardson didn't have that kind of bread to play with, and he pawned things, he stole from the evidence locker and fired other cops to cover his actions. He wrote bad checks but was able to cover them with winnings. It was those kinds of problems that led to his meeting with the mob.

He was into Lucky's for almost one hundred thousand dollars, and the casinos don't like that. You see, gambling debts couldn't be collected in normal ways. The casinos couldn't go to court or file liens, or anything like that, and although the mob wasn't tolerated in Nevada's gambling houses, they hung around, knew they could pick up some of their own action.

The pimps and madams at the Morning Star Ranch Brothel east of Reno, looked forward to Richardson's visits as well. He would often buy two or three of the prostitutes at a time, have them join him in a bubble bath, and then take him to a room and beat the hell out of him. He paid each of the girls several hundred dollars on each visit. His only rule; "Don't hit me in the face."

He would not be able to return to Ft. Bragg with black eyes and broken nose from a simple fishing trip. They beat him with fists, open hands, belts, shoes, anything they had. He never screamed, he never cried out in pain, he seemed to relish the beatings, and was always very polite and generous with the girls. Sometimes, after a particularly grueling session, he would be able to get an erection, but in all the years they knew Randy Richards at the Ranch, no girl was ever heard to say she got laid by him.

The frustration of such a situation was corrected through beatings and through gambling. These were expensive ways to conquer sexual hunger and frustration, and Richardson was an easy mark when he was approached by a representative of Alberto Pelligrini. Mr. Richards was staying on the seventeenth floor of Lucky's Hotel, and he had a visitor named Anthony Colletti.

"Mr. Richards, we have some things in common that need to be discussed. I work for a gentleman named Alberto Pelligrini, and Mr. Pelligrini doesn't like to see representatives of the police get in serious financial trouble, as you appear to be right at the moment."

Richardson was into the cashier's cage for well over eighty grand at the time, probably closer to one hundred thousand, and didn't know how he was going to be able to pick up the markers. "I'm not a policeman, Mr. Colletti. You must have the wrong person. I don't even gamble, so your Mr. Pelligrini has gotten some bad information somewhere." He didn't know how this bastard found out he was a cop, but he knew he would have to get out of this problem on his own.

"Well, Mr. Richards, you might want to take a look at some of these pictures I brought along," and Colletti handed Richardson a packet of snap shots. Some were of Richardson at Morning Star Ranch, naked as the day he was born, being beaten by three equally naked young ladies. Some of the pictures were of Richardson at the twenty-one tables and crap tables in the Reno casinos, and most telling, were pictures of the chief of police of Ft. Bragg in his patrol car and inside the station house.

"Good resemblance, don't you think?" Colletti was smiling, and took the photos back. "Now, chief, let's you and me have a nice long talk, shall we?" For the next two hours, Anthony Colletti, the mafia hit man from New York, did some persuasive selling of a bill of goods the Ft. Bragg police chief readily agreed to. "I didn't think you'd want this little package to turn up at the San Francisco Chronicle, or the newspaper in Ft. Bragg."

Colletti told Richardson that the only thing he was required to do was hire a couple of very special friends of Alberto Pelligrini, and not to get heavily involved in what those friends might do. One of them, Colletti assured Richardson, had a long and successful career in law enforcement.

"You'll like Owen Riley, Randall. It's OK if I call you Randall isn't it? Or would you rather I called you chief. Well, Owen Riley served on the force in San Juan, Puerto Rico, and with honors on the New Orleans police department. He's a very important part of Mr. Pelligrini's business, Randall, so treat your new chief of detectives properly."

Richardson's gambling debt was taken care of that night, in cash, and after returning to Ft. Bragg, with a package of fresh cod and some well-iced Dungeness Crab, Richardson had little time to think of the consequences of his actions. Owen Riley was in his office Monday morning, a packet of papers swearing to his past record in various police agencies, and an evil smile on his face.

"We'll get along fine, chief. Just give me free reign, don't ask questions, and let me hire a few people.

Everything will be all right, and you'll be treated right, yourself. Mr. Pelligrini always takes care of his own."

Suitcase loads of hundred dollar bills arrived on Richardson's desk one morning, and Riley along with them. "These are gifts from Mr. Pelligrini, chief. He has some business here, and if we allow that business to continue, then deliveries of these suitcases will continue."

Chief Richardson had let things go for a couple of weeks, watched Riley and didn't see anything out of line. He had hired a couple of people, including that big son of a bitch Anthony Colletti, but Richardson hadn't seen anything different happening within his department. "I've heard of things like this happening in other places, Riley, but not in a little jerk water town like Ft. Bragg." He opened the suitcases and counted out more than three hundred thousand dollars in well-used hundred dollar bills; packet after packet, each holding ten thousand dollars.

"Each of the suitcases we'll bring you will have the same amount, chief. Stay with us as you have been, and this will continue. Be against us, and I think Mr. Pelligrini just might let your little secrets out of the bag. It's your decision.

"Of course, with that kind of money, you could visit Reno just about any time you wanted." Riley was an evil person, and Richardson instantly hated the weasel, but, he had almost a half million dollars in cash sitting on his desk.

Richardson caved immediately, and Riley then used his position within the department to recruit others. With the chief of police already on the take, and hints about that to other cops, it didn't take long to put together a pretty good little cadre of narcotics dealers. Riley never took the lead position, always indicated that Richardson was the honcho. Riley ran everything, but only he and Colletti knew that. Pelligrini and Lopez started moving more and more product through the area, and many suitcases filled with hundred dollar bills found their way onto the chief's desk. It really was a sweet deal.

Richardson had shown in Reno he could be bought, but that first delivery of actual cash to him, not to pay off a debt, proved just how weak he really was. He was of course terrified that a leak to the press of his activities in Nevada would get out, and his life would be over. It didn't dawn on the man that what he was doing was also the end of his life if he crossed the Mafia and Cartel thugs.

He had a relationship of sorts with Owen Riley simply because Riley was supposed to be his chief of detectives. An interesting sidelight to Richardson's mind was the fact he always assumed Riley really was a cop. It never quite made it into his mind that Owen Riley might simply be a thug in a uniform. "Riley, you've served in other departments, doesn't this deception bother you? I know what I'm doing is illegal as hell, that if we get caught, it means federal prison, but do you ever find yourself not being able to look directly into a mirror?"

"You don't seem to have too much trouble looking in those brief cases when they're put on your desk, chief. Are you having second thoughts? If so, Mr. Pelligrini would be very upset with you."

"No second thoughts, Riley, I'm just trying to keep myself justified in my thinking, I guess." His mind wandered back a few years, back when life was so much easier. "I was a good cop, Riley. I was a good investigator. If you or Colletti had come to me with your proposals ten years ago, I probably would have had you arrested for attempted bribery, attempted conspiracy. Maybe other charges as well. Now, I let you run the department, and I collect the booty. How did this happen?"

"When a guy needs to get beat up to get his jollies, and can't stay away from the gambling joints, he ain't a good cop. Don't think about fucking us over, Richardson. You're in this up to your miserable balls, so let the money come in and keep your mouth shut."

The two men glared at each other for a minute before Richardson walked out of the office. "I'm so ashamed of myself," he was thinking. "I've corrupted the entire department, made a fool of myself in front of gangsters, sold my right to be called a man, more or less police officer. How did this come about? I'm so weak, and I need to be looked up to. The whores, I know, they do it because I pay them, but it feels so good when they tell me they need my attention, when they pretend they like me."

His mind flashed back to his high school days. "I was always trying to be the stud, the big man, but I couldn't get an erection, and tried to always hide that fact. It was little Brandi Bianchi who found out, and the word spread through the school. God, the bastards had a field day. 'Hey, limp dick,' they'd yell, and then laugh like hell, and that bitch Brandi led the cheers." He felt as low right now as he had twenty five years ago. What would lead a man down this path? More than likely a simple imbalance of chemicals as he changed from being a boy to being a man, but Richardson was never able to discuss facets of his personal life with his parents or with doctors.

"If Brandi Bianchi had fun humiliating me, I can imagine what my father would have done. That prick would have taken out a newspaper ad if he thought he could make me feel bad, could ridicule me in public." He remembered how his father taunted him when he failed to get a touchdown once, stood in the stands and booed his own son. That night, he was humiliated at home as well.

"You're the worst excuse for a son a man can have. I named you Randall out of respect for my own father, but you don't deserve that name. Get on the floor with the dog, you won't eat dinner at this table. Get on the floor and eat with the dog." Richardson never told anyone about this, never talked with a school counselor, never saw a doctor. The closest he ever came was one night talking with his wife.

"I know I can't satisfy you the way a man should. I'm so sorry about that, but I don't know what to do. What should I do?" It had been another in a long line of failed attempts at maintaining an erection, and his wife was once again denied.

"Your father's right. You're a poor excuse for a man, that's what. Have you ever thought you're probably queer as a three-dollar bill? That's it isn't it, Randall. You're queer."

"I'm not gay. I'm not." The thought had never entered his mind, and now his own wife was taunting him, humiliating him in his own bed. She made it worse the next day by going to his father and asking if he had shown any homosexual tendencies as a boy.

"I think that bastard's queer, that's what I think." And his father picked up on the claim immediately, chiding Richardson at every opportunity. The marriage ended at that point and Richardson moved out of the area, first to Sacramento. When his father died, he sent a note to his mother saying he was glad. Except for his phony bank accounts, he hadn't had contact with anyone in Crescent City since, and now he was in a position once again to face public humiliation.

"I should do the right thing. I should call the attorney general and spread the whole damned sordid thing out, but I can't. I can't stand the thought of seeing my whole life plastered in front page newspaper stories, stories saying what a bad cop I am. If I did that, if I blew the whistle, I'd have to kill myself, and I don't know if I could even do that." A weaker and more forlorn man couldn't have been found anywhere in California, and he could hear the jeering crowds.

Riley reported his conversation with Richardson to the Wiley Carpenter, who in turn informed Alberto Pelligrini. Chief Richardson was on thin ground, and Riley and Colletti were told to be prepared to kill the chief at any moment. Do not let him blow the sweetest deal the family had ever made.

"Riley, I want you to know that I won't blow this deal. It's just that sometimes I feel so low, so dirty. I've lived most of my life in some lie or another, and I'm more terrified of being found out than I am of dying, so you won't have to worry that I'll give all this up. I'll keep my nose out of whatever you and Mr. Pelligrini are doing." As good a cop as he had been at one time, Richardson wasn't aware of exactly what it was Riley was involved in.

***

It was Anthony Colletti, the hit man from New York's crime families who came up with the idea of creating diversions when a load of stuff came in. He and Riley were sitting around, drinking beer one day when he hit on it.

"You know, Owen, if we could divert the so-called good Ft. Bragg cops and county sheriff patrols away from the coast when we have a shipment coming in, it would be a lot safer. Some of these bastards here in town are getting wise to what we're doing, and they might just take the lid off the operation." A fear of both Colletti and Riley was that one of the few remaining good cops might blow the whistle on the whole business.

"Most of the department is with us, Owen, even that slime ball chief is pitching in, but some of those old guys might go to the feds or something." One of the insurance policies the felons had was the known fact that cops don't squeal on cops. But it had happened in the past, and it could happen again.

"I think you've got it Tony. Let's move Murphy into the communications post, and when we have something coming in, he can send patrols out of the area. Damn, that's good, Tony. That's really good. Vehicle wrecks always take two or three patrol cars, and fires do too. Problems between the logging operations and the conservationist fuckers always mean trouble.

"Oh, yeah, Tony, that's good."

That was the environment that Sami Bertorelli moved into, and much later, Jason Caldwell. To help keep the feds from the operation, was the job of The Deacon. Deacon could not keep Bertorelli out of the area without blowing his cover. Being well placed within the bureau, Deacon knew what was happening, and most importantly, when.

Petersen couldn't figure out how the drug runners knew where he was, but The Deacon knew, and that was passed on. From the outside, Ft. Bragg was a beautiful little town, swarming with tourists and no one knew it was also a drug dealing Mecca. Mobsters with New York ties, European ties, South American ties, and a completely corrupt police department, would have been the last thing on the minds of people coming for Mendocino's famous crab fests, or for rides on the Skunk Train.

Chapter Twelve

"You have a good voyage, Butterball, and stay warm and safe." There were tears in Katie's eyes, and she and Caldwell hugged and kissed each other before he boarded a skiff for the short run over to *D'Anne*. "I'll see you in Fort Bragg." She stood next to Eric Petersen on the bridge of the *Roosevelt*, and watched as Jason Caldwell got his trawler under way.

"Will he be okay? I'm worried about that other speed boat that we've heard about."

"He'll be okay Katie. He's one tough son of a bitch, isn't he." It was a statement Petersen made, not a question, and he felt strongly about it. "I'd like to have about a hundred little boats like his spread up and down the coast, with about a hundred tough old bastards like Jason on them. We'd end this war then.

"It must have been quite a sight to see him take out that armed speed boat. I've read his report several times now, and the guy is simply tough. I take it, you have a crush on the gentleman besides, eh?"

"You take that smirk off your face right now." Katie was smiling, and blushing, as she thought about the last almost week she and her Butterball had spent together. "He's about the exact opposite of what I figured would be the love of my life, Eric, but damned if he isn't. Older, balder, much heavier than what I always expected would be my life partner. And about as tough a son of a bitch as I've ever worked with. There wasn't the least hesitation when that fishing boat attacked him, he simply took it out. I mean, he blew that fucker completely out of the water.

"And then when The Deacon leveled off on him with his own rifle, he jumped right over the railing, and he said he could hear the bullet go past his head. That would have been a loss I would have a hard time living with."

Petersen gave the orders and the big cutter was underway, leaving *D'Anne* in its wake in just minutes, both boats blasted horns in each other's honor. Petersen sent Caldwell a well meant salute from his flying bridge, and received one back from the skipper of the little trawler.

When one was on board a fifty-one foot fishing trawler, one felt a sense of being on a large boat, capable of taking on some nasty seas, but when one was standing on the bridge of a large Coast Guard Cutter, the size of a destroyer escort class fighting ship, one saw a little fishing trawler. Perspective changed based on where one was at the time. Jason Caldwell would take on the world from his point of view aboard *D'Anne*, while Petersen felt just as secure aboard his large ship. Blue water sailors, alike.

A seaman handed Petersen a piece of paper. "Coded, sir. Should I interpret?"

"Not necessary, petty officer Johnson, I'll see to it. Agent Dollarhide, will you join me in the mess?" A quick glance and Petersen knew the message was actually for Katie Dollarhide and was from FBI headquarters in Virginia. "This is for you, Katie. I hope it's good news. We need some.

"This business of just waltzing into Fort Bragg and taking down an entire police department is pretty risky. What if we're wrong about those people? What if it just seems like the entire department is dealing drugs or at least protecting those that smuggle them into the country?"

Those same thoughts had been plaguing Katie as well. "My information is that some members of the department, and probably high ranking officers to boot, are behind these drug shipments and the smuggling operation. There is lots of money involved, Eric, lots of money. Enough to support Pelligrini in his lifestyle, enough to support Lopez in his. Enough to buy coastal freighters and fast little speed boats to deliver the shit, enough to buy cops for protection, and judges and attorneys and politicians.

"The one big question we have is who? Who is the man behind everything in Fort Bragg? Jason thinks it's Owen Riley. I'm more inclined to think it might even be the police chief himself, or again, it could be someone directing traffic from outside the department, but with full knowledge of the highest ranking officers.

"When we find out who, the operation will end." She settled in with one more in an endless line of sodas while Petersen decoded the message from Washington, worried that John Chandler might put a stop to her plan, or curtail it enough so it wouldn't be effective. Her thoughts were on what they would do, and how to get it done.

She outlined her argument to Petersen as if she were talking to Chandler. "Jason is going to meet us, I've already called for Betsy Contreras to be on the scene, we've got permission to use Francesca's cabin and we have people working out protection plans. I have my statement almost finished for the press. This isn't the time for Cold Feet, John Chandler."

Petersen didn't notice but Jason probably would have. She had one fist doubled up pounding, first the table, then an open palm. Jason spotted that little personal quirk soon after they met. To him, and to other very astute observers, it meant Katie Dollarhide was angry and was ready to go to war. It was a clue, not too subtle if one knew what to look for, to go into protect mode.

"Here we are. He says, 'Good Hunting.' Katie."

"That's all?" She saw the original paper, and there were lots of lines written on it. "Good hunting? That's all?"

"No, there's stuff here just for you. Go over it closely, and I'll meet you back on the bridge. We may have a bit of planning to do."

She took the decoded message, opened another soda and settled in with a yellow pad. The message was very favorable to her plans, and she could see Chandler's ideas were in the same vein as hers. The message was brief:

"I agree with your plan. There will be one hell of a stink, from politicians mostly, and from those who are part of the organization. I think you're right on the initial consequences of your plan. When you break the news, the top dogs may want to get the hell away fast. Fastest way out is by small boat to a freighter and then maybe an airplane, a seaplane.

"I'm working to authorize Coast Guard intervention with as many small fast boats as we can muster to patrol that part of the coast when you chop their tree house down. I want Commander Petersen to command the sea end of this intervention. He knows the people, he knows the coast better than most, and he has command experience. He's a good man. I've already cleared all this with the Coast Guard Commandant, so Commander Petersen will get his orders from the Coast Guard command.

"I've read the reports from both you and Caldwell. That must have been quite a battle he waged. You're right about how good he is going to be for the bureau. I had my doubts at first, I mean, after all, an egotistical Hollywood producer is not a candid picture of an FBI agent. On the other hand, neither is it a representative picture for an agent to work for drug lords.

"I don't have words to express how hurt I am that The Deacon was a mole, but you are to be commended for your fast action. You obviously saved Caldwell's life, and probably your own, but brought to the surface the fact that we have been infiltrated, and at a high level. I agree with you there is still at least one more prick bastard somewhere in my office.

"Good Hunting, Katie."

"So, we're going to war. Damn good. Damn good." The fist into the hand was going at a fast pace, and she took up the decoded papers and headed for the bridge to brief Petersen. Her smile lit her face and she could almost feel the rush of battle. "Damn good."

***

"Your Commandant is going to let us know what kind of boats we'll have at our disposal, and how many. This is what you've wanted, Eric. Now, you have your own navy, and if I'm right, you'll be taking prisoners within days, maybe hours, of when I make my presentation to the press and to the nation.

"We aren't going to win a war with this operation, but we will have a decisive battle, and we will put a dent in at least part of the Pelligrini and Lopez organization."

Katie and Petersen were having dinner in the officer's mess, a few of the other ship's personnel on hand, and the two were planning to let the crew know what they would be doing for the next several weeks, maybe months. Eric Petersen was primed, he had been asking for this kind of back up for years, and now he had it. A contingent of small fast boats would patrol the little dog coves of the northern coast of California, with his cutter a little farther out to sea, trying to keep an eye on the coastal freighters.

"These damn freighters just steam up and down the coast, sometimes coming from Asia, sometimes from Central America, sometimes from the Caribbean, and it's almost impossible to tell a drug smuggling freighter from one bringing coffee and bananas, or one bringing exotic Asian spices from one bringing a new load of high end pot. Container ships sometimes have a few containers filled with illegal aliens that are simply dropped in the brine, and hopefully towed to shore. But with the little coves covered, I can keep a much better eye on the freighters, see which ones slow down to drop a quick speed boat and wait for its return, and possibly be in a position for intervention.

"I've wanted this for a long time, and now, it looks like I'm going to have it, at least for the duration of this operation." He had been in a jolly good mood ever since decoding that message from John Chandler, and now he was going to pass on most of what he knew to his crew. He rapped his butter knife on a water glass and had the attention of his command staff.

"Ladies and gentlemen, I think you all know FBI Special Agent Katie Dollarhide. She's spent enough time on board the *Roosevelt* to almost be available for deck duty once in a while."

"Oh, no, Commander. The black gang in the engine room or nothing." There was lots of pride on this ship, and Katie knew it. She just endeared herself to the crew members who had what others considered the worst duty on board, but who, they knew, were the best of the best.

The officers at the table joined in the celebratory occasion, and toasted their guest. All the officers agreed, it was splendid that their Coast Guard Cutter was stationed out of Bodega Bay because the officer's mess often sported some of the finest of California's vintage for dinners like this one.

Katie spoke to the men and women at the table plainly and without the drama she felt. "Our war on drug smuggling just got a little hotter, thanks to some fine investigative work by several FBI agents. One in particular, and we'll miss her for the duration, Sami Bertorelli, who was slain in Fort Bragg, gave us enough information that it appears we might put a big dent in a big operation. Her work has introduced us to the major dealers in this area, and we know they are being fed by the Pelligrini family in the Mediterranean, and by the Lopez Cartel out of Colombia." She let her eyes roam about the table, coming to rest on Commander Petersen's.

Petersen picked up the thread, saying, "The goods are funneled onto the coast near Fort Bragg, and according to agent Dollarhide, the FBI believes the Fort Bragg Police Department is part of the operation. She and her agents are going to bust that gang, and when they do, we will be working the coast to grab the bastards when they try to run away."

Dollarhide watched as Petersen warmed to his subject. Like Caldwell, Katie often thought of Eric Petersen as a throwback Viking explorer and warrior. She watched his eyes as they surveyed the tables, surrounded by Coast Guard officers. "I wonder if he ever sees the ancient war lord when he looks in a mirror?" She turned her attention to the group of officers, and each one had only Eric Petersen in his or her view.

"Most of you have heard me bitch about not getting any support, and having to patrol a damned coast that's hundreds of miles long with hundreds of little coves and bays where the pricks can hide. Well, boys and girls, we are getting some help. The FBI is working with my boss, Admiral Morgenstern, to muster a covey of little speedboats to patrol in close, and we'll be overseeing from out a little further.

"We will be taking prisoners. This is very important. We want them alive if at all possible. Don't put yourself in jeopardy, but take them alive if at all possible. Lieutenant Oakley, Sam, you'll have the northern squadron, patrolling from off Fort Bragg to about Crescent City. Go north of that, but only if you need to. And Lieutenant Smalley, Sandra, you'll command the southern squadron, from Fort Bragg south to Monterey. You're authorized to go further south, but again, only if you feel it is absolutely necessary.

"That's a lot of ocean, and right now, I don't know how many boats I'm going to get. The FBI's Assistant Director, John Chandler, has a phrase that's famous within the bureau, and I think I'm going to steal it just this once. Good hunting, all of you."

***

"I'm not even going to dock, Katie. I'm going to send you ashore with Lt. Smalley. I wish there were words to say thank you. It doesn't sound like many, but eight fast little ocean going speedboats, filled to the waterline with electronics is going to make a big noise out here.

"Have Smalley open that little bastard up for you. You'll get a hell of a ride. Keep me posted."

"I will Eric. Remember, from today on, no codes, no subterfuge. We want them to know everything we're doing. We want them to be afraid, very afraid, and if they are, they'll try to run, or do something stupid. The airport at Fort Bragg is under heavy surveillance, as are most of the small little runways up and down the coast and in the interior valley. They won't try to use the highways, I don't think, but even if they do, we're watching. I think the sea will be their primary avenue of escape, and you're here to meet them. This is one damn good operation, Eric. Let's get the bastards."

Katie Dollarhide was on fire, and knew she was going to have to wait at least another three days for Jason to meet her. She'd have to soak her left hand in warm water and Epson salts tonight, considering the pommeling it was taking.

She was delighted to get a ride into Bodega Bay on a fast ocean going speedboat, but was also surprised at just how fast the boat was. "Damn, Sandra, this is one fast little son of a bitch. How the hell do you keep it under control?"

"It's all in the feel, Katie. You know the angle of the waves, you know the keel line of the boat, and between the throttle and the rudder, you go fast. Someday, I'll have command of a cutter, but until then, I want to work with Commander Petersen.

"Very few of the old line command officers will give command to a woman, but Petersen is different. This is the second time he's given me command of part of an operation."

There was a considerable age difference between the young Coast Guard Lieutenant and the FBI agent, but it was obvious the two shared a number of similarities. Despite hanging on for dear life, Katie Dollarhide was thrilled with the ride. "We're in the air as much as on the ocean, Sandra. People would pay a lot of money to get a ride like this," she laughed, brushing spray from her face. "I see fire in your eyes, and determination. You'll make a fine big ship's skipper someday."

Tears were streaming across Dollarhide's face from a combination of speed, spray kicked up by the fast little hot rod, and by her own exuberance. Her hair was streaming in the wind, tangled beyond help, and she was helplessly laughing and crying with the excitement. A look at Lt. Smalley, and she knew the young Coast

Guard officer felt the same way. "It's a good thing I wasn't introduced to things like this when I was younger, Sandra. I'd be in the Coast Guard instead of the FBI."

"You'd sure as hell be welcomed, Katie."

The little boat slowed to a crawl as it entered Bodega Bay, and Katie could see people fishing along the rugged coast line and inside the bay. The Coast Guard station was on a spit of sand dune on the south side of the bay, and Lt. Smalley brought her boat into the docking area, and her two crewmen tied it off quickly. "I think down the line, we'll be working together often, Lieutenant."

"I'm looking forward to it."

The trip from the *Roosevelt* to Bodega Bay was really fast, and Katie was breathing hard when she stepped onto the dock at the Coast Guard station. She didn't say it out loud, but she thought, "Sandra, you've got one hell of a set of balls."

A field agent from Sacramento greeted her on the dock and handed her the keys to her official car. "Thanks Jackson. After that ride in, I hope I can keep this thing under a hundred miles per hour."

Agent Jackson had no idea what she was talking about, but smiled anyway. "Chandler wants you to call him as soon as you reach Ft. Bragg."

***

She had just one small fight with her boss. Chandler wanted to inform the California Attorney General of what was being planned, but Dollarhide was dead set against that. "John, we don't know where this is going to lead. We already know we have some of their people on our own payroll, it's logical to think they may have people at the state level as well.

"No, please, John, don't do that. It could compromise the whole thing. The Fort Bragg Police

Department is filled with their people, and we know they have to be getting help from other agencies, probably the local sheriff's office, probably from some of the local judges.

"Let's not make it harder for us to bring these people down."

It was a passionate argument, and Chandler finally agreed to keep everything at the federal level. "One thing old girl, be prepared to hear lots of rhetoric about federal intervention, about state's rights, and about the arrogance of a federal agency simply taking over a local police agency. Those arguing will be loud and angry, Katie, so be prepared.

"Another thing to keep in mind is the international implications of drugs coming from abroad, brought by foreign interests. That is the one thing that makes this a federal project. The reason the FBI is involved is the national security issue, and don't be afraid to use that.

"Good hunting, Katie."

Chapter Thirteen

Winter along the northern coast of California was usually wet, with a combination of heavy rains and fog. It started raining while I was 50 miles off the coast, and 150 miles from the Golden Gate. It didn't let up for three days. In the summer, it was fog that wrapped the coast in damp tendrils of gauze, but in the winter, it was rain. Weather people called them storms, and I suppose that would be a fair statement, but they weren't the raging tempests the word storm brought to mind. Sure, the seas got up some, and there might be an increase in the wind, but not a 'tie yourself to the mast' frenzy. Actually, I liked these kinds of storms, with lots of rain to wash the air clean, and enough of a sea to keep me busy in the wheel house.

It was a little exciting coming in through the Golden Gate as the sea was up some and the tide was on the ebb. It made for lots of strange currents through that passage. I remember once, coming in from a fishing weekend, we simply couldn't get through the Gate. The outgoing tide was so strong and fast *D'Anne* couldn't fight it. I went back out to sea, found a large freighter coming in and jumped in its wake. We coasted in that time.

D'Anne had good strength in the engine, a strong center line, and moved easily with the water, but as I said, top speed was only about eleven knots, and an ebb tide through that narrow harbor entrance could overwhelm her. I didn't spill a drop of my coffee coming in today, and just as Petersen promised, my berth was waiting for me at the Oakland Marina.

It was days like that that I miss Sami so much. She loved storms, reveled in the strength of winds and waves, and begged me to go sailing when storm driven ocean waves would break across the bow of the *D'Anne*. She would go as far into the bow as possible, tie herself off and dare the waves to wash her off "her" boat. From her first cruise aboard *D'Anne*, way before we were married, the boat became hers.

On our first cruise of more than a day or two, we went north and had adventures in the waters of the San Juan Islands, watched killer whales dance on the surface, caught salmon and grilled them on the after deck, spent hours below decks during rain squalls, luxuriated in each other. Besides being probably the most intellectual person I had ever known, Sami was also the most romantic.

It's impossible for me to associate her with Katie. Katie pulled a gun, a semi-automatic pistol, and killed a man who was trying to kill me. Katie and Petersen kept telling me that Sami was the most effective agent they had, and yet, the Sami I knew and loved so much, was just the opposite of Katie. I couldn't conceive of her killing someone.

The first time we went to the kelp beds for a day of fishing, we made sour dough bread sandwiches of roasted peppers marinated in olive oil and garlic, and drank too much wine, spent two hours below decks, getting crumbs in the bed sheets, before we even wet a line, and then when Sami caught the first fish, she made me take it off the hook and put it back in the sea.

"I'd never eat a fish if I knew I'd killed it," she told me. It was all right with her to eat any fish I caught, but everything she caught went back into the sea. She could have been the poster girl for catch and release programs. And they keep telling me Sami was the meanest, finest, best agent the FBI had in their drug interdiction program.

Maybe it was just the rain pelting the wind screen in the wheel house, or the sound of the surf as it crashed across the bow, salt spray splashing and mingling with cascading sheets of rain, maybe it was the sighing of the wind as it blasted its way through the cables and lines holding things in place on the old boat, maybe it was just this old man's mind wanting to return to the peace I knew when I was with Sami. It was a regular weekend adventure every week for us. We left the dock as soon as she got home from school, and sometimes didn't tie up again until after sunrise on Monday. She was late for Monday's first class often enough that there was a comment about "Sailor Sami" in the school newspaper one week.

I guess I was just as big a softy as she was. I had that clipping framed and mounted in the wheelhouse. Katie had seen it, but she never commented on it. Was it possible that I was transferring my feelings for Sami, so deep I could feel her loss in my bones sometimes, was I transferring that to Katie? I didn't think so. The two women were so different, but my feelings for both were real.

Sami wore her emotions on her sleeve, demanded we all see them and knew what they meant. She would cry when sad, laugh when gay, dance and sing at the slightest provocation. Italian blood ran like syrup through her veins, as did her tremendous knowledge of the world.

Headlines in a newspaper would set her off on a crusade of righteousness that wouldn't end until the next emotional crisis arrived. Maybe it was her ability to react to her surroundings that made her a good undercover agent. She simply never gave the appearance of being anything like what one would expect a cloak-and-dagger, covert, operative to be, whatever the hell that was.

Katie on the other hand was able to maintain an even keel in the most devastating circumstances. Like blowing Deacon away without the slightest qualm. No, I was not trading one for the other, I did love Sami and always would, and I was feeling more and more that I would like to spend the rest of my days with Katie. I was sounding like a frivolous little teenager, but the questions bothered me.

I knew I shouldn't, but I wondered what life would have been like for us if Sami was still alive. I know we'd have made the trip down through the Caribbean, but would she have told me about her 'other' life? How would I have reacted? Those were serious questions that scared me. I was incredulous when Petersen and Katie told me about Sami that day on the high seas, a hundred miles off shore. I felt betrayed. How would I have reacted if Sami herself had told me these things?

What if she hadn't told me and we sailed into a trap like I did with those thugs off Costa Rica, then what? I didn't like it when my mind started playing these games with me, but these were questions that kept coming up, and the longer I knew Katie Dollarhide, the deeper I got into this investigation of drug dealers and distributors, the more the questions surfaced. I was very glad I was never faced with them in Sami's reality. They were tough enough this way. Sometimes the arrogant, egotistical Hollywood producer label was correct. I didn't want to think what I might have said to Sami, if her other life was slapped in my face along with some inherent danger.

My boat, my life, and two beautiful women have invaded every cell of my body, one alive, one blown away by bad guys. At least I had the pleasure of knowing

I might have something to do with the bad guys being put away or stopped.

***

I arrived in Ft. Bragg on a Wednesday, and according to plan, went right to the FBI/Justice Department offices in the Federal Building there. Be obvious, that was the name of the game. On the way, in my little rented piece of Japan, I passed some people I had known when Sami and I were together, and went out of my way to honk and wave to them. Clandestine I was not.

Our accommodations were at Francesca's homey old house just outside town, and after seeing to it that everyone at the FBI office knew I was in town, I headed out there. They gave me a 'company' car, but it didn't have government plates. It was called a Japanese import, something new for the end of the first decade of the 2000s. All wheel drive, and it had a tracking device built in. All I had to do was activate it, and those in the operation would know exactly where I was. Not just global positioning for the driver to know where he was, but the coordinates transmitted to FBI sources in Ft. Bragg. I loved the 21st century so far.

Petersen was not at the house when I arrived, and I really wasn't sure he would be in on the fun. Katie introduced me to a woman known in the agency as 'fingers,' but to us she was Betsy Contreras. Katie was being kind today and introduced me as Jason, not Butterball. More points, dear heart.

For Betsy's sake, it's a good thing I was head over heels in love with Katie. Betsy had long black hair, fiery brown eyes, and the body of an athlete. There probably wasn't 3% body fat, and she stood a good six feet tall. They called it 'hard-body', and it was true. Katie gave me the evil eye when I sized her up. Good for you, Blondie, you were getting to know me pretty good.

"What is it with the FBI, Katie? I didn't have this kind of beauty to draw on when I was making pictures." The evil eye returned, but there was also a hint of a smile on her gorgeous face. And Betsy simply said thank you.

"We called a press conference for 4:30 this afternoon, Jason. We've invited the local media along with wire services, and reps from San Francisco and Sacramento, so we could start seeing some kind of action at any time. For your information, there are four agents outside the house here, and they will be with us twenty four/seven. There are also some surveillance cameras they have set up, and only our three cars will be allowed in unrestricted. Others will be watched closely and physically stopped if there is any sign of trouble. If someone is coming to visit Francesca, I hope they stop when told, 'cause they'll be dead if they don't.

"You brought that nine millimeter I left for you on the boat, didn't you? You just might find it handy during the next few days or weeks. Until things get dicey, if it comes to that, I think we can all ride together in that quick little car you have, Jason.

"One other thing, and my speech making is over," She said. "No one here in Ft. Bragg, including me knows what our agent in the cop shop looks like, or what name he might be using. Any information he may pass on will go to Chandler in DC, and then to us. In other words, if he gets in trouble, we may not be able to help. There's a hell of a time lag here, but it is the safest considering we have already sniffed, and snuffed, one plant.

"According to Chandler, he knows there's a second traitor in the bureau in Washington, probably very close to him, but he hasn't forced the bastard to show himself yet. It's because of that, our man here is as far undercover as one can get. He only has one contact, and that's John Chandler."

Not the most positive speech I've ever heard Katie give, but at least we knew what the situation was. Once we announced our investigation of the Ft. Bragg Police Department, every cop would be a potential problem for us, and some of the old timers were not going to take kindly to our actions. Even though it appeared there was a problem within the department, some of those old guys would want to handle it themselves, and wouldn't want federal intervention. Police were an interesting breed, they stuck to themselves, protected the hell out of each other, and when one did go bad, the other cops wanted to do the reprimanding. Outside agencies were not tolerated.

For years, groups were formed to complain about federal intervention, and for years, I was a quiet supporter. Government had become intrusive to a point, and for many, intrusive was too mild a word. Militias had been formed, and often there had been armed conflicts between citizens and feds; Waco, Oklahoma City, Montana. We were going to stage a press conference and give the impression that the federal government, under the auspices of FBI and national security concerns, were going to take control of a local police agency. There would be howls of protest from coast to coast. I just hoped Katie and her troops had the kinds of evidence it would take to convince the general populace that we were taking the correct action.

We will have to prove that we were protecting them from the bad guys, and sometimes, when drugs were involved, many people didn't consider the dealers the bad guys. I was that way, in a sense, when this all started. Did you smoke a joint or two? What the hell? Did you stuff a little nose candy from time to time? Who cared if I didn't hurt someone? The answer was, simply, so many people were more than hurt, they were dead. Not from the drugs themselves maybe, but from the fights between the dealers, turf wars, gun battles with cops, and of course, things like the killing of my Sami.

For some, the concept of a man like Pelligrini having control of politicians was just not possible, that agencies that were designed to protect us being led by criminal elements couldn't happen. That wasn't naive, in their opinion, while in reality, it most certainly was.

Sami and I had talked about drugs, and it didn't surprise me that she was so adamantly against their use, and decidedly in favor of shutting off drug supplies. I look back and remember that I thought she was just a little naive schoolteacher who feared a student might be smoking pot after class. How differently I would have reacted if I had known she was at the top of her class in the FBI.

She had a strong sense of what was needed to stop drug importation, but she also understood that with our form of government, it was freedom that must take precedence over simply stopping criminal activity. Law and justice were more important to the overall picture, even if it meant some criminals would have greater access to their victims.

There was a depth to the questions that amazed me. Someone abusing his or her own body was being treated in the same way as that of a criminal organization that was working to disrupt society and the political system, as it killed, tortured, and maimed to get it done. I had to look at what we were doing as an answer to the second half of that question.

"It's impossible to think there would only be one gang family member who has infiltrated this department," I said. "Too many decisions were made during the Sami investigation that had to come from the upper echelons of the force. Every cop on the department has to be considered a suspect, everyone, from the chief down. And those who are on the take will be extremely defensive. Many people are already dead, and I'm afraid there will be more.

"Katie, I know this is mostly an FBI investigation, but has the DEA or any other agency found problems with this department? I'm thinking that since this coastline has so many little coves and bays, drug runners wouldn't have that much trouble smuggling their shit in. If they had help from a local police department, it sure would make the job easier.

"This whole thing has to be well planned, from very high sources within the crime families and the cartels. This has to be more than just a couple of dumb-fuck cops looking to make a few easy bucks. These guys have to have been on the take for years, and be involved in the planning and carrying out of the smuggling operations."

"There's no doubt, Jason." This was Betsy contributing to the conversation. Sweet and delightfully beautiful Betsy. Her brown eyes were on fire as she spoke. Every man-Jack she had ever worked with had to have had feelings of lust just being near her. "For the last year all I've done is go over records of known drops along the coast, and from a percentage standpoint, between sixty percent and sixty-five percent of the drops that we know of were along the part of the coast where the Ft. Bragg police could add protection. Maybe not within their jurisdiction as such, but where they could create a diversion and give some aid to the drop.

"There were quite a few false burglary reports and false automobile accidents that needed investigation at the same time a drop was scheduled. Fires were reported regularly, and reports of confrontations between logging interests and tree huggers were always taking place. At least according to police communication records. Most were false. According to DEA and Coast Guard informants, secret radio messages were sent just hours before a drop, and invariably, if the drop were in this vicinity, something would happen that would cause the various police agencies to be called away from coastal areas. Burglaries, wrecks, fires, even conflicts with ecologists and loggers were reported and needed follow-up by patrol units. Any ruse to draw real cops from the drop area was used.

"One other thing we know, the boats never actually stopped in the coves and bays. They would swing in, drop a bundle that would float, a small skiff or in some cases even Zodiacs, would zip out from shore, pick up the shit, and everyone would be gone in less than 10 minutes. No noise, no lights, no transferring of cargo. Just run through the bay, drop and run. These little coves are small, too small for large boats or ships to be able to maneuver. I think large ships off shore would dispatch fast motorboats into the coves, drop the merchandise, and be back at the mother ship within minutes. Eric Petersen thinks I'm right on this, too. This is one well-oiled machine, and when we break it up, hundreds of millions of dollars of lost revenue is what these bastards will be fighting for.

"Coastal traffic between points north, like Seattle, Alaska, even Japan, and San Francisco Bay, Los Angeles, or other southern ports is heavy, and Petersen is sure the freighters carrying the drugs simply look like coastal freighters. They become a part of the scenery so to speak, and let the fast little speedboats bring in the stuff.

"Keep in mind, this is not a ten-dollar pot operation. Hundreds of millions of dollars of cocaine and heroin, opium and meth come on shore within fifty miles of where we are sitting. The cops, distributors, dealers, growers, everyone involved in this are very rich, and they want to stay that way. This is going to be particularly dangerous.

"There's something else, too, Katie. While I've been on this end of the investigation, and I think Sami was getting into this before she was hit, along with the European and Colombian merger, it appears that several of the gangs that are responsible for Asian drugs are getting in on the program. A few names have cropped up that we recognize from Seattle and Vancouver operations. Just one more thing for us to worry about, I guess."

"Thank you, Becky," Katie said. "Chandler and the director both believe that we must treat our operation as part of the Homeland Security fight against terror and attempts to disrupt our government operations. These people own congressmen, own judges, and own police departments. They are a threat to our way of life, to our democracy."

There were only a few representatives of the press on hand at the Federal Building when we arrived, and they were thinking they had been sent on some stupid Justice Department story about who-knows-what. For a change, there hadn't been any leaks before our stupendous declarations. Katie walked out to the podium and took command of the situation at once.

"I want you to understand the gravity of what I'm about to tell you. My name is Katie Dollarhide, Special Agent in Charge, and I work directly for John Chandler, deputy director of the Bureau. I'm, providing packets of information for you outlining our charges and most of the evidence supporting those charges. The Fort Bragg Police Department is the most corrupt organization in this country, and the federal government is assuming its responsibilities." Gasps filled the small room as what she said was understood.

"Hundreds of millions of dollars of hard drugs are deposited on the shores near here and are distributed by this department. Shipments are protected by this department. FBI agents have died at the hands of this department." Looks of amazement, of dis-belief, even of anger flared through the gathered reporters as they listened to her comments.

Katie continued on for almost another half hour, outlining what was happening, how European and South American crime organizations had infiltrated the department, how Sami Bertorelli had been slaughtered, how FBI agent Deacon had been turned and in turn killed. She laid it on as thick and heavy as possible, and then distributed the hard copies of what she had said.

There was almost a stampede for the phones and for satellite feed trucks when we got through. The revelations brought headlines in every major newspaper in California and across the country. The Pelligrini connection, coupled to the Lopez Cartel operations guaranteed lots of ink and broadcast time. For the first time, the revelations from Carlos Lopez were used in public, which coupled the Colombian operations to European and North African gangs.

Since Chandler and his office in Washington headed up this operation, our stories often had a Washington lead, giving even more credence to the story. Network satellite feed trucks made Ft. Bragg their home, and evening news programs had feeds regularly. John Chandler laid it on thick, saying he felt operations of this type were not only in the public interest, but were a matter of national security. "Our very way of life is being threatened by the drugs coming into our lives. Good people, whole families, are being ruined, and that's personal.

"But from a national viewpoint, your personal security, the security of our nation, our ability to protect ourselves, our government, our way of life is threatened when members of police agencies are conscripted by these murderers. Money is at the root of course, and weak people will be turned by large amounts of cash. My job is to root out these weaklings and replace confidence in our police, in our politics, and in our way of life."

Newspaper reports, TV stories, and news magazines made the most of what we had disclosed, and of course, in Fort Bragg, we were either looked on as those who were going to clean up the mess, or we were agents of the federal government overstepping our positions.

***

Katie and I headed for the police station with a fistful of court orders and early subpoenas, giving us the right to every file in the department, and the right to talk to every employee of the department. We also had about fifteen agents and federal marshals with us, and the guarantee of others if we needed them.

"Funny, isn't it, that we had to get our judicial orders from federal judges? The local district judiciary might be in on this operation as well, Katie." It surprised the hell out of me that the FBI and the Justice Department couldn't get court orders and search warrants and seizure orders from the local judges. I guess I was pretty naive when it came to how these drug organizations were operated. Chandler wasn't wrong in saying that weak people could be bought easily. He should have included the fact that simply because a person might be in a high position in government doesn't mean he was bright. One could buy one's way in life.

Katie had told me about the influence Alberto Pelligrini had at the national level, senators, congressmen, federal employees, and others, and it should have been just another step for me to realize his gang members could have that kind of influence at this level as well.

"I know you've said that Pelligrini had ties nationally, but would he have had this kind of influence locally?" It still seemed incredible.

"My sweet, dear, naive Butterball. That fucker could stop governments if he wanted to, and I'm not joking. Before he was killed, he had that much power. I don't think even he realized it, and we're lucky for that. Through all his giving away money and gifts to the arts and education, he built a reputation just the opposite of a crime boss. His gifts of money and power and prestige to politicians extended far beyond just the national level. There are literally thousands of politicians who owe him big time.

"Jason, I don't doubt for a minute the local judiciary is on the payroll here, and it wouldn't surprise me if some in Sacramento are too. His tentacles were long and slimy.

"I called Chandler this morning and told him about our local problems with the courts, and he is passing all the information onto Justice. They'll have their own people here in no time. Like he said Butterball, large amounts of money can turn a lot of heads. We'll see too many heads fall around here, some of them highly respected local leaders."

"What I'm seeing, Blondie, is the whole damned area has been bought. Our drug lords, whoever they are, however many they are, seem to own Ft. Bragg and the entire county. It's so hard for me to accept, you know. I lived here. Sami and I had our home just down the road a piece at Noyo Harbor, and I always trusted the officials, the cops, the judges." Katie smiled at me, and I understood. I was just being naive.

Chapter Fourteen

Katie was on board a really fast salt water speed boat, Jason was coming through the Golden Gate, Petersen was on the prowl a few miles off the north coast of California, and they all thought they were going to surprise the bad guys in fort Bragg. They forgot a set of ears in Washington.

"Tony, listen hard. I just got a call from Sarah in DC, and the feds are coming to town, just like I feared. That Dollarhide woman, Bertorelli's husband, and another bitch, some Latina.

"According to Sarah, they're going to stay at a cabin just east of town, I'll get you the address. We need to hit them hard, with everything we have as soon as they get here. I'm trying to set it up so it looks like some of those puke pot growers did it, but get that Hummer out, get those fucking machine guns mounted, and make sure you have enough people to pull this off. I want everyone of those fuckers dead.

"They'll have some kind of protection close by, you can be sure of that, so do some scouting around there." Riley was worried about having a New York hit man on the team at first, but has come to depend on him. "What the fuck would some guy who spends his whole life walking on concrete know about how we live around here? But he's done good. He goes out to that little ranch, has learned to wear boots and jeans instead of silk suits and Italian leather shoes, even talks a little better. He'll never go back to New York. Not now."

As much as Pelligrini's people hated having to work with the Colombian Cartels, there were times it paid off handsomely for them. They own a large Hum-V military attack vehicle they "acquired" from some Central American despot, along with twin .50 caliber machine guns mounted on the roll bars. Known in civilian circles as a Hummer, these machines are four-wheel drive, high centered, powerful fighting weapons, first used extensively more than thirty-years-ago during what was called the Gulf War and of course in the Iraq and Afghanistan messes. They don't need roads or trails, can climb steep hillsides, don't turn over easily as the old Jeeps did, and can carry some serious armament.

Anthony Colletti drove north of Ft. Bragg, to an isolated little ranch, dropped off some steaks and fresh salmon for the caretaker, and a few grams of white powder to keep his nose and attitude in line, and serviced the Hummer. It was painted muted forest green, striped gently in various shades of brown, and had two evil looking muzzles fronting the working action of twin machine guns.

"Jerry, just look at this killing machine. I worked the streets of New York for Mr. Pelligrini for years, Jerry, and never had anything like this. A couple of dumb fuck automatic pistols, some lead saps, maybe a ball bat, but nothin' like this." Colletti's mind wasn't fast, but he knew perfection when he saw it.

"What a kick in the ass it would be to drive this fucker down Broadway, or into Jersey. Man, a guy could own territory with one of these things. Nobody, I mean nobody, would fuck with me if I had this thing.

"C'mon, you little fucker, help me get some fuel in it, and listen, Jerry, things are gonna heat up around here, so don't let anyone come onto this place. If it ain't Owen Riley, that asshole police chief or me, shoot the fuckers. You understand?" Jerry hadn't had a thought of his own for several years, and simply nodded yes as he hefted a five-gallon can of diesel up to Colletti.

It was Riley who brought Jerry to the ranch, or maybe it was Jerry who led Riley there, but Riley killed the little wanna-be hippies who were using the place to grow pot, put Jerry in charge of the place, and erased most outward evidence the place existed. A small dirt road led off the highway, but was left to overgrow, and it was Jerry's job to see to it that any trace of visits from Colletti or Riley or Richardson were erased. There was no power or phone service, no mail, and above all, no visitors. This was their safe house, to be protected from every source, and the best way to do that was to provide Jerry with good food, plenty of wine, and as much cocaine as he could stuff up his skinny little nose.

Colletti figured rightly the steaks and salmon would spoil, but the white powder would be used up in no time at all.

***

Owen Riley, along with everyone else at the Fort Bragg cop shop, knew the feds were on the way, and he was putting a plan together. He knew he had to do something drastic and had to do it now. "I've got to turn the heat off of us, get it on the tree huggers or maybe the pot growers." He called his communications officer into his office.

"As soon as we know where that broad Dollarhide and Bertorelli's dear widower are, you let me know. Also, get a handle on some of those pot growers around here, and when you hear from me, bust 'em. I don't care how or even if some of them die, just make sure they are charged with what's going to happen to the feds. Don't pull anyone off whatever detail Colletti has going on."

He settled in, his mind still working. Did he get rid of all the incriminating paperwork that's always around? Were there any pictures of the wrong people in any of the files? What the hell would we do if they wanted fingerprints? He couldn't slow it down, and could feel pangs of paranoia gripping as well. Would Colletti blab if they caught him? What about that fool Richardson? That bastard needed to die. He would cave in immediately. And Lopez? He had probably already given them every name he knew.

The young communications officer stuck his head in the office. "They're all bundled up at a cabin just out of town, Owen. I think it's the one owned by the broad that owns the coffee shop where that bitch Bertorelli got hers. I have roadblocks ready to go up, and Colletti has already sent in some ground people. The FBI has security on the grounds, so he figures to get rid of them immediately.

"Do you want me to contact Colletti?"

"No. You done good. Keep me posted on any changes of any kind, and don't let those feds hear anything we're doing. Get on those pot-heads right away. As soon as you know Colletti is making a move, send as many people as you have and bust those pot growers." Then he reached for his cell phone and called Tony Colletti.

"They're gonna tear this place to shreds, 'Tonio, but according to our patrols, the Fed pricks are holing up at that Ripoldi cabin. Now would be an excellent time for a strike. Hit those bastards with everything you've got and get the hell out. I don't want anybody left alive. Kill every one of those bastards. Dorsey will let you know when they're at the cabin. I'm sure they'll come here first, so you've got some time to get set up.

"I've got road blocks ready to go up, and people surrounding the place. Hit 'em, Colletti. Kill those fuckers." Riley was pleased with how Colletti was setting up the hit on the feds. "I was worried when the Wiley Carpenter sent me a New York hit man. What the hell does a city boy know about working in northern California, but he's OK.

"Mr. Pelligrini would be proud of all of us. It was only the stupidity of that asshole Lopez that blew this operation up. Hit a federal agent in the middle of your own fucking living room. Jesus. Now, we have to hit a whole army of the bastards, and then try to make it look like the work of some pot-heads.

"I don't think Mr. Pelligrini would like what's happening here. I've got to try and think like he would. Wiley would be a good man to have here right now, also, but he's got his hands full just trying to keep all the pipelines from getting shut off. If I could do it myself, I'd fly down to Costa Rica and kill that idiot Lopez."

***

"You remember what I said about visitors, Jerry. Kill anyone who shows up." He loved driving the Hummer and headed cross-country, through valleys and over mountains, around giant groves of redwood and oak trees, and came eventually to a little homestead where he picked up four uniformed officers of the FBPD.

"OK, shit head, here's how it is. The feds are going to bust our operation here if they can, and we're going to fuck with their plans. There are at least four FBI agents protecting the cabin where we're heading and they need to be taken out. Jensen, you've had training with the Army's special ops, think you can still slit a throat or two?"

"They'll never know I was there, Tony. I won't carry anything with me but my service weapon and my knife. Sure as hell don't want a radio to give me away."

"Good. Do you want someone with you?"

"No. If there are four of them, I can do it alone. No, don't send anyone with me."

"Freddy, I want you on those big guns. You've fired them before, do you have any questions?"

"No, boss, I know how to work those bastards."

"OK. I'm driving, Pete you ride shotgun alongside me, and help Freddy if he needs it. We're going right down their fucking driveway and blow that cabin to tooth picks. Everyone wear your damn Kevlar, we don't want people shot to hell, other than the feds.

"Now look, you assholes, this is do or die. We knock them out, kill everyone of the fuckers in that cabin, or we lose, and that means federal prison, or death. This isn't a training mission, so no fuck ups."

Chapter Fifteen

Betsy was working with the justice investigators, and starting the process of creating a federal grand jury to further the investigation. Our little army was expected, and the police chief, Randall F. Richardson, met us at the front door, and invited us in. He was very gracious, as we had expected.

Richardson was a born and raised north coaster hailing from Eureka, and later, Crescent City. He attended schools there and college at Berkeley. Katie had told us that he was a professional cop, had worked his way from patrol in San Jose to detective in Sacramento, and then chief in Ft. Bragg, beginning about 10 years ago. We anticipated a voice of reason from him, and it was starting out that way.

"These are extremely egregious charges, Special Agent Dollarhide. I hope you have something other than a hunch about this. I have always felt this was an upstanding department, and one I was very proud of. I sincerely hope, for your sake, this isn't just a case of federal intervention."

Katie was sure of herself, and handed the charges to the chief. "Take your time looking through this Chief Richardson. We have been investigating these serious charges for well over a year now, have had one of our own agents become a turncoat, had another agent gunned down in cold blood, in your community, and you have lost members of your department as well. We don't go into these things lightly or frivolously.

"Our preliminary investigation has led us straight to your department. How many of your people are actually involved, we don't know, but from what we do know, among those involved are officers of a high rank. FBI agents and Justice Department investigators will be combing your department, Chief, and we will expect your cooperation, along with the cooperation of your officers and staff. Yes, this is federal intervention Chief, but there is a reason for it, and we'll prove it."

Richardson was behind his desk now, holding several hundred pages of charges, reports, documentation, and the required federal court orders, which allowed us to complete our investigation. He picked up the phone and told his secretary to call a meeting of his deputy chiefs, the captains of various divisions, and the office staff. No one was exempt.

"I can guarantee my cooperation, Agent Dollarhide. Many of my top people have spent their entire lives building careers in law enforcement, many have attended the FBI training schools, as have I. We don't take charges like this lightly, either."

We sat with the chief as he outlined the charges and the investigation of his department to his staff and paid close attention to the faces of those in attendance. I could see both Katie and Contreras matching the names they knew with faces they could see, and little sparks of recognition told me we were dealing with known drug dealers.

Ten minutes into the proceeding, a secretary came in and told Owen Riley he had a call from Sarah Costello. Riley was agitated as hell, but went out and took the call. Afterward, Katie and I went over our own notes and the personnel records of the top people in the department. One name caught our attention immediately. Deputy Chief of Detectives was listed as Owen Riley. He had been in Ft. Bragg for about five years, coming from New Orleans, and San Juan, Puerto Rico before that. "That call he took was from Sarah Costello, Jason. That name, Sarah Costello is familiar to me and I don't know why. And now, Riley comes here from San Juan,"

"Is that a coincidence, Katie? Pelligrini was killed in San Juan. Lopez spent a great deal of time traveling all over the Caribbean, including Puerto Rico. Riley's the jerk that insisted that Sami was killed because of a robbery gone bad. He called me an egotistical Hollywood producer. Let's check this dude out. I'd love to write 'fini' to his career."

Katie called Betsy at the Federal Building and the wheels went into action. "We'll have an answer about his background right away. What does his personnel folder say?"

For the next couple of hours we poured over personnel records, particularly of the top men and women, and looked into the functions of the different divisions to see if there were discrepancies among the way each division functioned. Did patrol do the same as burglary, did accidents do the same as detectives, was there something different that stood out?

"It's getting late and dark, Blondie. Let's get back to the cabin. I'll feel a lot safer there, and besides, I'm hungry as hell." We packed up our papers, jumped in the quick little sedan and headed to what is now being called home. The rain had finally stopped, and there was a chill to the air. "This might be a good night for a fire in that roomy old fireplace.

"I think I've told you, Sami and I spent several weekends here, cuddled in front of that fireplace. There are some strong memories, Katie. I promise I won't let them intrude on us, but I want you to be aware."

She was washing a glass at the sink, had that wonderful smile plastered across her face, pinched me on my ample butt, sprinkled cold water at me with her finger tips, and nestled into my arms. "Sami is part of both our lives, Butterball, and she always will be. Your love for her was different than mine, but we both loved her, and we'll always miss her. Her memory should be part of our lives."

At about seven O'clock, the fax rattled off several pages on Owen Riley, former detective in San Juan, Puerto Rico, and chief investigator in New Orleans, only none of it matched. A picture of Riley from Puerto Rico showed a man in his forties, tall, thin, with lots of dark curly hair. A picture from Ft. Bragg showed a man in his forties, medium height, heavyweight, and bald as that proverbial billiard ball.

In a ten-year period it seems, Mr. Riley lost about ten years, grew considerably shorter, gained a hundred pounds, and lost all his hair. When the fax chattered again, there was a picture from New Orleans of the Owen Riley we knew in Ft. Bragg.

"So it appears we're right. We don't know if Riley is a Pelligrini plant or a Lopez man, but it's obvious to me the real Owen Riley was done away with and this dude has assumed his identity. I wonder who he really is?

"We need a finger print from our current Mr. Riley. How to do that, Jason?" Katie was already calling Betsy, and I figured we could ask each of the division heads to fill out a questionnaire, to get all their prints.

"I would bet the fingerprint records that are on file at the police station are false as hell. We can't use them at all. These guys, besides being drug dealers and killers, are also trained cops. I don't think they'd have legitimate fingerprints on their records."

After Katie finished talking with Betsy, she remembered why the name Sarah Costello meant something to her. Costello was a secretary in John Chandler's office in Washington, DC.

"First things first, Jason. I've got to call John. It's not midnight yet in DC, I'm sure I can find him. Shit,

Costello has been one of his secretaries for so long, she probably knows more about what we're doing than John, himself.

"What's with the fucking phone, now." She was standing there with the phone in her hand, trying to call Chandler, and the tension of what had happened today was coming out in frustration. She looked like she might destroy the telephone in her hand. This had been a hectic, frightening day for all of us, but for Katie in particular. She was the agent in charge, she was the one who would have her head on the chopping block if anything went wrong, and right now, she was going to take her frustrations out on a telephone.

I wanted to laugh at what was happening, but that and my idea about fingerprints, and Katie's thoughts about Sarah Costello would have to wait. We didn't get a chance to talk about it. Full automatic fire from something larger than an Uzi or AK 47 blasted the front of our cabin, tore great holes in the walls, broke windows, and smashed trinkets, knickknacks, furniture, and pictures inside. Big heavy bullets whined off the rock fireplace and plowed through furniture. The noise was fearsome. Katie and I were on the deck behind the couch, tried to get even lower to the ground. Our handguns seemed like pitiful little toys at this point. Pop guns at best.

"That sounds an awful lot like an M-60, Katie. That's the kind of armament armies use, not cops. That's the sound of the guns that were fired at *D'Anne*, Katie. Those are military machine guns. Listen to that." The heavy rattle of the big guns was mixed with the fury of large projectiles bouncing off of or breaking through our cabin.

"Where the hell are those four assholes that are supposed to be protecting this place?" I howled. "Jesus, listen to that thing. It sounds like it's mounted on some kind of vehicle. What do they have, a tank?" I crawled on my belly into one of the bedrooms to see if I could see something. All the shots were going into rooms with lights on. And then it got quiet.

I watched a big wide Hummer, that's the civilian model of what the military calls a Hum-V, a huge four wheel drive vehicle with massive amounts of ground clearance and a very wide track, this one with a pair of military machine guns, as it raced out of our driveway.

I popped off a couple of shots from my little peashooter and hollered for Katie. "I think we woke 'em up, Blondie. The vehicle left, but I never did hear any shots or noise from our own agents. We have to be really careful now, there may be more of those assholes on the ground out there." We cut what few lights were still on and carefully went from room to room, not surveying the damage, but trying to see if anyone was moving around outside. The cabin was built in such a manner that various windows gave us a 360-degree look about the place.

"This is really strange, Butterball. They had us, but left. Why?" The two of us searched the grounds for our defenders and found them, throats slashed and dumped in a ravine about thirty yards from the house. This was a big-time hit. To take out four well trained FBI agents on guard duty without a sound, cut the telephone wires, and then bring a Hummer with mounted machine guns up a public roadway without having to worry about being discovered, told me we had definitely awakened a very mean beast.

A movement in the brush caught our attention, and in our flashlight beams, we found a Fort Bragg cop, gun in one hand, a bloody knife in the other. "F.B.I. Freeze, fucker, and you'll live." Katie was already aiming her 9mm right at the guy, but he wouldn't stop. He drew down on her and she fired two quick shots, killing him instantly. "Shit. I wanted a prisoner. Damn it. I had to kill him, Jason, I couldn't take a chance on just trying to wound the prick." We knew he had not been at the station when we were there, and we had to find his personnel records as quick as possible.

"This guy might give us a clue as to who we're looking for. We know Owen Riley is a big time suspect in this, but which division this guy is assigned, might tell us even more."

We were trying to find our way through the mess in the cabin when a contingent of agents and investigators arrived, led by Betsy, and started gathering as much evidence as they could. "How did you know to come, Betsy?" Katie asked the question that hadn't dawned on me.

"We got an anonymous call that you were in danger. It came from a cell phone, so there was no caller ID."

"I bet that's why those bastards lit out of here. If that call came from our man inside, he's probably already dead, or in big danger of being dead very soon." Katie was well past the point of being furious. "This is war, now. War, Jason. Those bastards are down and dead, Butterball. They just don't know it yet."

Her little fist was drumming a war dance into an open hand, on her thigh, even threatening a few pieces of furniture. Her eyes were narrowed and ugly, not the bright, shiny eyes I can remember from our days on *D'Anne*. This was a mean woman right now, mean, nasty, and ready for one hell of a fight.

This was a personality change I hadn't seen before, and it frightened me. Katie is still a soft, sensuous woman flitting about the afterdeck of *D'Anne*, sans clothing, thank you very much, but I was looking at a face filled with hate and anger. And hurt.

"I've just lost four trusted agents, Jason. Those filthy bastards killed four of my agents. Many people will pay for this, and I hope pay with their lives." She reloaded the clip for her pistol, slammed it into the piece, and wept. "Those men were our front line of defense, Jason, brave, virtuous FBI field agents. They will be avenged."

At least some of the lights still worked. "Katie, with that kind of firepower, that kind of noise, doesn't it seem strange to you that we haven't seen either the Ft. Bragg police or the county sheriff? What the hell are we up against here?"

"There was a contingent of police cars and sheriff patrol cars heading back into town as I came up here. We had the portable emergency red flashers on top of our cars, Katie, and they wouldn't move aside for us. There is a level of arrogance in this police department I haven't seen in all my years traveling around the world for the Bureau. They really think we're going to roll over and play dead.

"They must have had all the access roads up here blocked off so that hit team could simply roll in. I wonder why they didn't stop to finish you two off? They killed the four security agents, blew the damned cabin to bits, but didn't check to see if you had been killed in the assault. Strange. It must have been that call." She didn't finish her thoughts, just appeared to let her mind drift into another pattern. All I could think of, this was not as safe a place as I thought it would be. Of course, we weren't thinking of being attacked by military weapons either.

"The only thing they didn't use, Betsy, were grenades and mortars. I wonder if that's next?"

Katie was on her cell phone to her boss in Washington, who just happened to be the number two man at the agency. I heard as she described the hit, told about Costello, and her fear of our man inside the Ft. Bragg police station. I was completely amazed, sat in disbelief as I heard her ask for military protection.

"Sir, this is no longer a criminal investigation, this is the complete takeover of civilian police agencies and the local judicial system, by criminal, probably foreign interests. I will call it criminal terrorism if need be, John. I recommend in the strongest possible terms, sending in the Army."

She listened for a moment, drummed her fingers and scowled at the cell phone before continuing. "I can no longer guarantee the safety of anyone connected with the federal government in this area of Northern California. To the best of my knowledge, the local population is not being threatened, but I feel that might just be a matter of time.

"John, does Sarah Costello still work for you? She tried to contact one of the cops while we were in the station this afternoon. She's your mole, John."

She listened, did a couple of uh huhs, scowled a bit, and hung up her cell phone. "There will be a plane load of agents and investigators from the Justice Department, and the Treasury Department arriving later tonight. Let's move out of here and set up camp in the Federal Building downtown. We're no longer safe here." Francesca will not appreciate the condition we're leaving her little cabin.

We moved out in a convoy, red lights and sirens screaming, and purposefully swung past the cop shop on the way to our new home. It was out of the way, but sometimes one must simply be an egotistical Hollywood type. Arrogance was our answer to their arrogance.

According to the police radio scanner we had with us, a fire had erupted at a cabin just out of town within five minutes of our leaving. Those bastards had people in the area and watched as our investigators went over the place. As the bodies of the four agents were removed. As the body of one of their own was taken away, members of the drug conspiracy moved in and torched Francesca's cabin.

"Blondie, how the hell many people are we dealing with here? If Betsy was passed by a contingent of police vehicles, and we know it took at least two men to operate that big assault vehicle, and more men on the ground to assassinate the agents, now we find others have burned the damn cabin. How the hell many in the police department are we going to be fighting?"

"We won't be getting the Army, Jason, but these guys coming in tonight are bringing some pretty impressive firepower of their own. Holy shit, did we open up this can of worms, or what?" Her smile challenged the sun, and she laughed long and loud. This was the Katie I loved. "When I make a plan to bring someone into the open, I bring them into the open."

She was sitting quiet for a moment. "You know, first I learn that Deacon is a traitor, and now I find out Sarah Costello is also. I never worked much with Costello, she worked as one of John's secretaries, but she sure would have had access to all the information passing through his office. God, Jason, these guys have people planted everywhere." She had the mental picture of Costello going through Jason's file that morning in Chandler's office.

When I looked over I could see that little fist of hers doubled up, released, and then doubled up again. I would not want to be on the wrong side of a round-house punch by that charming and lovely lady. She had a nasty look on her face, and I pitied any little mechanical device that might get in the way of her frustration.

Chapter Sixteen

The FBI director was with the Attorney General, discussing how to implement martial law at the Ft. Bragg Police Department, and had gone to the chief of staff at the White House with the problem. Chandler couldn't authorize such a thing on his own, as he had explained to Dollarhide, but that thought wouldn't go out of his mind. "These people were attacked by a military vehicle armed with twin machine guns, and found a member of that rotten police department with a bloody knife and four dead FBI agents. We need as much help as it is possible to get, sir."

Alberto Pelligrini, although very dead, had long fingers that reached into high government places. The White House gave its approval, the Attorney General himself called the Justice Department head in California, who went straight to the governor of the Golden State.

Chandler had called the White House as soon as he hung up with Katie. He also called his boss, the FBI director, and the Attorney General. The meeting was set up for midnight, eastern time. That was fast considering most of those involved were bureaucrats. Because of the press conference that had been held in Ft. Bragg, and the statements being issued by the FBI and the Justice Department in Washington, the press was onto the meeting immediately.

Chandler had a unique position within the bureau, and wasn't afraid to use it to his best advantage. He and President Marcus Kipling had been far more than just acquaintances over the years, the two families had been very close. Both Chandler and the president were avid fishermen, in particular fly fishing, and had traveled to some pretty exotic waters together. They had been to Canada, to the western states, to the waters of the Florida Keys, even once to Ireland. Fishing was a way of life to the two, and it made for a strong friendship.

Before his appointment to the FBI, Chandler was a well respected attorney who specialized in big business and politicians. He had done considerable work for Kipling, and the wives of the two men hit it off exceptionally well also. Chandler's wife was a professional fly tier, with a thriving coast-to-coast Internet and mail order business.

Chandler had joined the FBI in a unique position following the tragic death of his wife. He worked specifically in the National Security division, coordinating efforts of the mingled agencies working in drug interdiction and national security.

"John," Kipling had called Chandler to the White House within weeks of his election. "John, I think you'd be a fine FBI director. I'd like to submit your name to the Senate."

"No, Mr. President, I have a better idea. The director we have now is doing an excellent job, and this position shouldn't be political, it should be in the best interest of the Bureau and law enforcement. I like Harold Collins, and he's doing a fine job.

"No, what I think is needed is a direct link between the bureau and the White House. Right now, we have to funnel everything through all the levels of the Justice Department, and there are times that bureaucratic nonsense obstructs our needs, forces us to a seriously slow crawl. As you know, the FBI works closely with military intelligence, and one of our main concerns is national security.

"If you feel you have to appoint me to something, Marcus, have a long talk with Collins and set up another position, answerable to the bureau director, but with a direct line to the White House." John Chandler had found his calling, and when the president started making it known he felt the crime families and drug cartels were a threat to national security, Director Collins appointed Chandler to hold that position as well.

With agents like Katie Dollarhide and Sami Bertorelli in the field, The Deacon at headquarters, and access to the Coast Guard, Chandler felt he was making progress in his own war on drugs. "This so-called war is so much more than that, Mr. President. We have international crime families involved, and the internal security of this country is being jeopardized. A national security threat exists, sir, and I think we are at least getting a handle on it."

He had talked many times with President Kipling about the idea that drugs and other crime coming onto U.S. shores from overseas was a threat to the nation, and the president agreed on most issues. Chandler had the president's ear, and that should have frightened the crime families and cartels. It didn't.

"Marcus, what we've feared for so long is happening right now in California. Crime families from all the major drug areas of the world have infiltrated the police and justice systems in Ft. Bragg. You've read the headlines, and the stories behind them are even more gruesome.

"These crime families, some from Italy and Greece, some from North Africa have joined forces with cartels from South America, and we believe that Asian gangs are also in on the feeding frenzy, and they have interests at the national level as well.

"You will be contacted by some very influential people to slow down what we're doing, but it is essential that we finish this job. This is the first time we know that major crime organizations have literally taken over a political system, the entire county-wide police and justice system, Marcus, and we have an opportunity to crush them.

"I have fine agents on the scene, I have justification for an all out federal take over of the county, Mr. President. Please read these reports carefully, and you'll see we have, for the first time, a chance to end a major threat to our way of life.

"Mr. President, if crime gangs like these can infiltrate an entire county, it is very possible they have already made inroads in state government, and in federal agencies. I have discovered two gang moles in top positions at the FBI. One is dead, the other is about to be in custody. Are there more? Probably, and not just in the FBI.

"We're dealing with so much money, so much power, so much control, it wouldn't surprise me to learn crime family members are in every part of our government, including congress." Too often at the higher echelons of government, the word gang means sleazy street types with Saturday night specials, robbing liquor stores and dealing small potatoes in drugs. Chandler used the word gang in a world-wide sense. "I call them gangs, Mr. President, not in a street related meaning, but to indicate they are not fettered by law, by morals, or by allegiance to anything other than their own family."

It bothered Chandler a great deal when he learned that Deacon had been a member of the drug mob, mostly because he had never suspected him of anything other than being a good agent, a good investigator. He had even given him a good review in his record, not long before he was discovered.

"Katie, that son of a bitch has been to dinner at my house, eaten at my table, been given Christmas presents by me. I'm sorry when anyone has to die by violence, but I'm also giving you a commendation for doing a fine service for the Bureau and for our country.

What the hell is this coming to, Katie? A former Coast Guard officer, FBI special agent, member of our drug interdiction program, is a member of one of the world's largest drug smuggling operations? Unbelievable."

He had made that speech to Katie Dollarhide while we were still at sea, and now he gave an almost identical speech to the President of the United States. "Marcus, this agent, we called him Deacon, had every credential an agent could carry, and another agent had to shoot him dead, or die herself. Now I find out one of my most trusted secretaries is also a turncoat, a mole, an informer, a traitor. She has been with the department for more than ten years, Mr. President. Ten years.

"We must stop these people now, and we have a chance to do it. Please, let us declare a national emergency, and let us find every son of a bitch in that organization. We have now lost one agent, one of the best who ever worked in our drug interdiction, national security, division of the Bureau. She died violently at the hands of two punks, outlaws hired by Pelligrini and Lopez. We have lost another agent who turned to crime, was found out, and died violently at the hands of another agent. An agent in Costa Rica died getting us the information on a hit on another agent, and four brave agents died tonight, their throats slashed by a renegade cop. And now, we have a trusted employee in custody.

"The cost is getting very high, Mr. President, and we can stop it now."

***

"Following the death of Alberto Pelligrini, the Justice Department had received some interesting calls, most wondered why a man with Pelligrini's background as an upstanding international philanthropist, would be gunned down near a seedy little bar in San Juan, Puerto Rico." The Attorney General had been briefed on the investigation from the day Sami Bertorelli was assassinated. He didn't like his people being wiped out gangland style.

"I've told many of the callers the Pelligrini they thought they knew was one of the world's most dangerous drug dealers and assassins, and he was in the process of being arrested when he was killed. The president has even received calls, gentlemen, so Pelligrini is a big fish no more."

Chandler spent the next half hour outlining what Dollarhide had told him in her call, and what was going on in Ft. Bragg, California. He finished it off emphatically calling for federal takeover of police duties in the north coast area, for the second time, to the second high-ranking federal official. "Agent Dollarhide specifically said she can no longer provide for the safety of our own people there, more or less the civilian population. It takes a big decree to enforce military rule, but there will be lots of blood on the ground if we don't." His mind was actively finishing off what he had just said out loud. "Such a pretty little town, and now almost a war zone. I might have expected serious problems to crop up between logging interests and environmentalists, but not this."

Chandler continued with his briefing. "While agent Dollarhide was in the Ft. Bragg police station, a member of my own staff called one of the suspect police officers, to brief him on what we were planning. My own staff, gentlemen.

"These are desperate people, and they will do everything in their power to protect themselves and their operations."

What Chandler did not tell the group was how he expected the governor of California to react. Samuel Dunbar had been a thorn in the side of almost every federal agency in Washington, threatening to cut off all communication with federal housing people, with emergency management officials, even with the weather bureau.

He hated the Department of Transportation, HUD, and virtually every other agency, in particular, the Department of Defense. Dunbar was radical in the extreme, had campaigned on the idea of being radical, of forcing Washington out of the lives of Californians, and he would be a serious problem in Ft. Bragg. "I think the best bet will be for Katie Dollarhide to face off with him, one on one. She's about as tough an agent as I have, and she'll keep that pecker head in line."

His train of thought was interrupted by President Marcus Kipling. "I have just been briefed on this situation, and I heard enough of what you were saying Chandler, that I can make a decision right now. I am sending a message to the governor of California asking him to mobilize the National Guard.

"Tell your people to continue their investigation. We were right, weren't we, when we said this drug situation was going to be of considerable national security proportions?

"I've also contacted leaders of both parties in congress, and many will be joining me for breakfast here in the White House shortly. I will also meet with the press immediately after that meeting. Insurrection, that's what it is, and it won't happen while I'm president."

Some in the press had thought that Kipling might have been just a bit soft on drug related crimes, but this speech certainly changed that. Kipling had said during his campaign that he had smoked some pot as a younger man, but he had never used anything stronger. He hinted that he thought marijuana use should not be treated the same as heroin or opium, or some of the stronger cocaine based narcotics. "Maybe," he said once, "Marijuana laws need to be restructured. Some states are in that process right now.

"Some of the laws relating to drug use might be rewritten to take advantage of all that is known today. Free-basing with cocaine can't be put in the same category as smoking a joint. Crack cocaine, heroin, opium; these are very dangerous drugs. Methamphetamine use is skyrocketing and tearing families apart. They buy the damn stuff with food stamps. The problem with marijuana is it has been put in the same drawer as these others, and just maybe it shouldn't have been."

This is the same man who when elected, said drugs and their criminal elements were a national security threat. He didn't think there was a problem with his views. "I'm much more interested in the justice of the situation, and when criminal elements are seeking to dismantle the very fabric of American life, then it is a national security problem."

The group talked for another hour among themselves, and watched as the sun rose over Washington. "I'll have breakfast with the congressional leaders, gentlemen, and then meet with the press. So far, and this is important, congress is treating this as a bipartisan problem, and I want to keep it that way. This isn't political, it's criminal action designed to alter the American way of life, and that's the way I want it handled."

The Attorney General, the Homeland Security boss, the Secretary of the Treasury, and the various agency heads under them left the White House for their respective bureaus, and more meetings. Chandler and his boss headed for FBI headquarters. "John, this is a threat of immense proportions, and I'm very proud of the way you've handled things so far. Keep up the good work.

You have my complete confidence, and you have free reign right now. Do what has to be done."

"Thank you, Harold. There is one problem I haven't brought up yet."

Chandler was cut off by Collins. "Yes, I know. The governor of California. The strangest man I've ever met, John. Can your people out there cope?" It was a fair question, Chandler knew.

"Katie Dollarhide can probably take the little bastard on his own terms, Harold, I just hope she understands she has that authority."

"You call her John, and you tell her she has that authority."

Seven o'clock in the morning in Washington, DC, is four o'clock on the west coast, but Chandler didn't even hesitate, and called Katie Dollarhide at the federal building. He wasn't surprised that she was already up, despite the harrowing experiences of the night before. He watched out the window of his office as bright early winter sunshine glowed on marble monuments to democracy, and felt he was doing the right thing to protect his country.

His mind played with what might have been if Kathy had lived, where he would be, what he would be doing. He couldn't focus, he was so deep in the present. His reverie ended when Katie came on the line.

"Katie, I knew all four of those agents. I'm sending, under the president's own signature, condolences to all the families. Is there anything we could have done to protect them any more than what we did?" Chandler was devastated by the death of four agents, and furiously angry that their deaths came at the apparent hands of police officers. "I'm sick to my stomach just thinking about this entire situation, Katie. We've now lost six brave, patriotic agents to a rogue police department, have had to kill one of our own because he was turned, and we are still faced with the possibility that another traitor is in our midst, right here in bureau headquarters. Do you think Costello is the only one? I don't.

"The director just told me I am to do what is necessary to bring an end to this rebellion, Katie. I'm passing that on to you. You're getting what you asked for old girl. The president is declaring an emergency and the California National Guard is being mobilized. The first contingents should be in town within the hour, and of course, more will follow. You're the senior agent on the scene, but more than that, you are now the director of operations for the federal intervention, at my command, with the full backing of the director, and the Attorney General.

"I want this ended as soon as possible. I'm not saying walk into that station house with guns blazing, but do not put any more of our agents in a position of serious jeopardy. If they have to use force, then I want them to use maximum force, is that completely understood?"

Katie was elated, was beaming at the news, but also, she had never heard John Chandler as angry or as hurt as he sounded at this moment. In all the years of her service to the agency, in all the years she had worked in the field and in headquarters, there had never been an operation in which six agents died, and in which there were two known traitors working within the bureau.

"John, I understand fully. Please send copies of your orders to every federal office in the country. I don't want there to be any questions to my authority, or to the conclusion of this operation.

"For your information, the best thing we ever did was turn Jason Caldwell. He is a born leader, smarter than most people I've worked with, and seems to be absolutely fearless. He's still Butterball, though. He just doesn't lose any weight, no matter what we do.

"I really didn't want to kill that cop last night, John. It would have been in our best interest to have a prisoner, but it was him or us. Your thinking is right on the money. This is insurrection, not just drug smuggling. These bastards own this part of the country.

"I'll keep you posted on what's happening here, and I know you'll keep me filled in on what the Washington scene is. This will end soon, John. We woke them up, they took their best shot, and now they go down. We have leads on three traitors in the department, but I have to believe there are many more than that involved in this drug operation.

"One, Owen Riley is the name he's using here, is a hired Pelligrini killer from San Juan, another, calling himself Anthony Colletti, is actually from New York, and worked as a hired gun for several mob families. They did a good job of infiltrating the department here. It may turn out to be some serious infiltration of the department rather than the entire Ft. Bragg Police Department becoming drug dealers. But, we can't forget this, they have judicial backing as well, so they have infiltrated the cop shop and the court room.

"Everyone here is carrying full automatic weapons, John, and we always move in groups of two or more. These guys are armed to the teeth with heavy weaponry, and we intend to respond in kind. One shot, we blow up the building. That's just a comment, not current tactics, but you get the idea."

For the first time in a couple of days Chandler was able to get a smile started. "That's quite a picture you paint, Katie. I can see the headlines now: FBI razes police department headquarters following a back fire from a local pick up truck." The two laughed out loud over that.

"If you get a chance, Katie, watch the president at his press conference. I'll call again in a few hours. You'll be going up against California's best shortly. Governor Samuel Dunbar is as radical as they get, and he'll fight you toe to toe over federal intervention. You're working for the president on this, so don't take any of his shit. Good hunting, Katie."

***

Ft. Bragg Police Chief Richardson was sitting at his breakfast table, his pajamas soaked in sweat from a nightmare he had been enduring when the phone woke him. "Are you telling me that members of my department attacked the FBI contingent inside our own town? Riley, what the hell were you thinking? My God, they'll bring the whole damn army in now."

The nightmare had to do with headlines in a newspaper naming him as a turncoat cop, a sexual deviate, and soon, a prison inmate. Headlines saying he was a member of an international gang of drug runners, the leader of the police agency responsible for apprehending drug runners, not being one.

"Listen to me chief. I got this all figured out. We brought in some of those hippy types that grow pot, and we're going to put the blame on them. Keep your cool Richardson, we got it all figured out."

"You haven't got shit figured out, Riley. You said they used machine guns on those agents, that four of them are dead? Where the hell would a hippy get a fucking machine gun?"

"Just keep your fucking cool, chief. Don't get all screwed up over this. We got it under control. You don't want me or Colletti to find out you're losing your cool. Just go to the cop shop this morning the same as usual."

Richardson was shaking all over, couldn't get the coffee cup to his mouth. He got up and walked into his bedroom, pulled his police service revolver from its holster, even cocked the hammer, but fell to the bed sobbing, heaving great sighs, screaming his agony. Before he could put the gun to his head and fire the shot he caved in to his rattled emotions. "It's all over. My life is over, but I'm not strong enough to make it end. How will I be able to face anyone knowing men from my own department killed four federal agents, maybe more."

He tried again to bring the pistol to his head, but wasn't able to and broke into moaning sobs and threw the piece across the room. He wallowed in violent fits of crying and sobbing, screaming his fear, and finally, well before sunrise, tried to make himself presentable. "Presentable. There's a word for me. Make myself presentable for a firing squad."

***

"Good hunting, Katie, is what he said, Jason, and that's what we're going to be doing. I've been so busy with all this, with so much death and blood, I'm sorry I've neglected us. For the first time in my life, I actually love someone, not something, as I feel about the Bureau, but someone.

"You, Jason, you. Yes you old fat bastard, I love you. Do you know how you got that name, Butterball? I gave it to you. I told them at headquarters that you were just about fifty pounds overweight and looked like a turkey ready for the oven. A Butterball, Jason."

Laughter echoed down the halls of the Federal Building. "I said this before, but I really mean it. When this is over, it's over for me too. I'm resigning from the FBI, and I want us to travel the world on board *D'Anne*. Just you and me, acres of tuna, a freezer full of exotic fish and fowl, a breeze at our back and blue water. That's what I want Jason."

Her face was glowing as she said all this, probably as much from releasing the tension and frustration as from actually saying these things out loud.

Katie Dollarhide had just been given the biggest job in the Bureau, and the weight of that, coupled with her innermost feelings, begged for serious emotional release.

"When I met you, Blondie, I hated you so much. You told me my wife had lied to me, had cheated on our vows, was someone she wasn't, at least to me. I would gladly have thrown both you and Petersen to the wolves, to the sharks, but because of you, I've learned what a magnificent person Sami was, how I was so lucky to have known her, even for such a short time.

"If all this ends wrong, it's important we know how much we mean to each other. I'm terribly sorry Sami and I never had a chance to be completely honest with each other, and I've fretted, worried, how I would have reacted had she been honest, but with us, we have built memories no one can take from us. You saved my life by killing another person, that's about as impressive as a man could ever ask, and you've allowed me to be in on an investigation that will bring an end to my grieving for Sami.

"More than that, you tough little shit, I love you. We might be dead in the next few minutes or days, but you must know, I love you. When it's over, if we're still here, I'll take us places where the fish will jump into the boat on their own, where the surf runs high, where a safe harbor is only that, not where blue water sailors want to be." Ragged, raw edged emotions, squared. Soldiers hugged, kissed, and looked deep into each other's eyes.

**

At seven thirty in the morning, five tanks, two hundred fifty men and women with their respective weapons, five gun ship helicopters, and the governor arrived on the steps of the Ft. Bragg Police Department. Well, they were at least in proximity to the steps of the police department. Every person inside was disarmed and sent home. Every one of them was followed by at least three federal agents or National Guard troopers, in different cars. This was a massive takeover. Katie and Jason, along with Betsy Contreras and other top agents on the scene met the Governor of the Golden State, Samuel Dunbar.

"So, you're the agent trying to destroy this pretty little town. Well, I for one am willing to believe there are some bad apples in this department, but I'm not sure this kind of response is needed. For God's sake, woman, you have enough fire power here to start a war." Katie agreed totally because that was her intention.

Dunbar was one of those who had called the Attorney General questioning whether or not Alberto Pelligrini should have been gunned down. Pelligrini had given several million of his drug dollars to various state institutions, in particular, art museums, and education facilities, and he was a large contributor to Dunbar's political career.

"I can't believe the federal agents had to shoot Mr. Pelligrini as if he was a common house burglar. I intend to talk with our congressional delegation about this. The federal government is being seriously intrusive in what should be a California state matter."

Katie stood her ground. "Governor, a military attack vehicle with two machine guns mounted on it attacked my headquarters last night. Right here in this pretty little town. In the operation, four FBI agents were slaughtered. Would you like to see the pictures of what those machine guns did to that cabin, and what the fire did later? Would you like to see pictures of the four federal agents with their throats slashed? Governor Dunbar, you think because Pelligrini gave this state some money, that his drug running operation is OK?

"There are hundreds of thousands of people who are being affected because of this criminal operation

Governor. Some are junkies, some are families of junkies, some are citizens of this pretty little town, now without proper police protection, some are politicians and cops on the take. These are just a few of those whose lives have been affected by this affront.

"There are men working in this police department with known connections to both the Mafia crime families and Colombian drug cartels. An agent working undercover was murdered here in this pretty little town, slightly more than a year ago, and there are two known traitors working within the FBI itself. I killed one of them personally, Mr. Governor."

Her eyes were narrowed, her fists were clenched, there was controlled anger flowing through her body, and the Governor of the Golden State took a small step backward. She was angry, but this time I didn't see the hate that had clouded her features last night. I was glad for that because it frightened me more than anything that's happened since this whole thing started. Katie was tying this conspiracy down in terms anyone could understand, but wasn't showing that terrible hate I had seen.

"In my opinion, Governor, I wouldn't argue about seeing an entire division of Marines on hand right now. If you have second thoughts about providing this operation with the necessary protection we have asked for, I will pass that on to the president. At this time, I am working under the authority of the Director of the FBI, under the auspices of the Attorney General of the United States, with the complete authority of the president.

"If that isn't clear enough for you, I have the authority to declare a military emergency, and if you're unwilling to participate in our operation, you can leave right now."

Her eyes were blazing, her fists were doubled up as if to deck the governor, and on top of that, she cradled a vicious little machine gun in the crook of her arm. Katie Dollarhide was in charge, and damn the torpedoes. The governor made a couple of little stupid remarks about the federal government, and then stepped away from Katie.

Before descending the steps, his eye took in the scene before him, and later recalled the sight to an aide. "General Sappenfield in combat fatigues, his stars muted in the early morning light, standing next to the FBI bitch, and surrounded by colonels and majors, all armed to the teeth. Out front, two tanks, two armored personnel carriers, two Bradley Fighting Machines, with armed troopers nearby, arrayed in platoon formation, fronted by lieutenants and captains, row after row, standing at Parade Rest, cradling automatic rifles, their suspenders bristling with hand grenades, and overhead, the distinctive sound of helicopter gunships.

"I tell you, it was an impressive sight, but one I didn't think I'd ever witness on the streets of a California town."

On the street corners, Governor Dunbar could see Military Police, dressed in Class A uniforms, but with helmets and bloused trousers in their combat boots. "Federal Police now patrolling this pretty little town. All because of marijuana?"

The federal government had called his bluff, and they were holding a royal flush. There was a sea of combat trained troops surrounding his position, and his only move was retreat, retreat as gracefully as possible.

"You'll hear more from me, Agent Dollarhide, you can bet on it. Federal intervention of this magnitude won't be tolerated. You'll hear more from me."

Dunbar retreated to his limousine and drove from Ft. Bragg, talking to a couple of aides. "She's a bitch, eh? Tough little bitch. Probably a ball buster, too. Anyway, boys, we can't stop this now, so let's go back to Sacramento and start working to protect what we have left of California. These damned feds want to run the lives of every single person in the country, one on one."

Newspapers up and down the coast had been asking the question, how had this happened and why hadn't the state done something about it? Federal intervention was extreme at worst, and the current scenario was more than Dunbar's agencies could handle. Many question if, one; did any of the state agencies have any idea of this drug conspiracy? And, two; if they did, why hadn't something been done prior to federal intervention?

A native of the Golden State, even though from the south part, Governor Dunbar was always a supporter of the individual, even while in school. Way back when he was just a child, he took part in demonstrations against our involvement in Viet Nam, was a leader of the most conservative political organizations during university, and after law school, gravitated to politics without a stop in private practice.

"Hell yes, I was just twenty five when I ran for District Attorney, and by damn, I won. We won. It was the people telling me, they wanted control of their lives back, and for the last thirty years, I've worked for that.

"Little fucking FBI bitch with a machine gun tells me I can't make the decisions about the state I was elected to lead. I'm demanding a congressional investigation of this operation right now. Jackson, as soon as this fucking car stops in Sacramento, you get on the phone to our delegation in congress, and you force them to call for an investigation. This is pure politics from the president, and from those federal agency heads he put in office.

"I want this to become the political football of the new century, boys. I want this to carry me to the White

House, and I want this to be the end of federal intervention in private lives."

Jackson nodded, but couldn't help but wonder what the governor was thinking. He was of one party, the entire California congressional delegation was of the other party, the same as the president.

"I'll do what I can, Governor," was all he said.

***

Katie, in the meantime, took command, called the commanding officer of the National Guard and explained the entire situation. When he heard Hummer with twin machine guns mounted, his mouth dropped.

It was getting late, and Katie wanted to get back to the federal building and see President Kipling's press conference. She had just gone head to head with the California governor, in front of hundreds of representatives of the press, but was more interested in seeing and hearing what the president had to say. I don't believe she was even aware of how strong a position she currently commanded.

When we arrived, there was a call from John Chandler. "What the hell did you say to Governor Dunbar, Katie? He actually called the director and demanded you be fired. Good work. We passed all of this to the Attorney General, and he's getting word of it to the president. That news conference is coming up in about half an hour, and should be a good one."

"Well, Butterball, we have raised the level one more notch. Governor Dunbar complained to the director about me, and I just got commended for it. Neat." Sometimes Katie could be a little kid, and this was one of those times. She was primed for a war, and she was in command. Just maybe, she did understand.

President Kipling looked tired when the news conference started, and he spent several minutes outlining what had happened over the course of the FBI investigation. When he talked about agents having their throats slashed, and military attack vehicles with machine guns used to strike at an FBI manned complex, he showed visible signs of anger.

He went into great detail on the charges against the Ft. Bragg police department, and in particular, the men we had singled out as being a part of the covert drug operation. "These men have been strutting about as protectors of the city and its residents, as proud members of a police department that has a wonderful history. They have vilified everything an officer of the law stands for. To serve and protect? No. In this case, it's to serve and deceive.

"Agents of the FBI, and other federal agencies, have found them out, and in so doing, six FBI agents, brave men and women, are dead. I have just sent a personal letter to the governor of the state of California outlining my displeasure at his behavior this morning. He feels our intrusion into the picture is another example of federal intervention going overboard.

"Mr. Governor, this operation has roots in Italy, in Greece, in Colombia, in Costa Rica, throughout the Caribbean, and is partially headquartered in the central station of the Ft. Bragg Police Department. You are damned correct sir, this is federal intervention.

"At this moment, I have ordered tanks, helicopters, and troops to Ft. Bragg. They are brave and patriotic members of the National Guard under the direction of General Frederick Sappenfield. His orders are very simple. Keep the peace. My FBI agent in charge is Special Agent Katie Dollarhide who has led this investigation from day one, and who is responsible for bringing this international conspiracy to an end."

There were a few more comments, just a very few questions were accepted from members of the press, and the show was over.

"Yes, Ma'am, Ms. Special Agent Katie Dollarhide, you do know how to light a fire. The rats will be running in every direction from now on." We were hanging on to each other, almost in desperation. "I've never been so scared in my whole life, Katie, and at the same time, I'm so comfortable knowing you and I are doing this together. I'm so proud of you.

"We're going to win, Katie, I just hope the price doesn't get any higher. I couldn't stand losing you. I couldn't stand it."

"Butterball, you're the most incredible man I've ever met. I was serious about what I told you before. When this is over, I'm giving my resignation. I'm a trained investigator, and remember, an attorney. There are a lot of places we could go, we could set up shop so to speak, and be very happy.

"You know, Mr. big shot, egotistical Hollywood producer, that was really fun standing up to that ignorant fucker of a governor. Did you see him when I got really angry? He kept eying my little machine gun. He didn't know if I would shoot him or not.

"To tell you the truth, Jason, I had it in the back of my mind he was going to try something really stupid and get physical with me. I just thought he might."

"He would never have made the first move, Katie Dollarhide. You know, retired movie producers are pretty tough too, even if they are a bit overweight."

And our Owen Riley did exactly what Katie said he would do. He drove straight to a little dog cove south of Mendocino where a fast speedboat was waiting for him.

But so was Commander Eric Petersen. According to seamen on duty, it took less than ten minutes to run down the speed boat Riley was on, and not a shot had to be fired. Owen Riley just sat in the boat, and armed Coast Guardsmen took him into custody. Riley spilled his guts to his interrogators, sobbing like a baby during his questioning. Petersen called to tell us about it.

"Did you video tape his confession, Eric? In particular, did you get any video of him crying, blubbering, sobbing like a big old school yard baby, because if you did, I'd like you to release the tapes to the press. It would be a wonderful sight for the public to see just how tough and mean these bastards are.

"And while we're at it, sample a still shot out, one that shows what a perfect little wimp this Riley is, and release it to the wire services. I'd like this to go world wide." I may be retired, and I may have worked primarily in movies, but marketing is in my blood. It was Owen Riley who said the wrong thing to me when Sami was murdered. I wanted him to pay for that too.

"Katie, there's still a bit of the movie producer in me, and we can use this kind of press to bring the public to our side. We'll run this just as we would for a new crime movie, with pictures of the bad guys showing what wimps they are, and we need a picture of you with that machine gun facing down the governor. A picture of our Viking on the bridge of his cutter will be perfect, and we need a picture of Sandra in her quick little speedboat going hell bent through the surf. Oh, this is perfect. We'll make those fuckers wish they'd never met this egotistical and arrogant movie producer.

"So far, there hasn't been the public outcry I expected, and I don't know if that's good or not. Let me get with Chandler and see if we can release pictures of the dead agents, not just head shots, but family shots, showing what a terrible loss this is. We need to win the hearts of the general public to win this war."

It went even better than I had thought, and the press kit we put together was published around the world. The national press loved it, and Chandler or his boss were on every Sunday show, discussing just how a national emergency was averted because of the FBI, and what a terrible loss the Bureau was enduring.

For two weeks, National Guard units, federal agents of every stripe, worked the north coast of California, from Monterey Bay on the south, to Crescent City in the north, rounding up the largest police infiltration gang in the history of the U.S. There were more than twenty Ft. Bragg police officers directly involved, and another ten or so members of the department who at least had some inkling of what was going on.

From my point of view, the most difficult to understand were how many members of the judiciary were involved. Prosecutors in DA offices, judges, even elected members of city councils and county supervisors. Members of the gang not police officers were spread to the extremes of the coast, outside the Fort Bragg jurisdiction. There were almost as many federal agents along the coast of California as there were tourists this time of year.

Judges were named in indictments after some of the cops ratted on parts of the operation, and in particular, what Owen Riley had said. Between Riley and Lopez, agents knew most of what the operation was, both on a world scale, and in the Fort Bragg area.

"You know Jason, the way I see it, this will make Fort Bragg one of the nicest and cleanest towns in California. So many of the local elected people, in particular in the court system, will have to be replaced, and you know the electorate will be very careful who they vote for."

"I agree with that, Blondie, but it also means the feds will have to run things around here for a while. I hope the locals come to understand and support everything that's happening."

"When they see pictures of their current leaders being hauled off to jail, they'll understand."

Police chief Randall Richardson's name never came up in all the interrogations. He was well insulated by Riley and Colletti. "Richardson has to know what is going on here, but not one of these cops is putting a finger on him. He's not stupid, Jason, we've talked to him, but there is something missing. He has to be involved some way. It would be natural to have Richardson in charge, Riley as his chief of detectives as number two, and Colletti right in the middle.

"We have Riley, and he's telling us about most of the organization, but even when we scare him shitless, he isn't giving all the story. Richardson, the fucking chief of police, Jason. He has to be as involved as Riley or Colletti, but Riley simply won't implicate him. Him or Colletti."

"Also, dear heart, we don't have any idea where Colletti might be. Richardson is such a public figure, he has stayed where we can talk to him, but that big dumb New York hit man isn't. Two bits says he's the brains behind the hit on us.

"Where will we find this asshole Colletti? He seems to be the third in command, right behind Riley. I'll bet we find a Hummer with a pair of fifty caliber machine guns mounted on it when we do." The National Guard and all the other agency people in the area had not been able to locate that vehicle anywhere.

Searches were conducted from the air, all the little tiny roads and paths in the area around the north coast were searched, and the Hummer couldn't be found. The forests in northern California are thick with vegetation, and to hide a single camouflaged vehicle really wouldn't be that difficult. Tall redwood trees, dense patches of ferns, magnificent forests of oak, madrone, fir, and an element of locals that might be willing to hide a brother dealer, an outlaw like themselves.

***

The nightmares were coming every night, and now, even when he closed his eyes to rest a minute. "Headlines in newspapers. Pictures of me with the whores. I can see my whole life going away. Pictures of me behind bars wearing prison clothing, pictures of me standing in front of a hangman's noose. I'm going mad, and I know I have to run away, but I don't know where.

"Criminals almost always run to somewhere they've been before, and that's why they're caught, but I've never been faced with having to run. Where would I go? I wish I had a passport. That's what I should have done years ago. I could have gotten one in a different name. Then I could run away.

"Riley is gone and only Colletti is still here, but I don't know where. He scares me as much as prison, but he might be a way out. If I knew where he was." It took a couple of minutes for the fear to subside a little and allow the chief to think.

"I do know where he is. He told me."

***

Katie was going over all the paperwork we had, but I was looking at a map instead. I'll bet if we went north, to where Highway 1 turned inland to meet with Highway 101, we would either find Colletti, or the Hummer, or some indication of one or the other. There was a real wilderness coast along there, supposedly no roads and no civilization. Hummers were good at cross-country travel. My thoughts were interrupted by Betsy.

"Richardson is missing, Katie. The agents covering him have lost him. At some point overnight, he slipped out. He had a motorcycle hidden in the bushes behind his house. I guess they never spotted it, but he went cross-country, and they couldn't follow. He's gone, Katie." She related the story as she had heard it, and felt in her own mind, none of the agents or members of the National Guard had been compromised, just outwitted.

"That little pecker head did us, Katie. I want to be the one to arrest him and put that smug little face in bandages."

"We'll get him, Betsy. He might just lead us to Colletti or others. Let's see if he left a trail." She was furious, but letting everyone know that wouldn't gain her a thing. After Betsy left, She unloaded.

"Butterball, I want you to horse whip me. What a fool I've been, and I'm supposed to be the damned leader. You drive a four wheel drive little car that could have followed Richardson, but what do the rest of the agents have? None of them have four-wheel drive pickups, SUVs, or wagons. They are driving Bureau issued cars. I'm so fucking stupid." She was so mad at herself for failing to anticipate the problem she was pounding one fist into the other strong enough to raise a bruise. I was very smart and kept very quiet.

Chapter Seventeen

As soon as all the Federales had departed the police station, Colletti and Riley put their own plans into action. Riley was heading for a cove not too far south of Mendocino where a quick little boat would pick him up and whisk him to a trawler that was standing by off the coast. A trawler on the outside, an ocean going speedster on the inside. Again, the Pelligrini men had to admit, the South American cartel boss, Lopez, had the answers. A fishing trawler with twin gasoline powered hot rod engines, similar to the one Caldwell blew up, and a Hummer.

"Those twin engines can really turn that old tub into a mean machine, John. Why not come with me? We'll be in Honduras in just a few days, and out of here."

"No way, shit head. I'm heading for that place up north, grab the Hummer and drive along the coast to Petrolia. I can get out of there without being seen. Besides, with my New York people, I'll have a new identity inside of a week and will be able to get back to New York, or maybe Italy."

Riley left immediately and Colletti walked into Richardson's office. "Time to leave, chief. You won't see any more suit cases filled with goodies, but it was a good run while it lasted.

"I figure it'll take about a year or two before we can get this pipeline reopened, so your best bet is to get as far away as possible. Feds don't fuck around, and they'll pin the whole operation on you. Maybe life, but too many dead people to think about parole, I think."

"Take me with you, Colletti. I'm dead meat staying here, and I wouldn't even know how to go on the run. Take me with you. I'm damn good with a gun, I'm not afraid of just about anyone, but I don't want to rot in prison." It was the first time he had actually spoken out loud about where his actions might lead. Prison. Shot dead. His mind was not quick, he had not a clue of where to go or what to do. For several years he had simply gone along with whatever Riley or Colletti wanted, never made a real decision about anything, and now his world was ended.

He had some money, actually lots of money, tucked away in various bank accounts, under several names and identities, even a few businesses he had fictionalized, but he didn't have the slightest idea of how to get any of the money or what to do if he did get it. His name and picture had been plastered in every front-page account of the story for weeks now, his name almost a household name, and what would he do, just walk into a bank and withdraw his funds? And then what?

"You know where the ranch is north of here. I've got the Hummer stashed up there, and I'm going to hide out for a week, maybe, and then head north. Stay visible for a week or so, then head up to the ranch. Come up late at night, and don't bring anything except the clothes on your back, your pistol, and ammunition. For God sake don't bring a fucking car. Use that little dirt bike of yours and come cross country. There's only a couple of guys who know where that ranch is, besides us, so it might be some time before the feds find out about it."

He turned and stomped out the door, headed out the front door of the station and walked to his car. Two feds moved right along with him, and tailed him several miles south before he turned cross-country and lost his shadows. He smiled as he saw them bog down. "There was a reason I bought a four-wheel drive car, you idiots." Katie didn't find out about this episode.

He used old logging roads, sometimes no roads, he worked his way back north, around Ft. Bragg and came to a small little five acre 'ranch' which he had taken from a pot head the year before. "Me, Riley, Richardson, and Jerry Polk are the only ones who know about this place." The doper who lived at the place, watchman is what he called himself, met Colletti when he came rolling in.

"'Mornin' Mr. Colletti. Didn't expect to see you, what with all the FBI people swarming around Ft. Bragg."

"Open the barn, asshole."

"Right away, sir."

Colletti pulled the car into the garage and parked right next to one big Hummer with twin fifty caliber machine guns mounted on the roll bars, a safety belt for the gunner, and several large boxes of belted ammunition. As he stepped out of the car, he called for the druggie to come in, shot him in the head, and rolled his body into a corner of the garage.

"Didn't like the fucker anyway." He went into the cabin and brought everything in it to the center of the room. Everything, clothes, papers, bedding, books, even paper plates and plastic forks and spoons. "I ain't leaving those bastards anything to look through."

He'd been planning this for some time, knowing that eventually, some dumb fuck cop would stumble on what they had going and make trouble. "Jesus, the trouble. That fucking woman brought a whole army with her. I hope Richardson doesn't cave before I'm out 'a here." The only thing not ready for his bon fire was his cell phone, and he was using it.

Cell phone calls can be traced, to a degree, but clone phones, as they're called, make the trail very difficult to follow. Colletti had three of them, taken from others by way of his badge and gun.

"Let me talk to Carpenter. Don't give me any shit, this is Colletti." Colletti was growling and needed to pass on what was happening. "Wiley, this is John. The whole fucking show is over here. FBI, National Guard, DEA, tanks, helicopters, everything. ATF guys swaggering around in their black pajamas, pointing machine guns at everybody.

"The place is crazy. Riley is on his way to Honduras, and I'm going north. See if you can get me some kind of ID so I can get back to New York."

"Shut up for a minute, John. Pelligrini is dead, that fucker Lopez is spilling his guts about everything on our end. Bastard's even using names. Don't come here, John, instead, I'm coming there. Riley didn't make it south, they picked him up at sea, and the fucker is telling the world about us. I've got a hit order on Lopez and Riley, but who knows when we'll be able to get to either of them. Stay at your ranch another couple of days and I'll meet you. If we can make it to Seattle, some of our Asian Gumbas will get us out.

"I'll see you tomorrow."

The phone went dead that fast leaving Colletti in a muddle. "Riley was caught? That little prick always talked so tough, I should have realized he was a shit head. They'll have to kill me. I won't be caught, and I know Carpenter feels the same way. I'm worried about that ass hole chief. Richardson has never been on the other side of an interrogation."

***

The Wiley Carpenter was true to his word, and arrived just before midnight, 48-hours later. "I hope you know your way out of here. This place isn't a hideout, John, it almost doesn't exist. How the hell did you find this place?"

"There were a couple of dopers growing an acre or so of marijuana, I stumbled into the place looking for a good area to hide our big guns, killed the bastards and took over.

"We've got to move right away. Two or three helicopters flew over today, and I've heard some rumbling from ground vehicles also. According to my maps, we can make it a long way up the coast by dropping down to the tide line and following the sand, almost to Cape Mendocino. We'll have to ditch the Hummer and get something else when we get there, but that won't be hard.

"Seattle's a long way, Carpenter. There's a lot of lonely water just north of the California-Oregon border. It might be better if we got picked up by a fast boat or something. Can we make that connection?" Colletti picked up one phone and called Ft. Bragg Police Chief Richardson, while the Wiley Carpenter used another to try and make a call to his Asian ally.

"What the fuck you bringing Richardson along for?" Carpenter could plan big time for the crime family, but he didn't have the instinct of a killer, Colletti did. That's what they paid him for, to kill, to wipe the highway clean of pot holes.

An hour later, they heard the motorcycle approach the cabin, and let Richardson walk in. Colletti smiled at him, introduced Carpenter, and as the chief reached to shake hands, fell to the floor with a bullet through his brain. "Dead men don't talk, Carpenter. Help me bring another body in here, get the Hummer out of the barn, and you and me will get out of Dodge."

There were two bodies on the pile of shit Colletti had in the middle of the cabin's living room, now soaked with five gallons of gasoline. Another five gallons were poured inside the four wheel drive car Colletti had brought to the ranch, and both fires were lit and burning as the Hummer, followed by a dirt bike roared into the early morning darkness.

They followed Highway 1 for a short distance and turned onto a seldom used trail that dropped off a steep cliff, the two vehicles headed north on open sand along the coast.

About fifteen miles down the beach, Carpenter ran out of gas and dumped the motorcycle into the surf. Colletti and Wiley then continued at about fifty-miles-per-hour up the coast. It was rapidly approaching sunrise.

They followed the coast along a wilderness section of northern California, driving just above the water line on firm sand. The Hummer was an ideal vehicle for this and they neither saw anyone nor were they seen.

"When we get almost to Petrolia, we'll dump this fucker, steal a car, and head for Oregon. There's some really rugged coast line near the border where we can hide and wait for a boat ride." His only worry was leaving so many tracks. "This damned truck leaves a track that can be seen for miles, Wiley. One thing in our favor, the next tide change will wipe out our prints."

"Fuck John, that's a chopper coming right at us." Carpenter was pointing at a helicopter, maybe a hundred and fifty feet in the air, drawing a bead on the Hummer.

"Get on that gun, Carpenter. Get that fucker. Shoot the son of a bitch. Shoot, God damn it, shoot."

Carpenter scrambled into the back of the Hummer, grabbed the pistol grips of the big guns, jacked a belt into place, and started shooting. The National Guard Huey banked hard to the right and took a full load along the left side, killing the co-pilot, an observer at the door, and wiping out the bird's transmission, the only reason a helicopter can fly.

The big National Guard helicopter went into a wild frenzy of uncontrolled spinning, its jet engine screaming out of control, and exploded just before crashing into the surf, several hundred feet off shore.

"If those bastards had a chance to use their radio, John, we'll be running into a whole army if we keep going north. Let's find a way out of here. Up those cliffs, or something." Carpenter stayed at the triggers of the machine gun while Colletti jockeyed the big rig around, and the two headed south again.

"That actually felt pretty good," Wiley Carpenter said with an evil smile plastered across his face. "I've never fired anything like this before. It's something I could get used to. Too much time in friggin' office work Colletti. I wonder if Mr. Pelligrini ever got a chance to shoot anything like this?"

"There's a spot about ten miles back, I think, where we can get off the beach. As soon as we get close to a road, we'll ditch this fucker and jack a car or pick up. I've never fought a whole fucking army before. Jesus, Carpenter, they sent a damned Huey gun ship after us. What'll we see next, a fucking tank?"

Two of the world's highest ranking criminals, one a direct representative of an international crime family, one from the ranks of American crime families, were on the run, in a well armed four wheel drive vehicle, trying desperately to get another couple of hundred miles north. They were to meet with criminals from Asia, and be able to get free of a fast closing net.

There was nothing in the world more frightening than having to face a vicious animal when it was cornered, and these men were slowly being cornered. Both had killed many times, so the thought of killing again was not something to worry themselves with, and both had the fear of prison or the death penalty boiling in their blood. The thought of interrogation by the feds terrified Carpenter. Both men, in particular the Wiley Carpenter, had lived the life of luxury, had money, women, booze in quantities unknown to most people, and neither was willing to give that life up.

"I wonder just how hard it will be to get this pipeline reopened, Wiley? Man, most of our people locally have gone down, Mr. Pelligrini is dead, that little fucker Lopez won't be available. Riley might as well be dead. We've got our work cut out."

Neither man was thinking of escape, but thought of continuing their illegal drug operations. How strange was the criminal mind? Several hundred members of the California National Guard, along with hundreds of federal law enforcement agents were searching for these two, representatives of every federal prosecuting agency were planning their days in court, they just burned a building containing two bodies of people they killed, former associates, they just blew a helicopter out of the sky, killed all aboard, and their thoughts were of continuing their illicit drug running.

If Special Agent Katie Dollarhide was angry when she faced off with California's governor, she would be livid if she knew what was in the minds of the two men she was bent on destroying.

***

John Chandler was sitting in his office, tired as an old dog he just told the director, but unwilling to head for home and a deserved nap. "No, I've got people in the field who have put their heads in the blocks, and I am the only one they can trust right at the moment.

"Special Agent Dollarhide told me the defection of The Deacon, and now the knowledge that Sarah is also a traitor, has put their operation in jeopardy. Katie is sure there are more of Pelligrini's people in our midst, and to the best of my knowledge, we don't know if Lopez, or any of the other cartels had any people burrowed into our operations. No, I have to stay right here. I guess you could call me a traffic cop."

He called a press conference for later in the day and planned to release all the photographic evidence they had on the interrogation and confession by Owen Riley. He spread some of the stills on his desk for the director to see. "What I like best, about these pictures and videos? Look at him, crying like the sniveling little baby he is, and there's not a mark on him. No bruises, no bloody nose, no broken ribs or black eyes. The fucking little weasel is sitting there in soiled underpants, tears running down his cheeks, and represents nothing. He's nothing but a wimp, and he'll fry. We're going to charge him with the deaths of every single person involved in this operation.

"Everyone. Sami Bertorelli, the Ft. Bragg cops, the two hoods, The Deacon, the four brave FBI agents with slashed throats, Carmen Santiago, and anyone else who ends up dead because of this. We can probably even add the death of Alberto Pelligrini to the list. After all, Pelligrini wouldn't be dead if it wasn't for Owen Riley and the bumbling efforts of his mob in Ft. Bragg."

Under other circumstances, that comment would have brought a chuckle to both men, but Chandler was fuming with anger, and before he hosted his press conference, he was advised of the National Guard helicopter shot down by two men in a Hummer. It was a grim and determined John Chandler who met with virtually the entire Washington, DC press corps.

He had made his opening statement and was about to go into some detail when the conference was interrupted by none other than the President of the United States. Kipling strode onto the raised platform, shook hands with his old fishing partner, and immediately started talking. He had written some notes on the quick drive to FBI headquarters, but never looked at them. Kipling was a large man, in remarkable shape considering he had spent way too much of his life behind a desk, and now, as he stood before representatives of the working press, was intimidating. His scowl, so effective during presidential election debates, was even more so now. His eyebrows were drawn together, big, black, and bushy, his jowls actually quivered with anger, and the moustache his aides were always trying to get him to shave off, bristled. Kipling was a force as he spoke.

"Ladies and gentlemen, as Mr. Chandler just told you, men representing this international conspiracy, have shot down a United States Armed Forces helicopter, killing the entire crew. If there ever was a question in anyone's mind that these people were a risk to United States security, this reprehensible action should set that aside.

"I have invoked a seldom used right of the president and have declared that those who are found guilty of any portion of this current situation in California, be declared traitors of the state. These actions by crime families from South America, Europe, The Near East, and Asia are seditious in every sense of the word. If any of those found guilty are American citizens, they will be charged as traitors. Those who are not citizens will be charged as international terrorists.

"In every case, ladies and gentlemen, I have instructed the Attorney General to seek the death penalty for everyone charged. This is to be considered a direct attack on the government of the United States in an effort to overthrow the legal right of all citizens to lawful protection."

He didn't ask for questions, took Chandler by the shoulders, and the two walked off the stage, leaving questions for a couple of agents and a representative of the president.

"Do you still keep a bottle of that fine Kentucky in your desk, John? I could use just a small snort."

"That was quite a show, Mr. President, thank you. I have the good stuff, the kind you like. When this ends, and it will, I'm going to take a short trip up to Montana. I have an extra supply of Kathy's Killers if you'd care to join me." The two long time friends sat in Chandler's office for the next several hours, sipping some fine Kentucky whiskey, talking about fly fishing. Both men wanted to talk about what was happening, and both knew they simply couldn't at this point.

"Someday, John. Someday."

Chapter Eighteen

You could almost see it in her eyes. She didn't actually mouth the words, but I've been watching her mental processes for some time now. She wasn't sad about this at all. Richardson would lead us to Colletti, and Katie would either capture or kill both of them. Her eyes were narrowed, her mouth grim, and those little fists were doubled up again. "OK, Betsy. Get all the details from whoever let him go. If you have any doubt that it was done on purpose, don't hesitate. I don't care if that person was with the bureau or not, arrest him. Shoot the fucker if you want.

"Well, Butterball, here's your chance to prove your theory. If Richardson is looking to join Colletti, and if you're right, all we have to do is go north, young man, go north. I love it when I say things like that." Ever since she faced off with the governor, Katie's whole persona had changed. She was only seeing this come to an end, and her sense of humor was wonderful.

"How the hell will we know if we do find their tracks? Christ, Jason, every bastard up here owns a motorcycle or four-wheeler. What the hell are we looking for?

"You drive, Blondie. A Hummer is unlike any other vehicle on the road, with a wide track, really wide. If they are in it, when they leave the pavement, and they'll have to, with machine guns bristling from on top, it will stand out like a fucking tank, we'll see their tracks. Even if that big overgrown SUV had taken a dirt road off the main highway, its wide stance would leave a trail that could be seen. It's been two weeks Katie, and no rain, so a trail should be seen. If someone was in a serious hurry, late at night on a dirt bike, he too would leave a tell tale mark on the side of the road.

"You know, Katie, Hummers can be bought through regular dealers, they are sold just like any other truck or vehicle, but not twin military machine guns. That national guard commander appeared to be shocked when he learned they had them. I wonder where they got them?" This had been bothering me for some time. Of course, military theft was not uncommon, but the theft of something like that should have rung a bell somewhere. No one seemed to know where those guns came from."

"I have agents looking into that right now, Jason. That's heavy armament for any military group to lose, so, unless the fuckers have infiltrated the military also, we should find out soon where they got the damn thing. I doubt if that will help us find whoever did it, but at least we'll know where it came from."

"There, look. Right off the side, and down that steep hillside. That's almost a cliff, Katie. Heading right to the water." The trail left by the Hummer stood out like a beacon, and right between the two tracks, motorcycle tracks. "The two are going in the same direction, Katie. If they got on hard sand, they could be in Shelter Cove in quick time. From there, they could make it to Petrolia and possibly get away."

Katie grabbed the radio. "Fort Bragg National Guard, this is FBI One. Set up road blocks on the north, around Petrolia. I've found tracks leading to the coast-line off Highway One. Follow the coast back south, toward Upper Mattole and Honeydew. Confirm, please."

"This is Fort Bragg National Guard. We confirm, FBI One. Roadblocks will be established near Petrolia, and units will proceed south along the coast-line. I will also dispatch units to move north from here. Over."

"Thanks, National Guard. FBI One clear."

We didn't know it at the time, but the National Guard general was so pissed at his California governor, and so taken with the authority of Katie Dollarhide, he authorized use of a Huey gun ship to run a course down the coast from the Mendocino Cape south to Ft. Bragg. The guardsman on the radio wasn't aware either, or I'm sure he would have informed us.

"This is one hell of a trail, Butterball." Treacherous non-trail would be a better description, but Katie was doing a fine job negotiating our way toward the sand. One thing we didn't know was when this trail had been made. They might be in Oregon or Colombia by now. "Stop for just a minute, Katie."

"This is no time to take a whiz, big boy."

"Just want to look at these tracks. The motorcycle and the Hummer came through here very recently. See here. The sand is loose around the track. It hasn't had time to harden up, or be affected by overnight fog. Now, we need to know where they're going."

Did the Hummer and the dirt bike leave their trail within hours last night, or was Richardson following along behind, maybe days behind whoever was driving the Hummer? Was the motorcycle track actually made by the same bike that Richardson was thought to have used to escape? "So many questions, Katie. Who are we following, when were these tracks made? We need a damn crystal ball to figure it out." I could feel frustration building, and this trail wasn't helping.

"I wish we had a Hummer right now." Katie was doing a good job working overland and getting us down toward the water. "We will have a hell of a time getting across that sand when we get down there." She wasn't kidding. The sand was soft and deep, and our tires tried to dig holes as soon as we got there.

"Hold it up, Blondie." I got out and let most of the air out of all the tires, which made for four large paddle wheels. "If we end up back on the pavement, we'll be dead in the water, dear heart, but for the next many miles we should be able to move along OK."

My mind was telling someone thanks for getting us a four wheel drive vehicle. There may be a few little dirt roads that lead down onto this wild coast, and we would have to watch for tracks leading back out of the sand.

"Drive down to the wet sand area, and then go as fast as you dare. That Hummer has been making some serious time, but he won't be able to back track with us here. If we see either of those vehicles coming this way, stop as quickly as possible and get the hell out of the car. Those twin machine guns will chew this little car to a shred, and whatever's in it." My mind was on fire knowing we were on the trail. I won't lose you Katie. I would take on the whole damned gangster world before I would lose you. Chandler said it. 'Good Hunting.' That was where we were, hunting one big vicious varmint.

The radio chattered, and Betsy came on. "There's been a fire, a big one at a ranch several miles out of town. When the fire fighters finally got to the place, a cabin and a barn had been destroyed, and they found two bodies in the ashes. According to our people, both had died from gunshot wounds to the head. A four wheel drive car was in the barn, burned out, but tracks from a Hummer and a motorcycle were evident."

"Roger that, Betsy," Katie Dollarhide said, "and thank you. I think we're following those tracks at this time. Did you get an ID on the bodies?"

"Negative, Katie, but people are working on it. I'll keep you posted."

"Your boys are scared, Butterball. If they come back this way, I hope we can fight 'em off."

"Our best bet will be to get out of this car, stay in the sand and as low as possible, and take well aimed shots at the assholes. The Hummer is wide open, and the guns are mounted on a roll bar set up. One person can't drive and shoot, so we are going to have to assume the two got together. If we see them."

Well, it sounded good. We had no idea at this point, if Colletti was alone or with Richardson, and that would change the picture immediately. "Who do you suppose those bodies were? Did they have hostages we don't know about? This just gets more and more frustrating, Blondie." An enigma of this proportion can be overwhelming, and I had to fight to keep a clear mind. "Work your magic on me Blondie. Make me think. I'm really frustrated right now."

"No problem, Butterball. Look, all we know is we're following a vehicle that is probably the one used to blow up Francesca's little cabin, probably occupied by at least one, maybe more, of the assholes who killed our fellow agents, probably the fuckers responsible for Sami's death, probably getting their information from spies within the Bureau. Now. Does that make it clear?"

"I needed that." She had given me tongue lashings before, but this one cut through all the fog, all the shit, and laid the project on the table. "Thanks."

There was a long stretch of white sand, undulating like massive swells for miles along this part of the coast. To the east, the sand led to steep, rocky cliffs, the beginnings of the King Mountain Range. The area was supposed to be off limits to motorized vehicles, but I considered this trip a perfect example of mitigating circumstances. And of course, the criminals in front of us didn't give a damn, anyway.

Katie got us down to the harder wet sand and really put her foot in it. "She'll go out of control with little warning, Jason, so tighten up those belts. If I lose it, we'll roll several times." She was following the trail laid out by the Hummer, a trail too wide for us to fit in.

"Look at this trail, Katie. That vehicle has been here since the last tide change. There's only twelve hours or less since he was through here. If your agents get set up north, they could get him, or force him to turn back this way." We were watching as far ahead as we could see, but of course, we were in wet sand and that wasn't like driving on dry ground. There was no telltale dust. This would be the right time for me to have some of my radar gear from *D'Anne*. We would be able to see a long way in front.

"We know that Richardson went to meet with whoever is driving the Hummer, and I'd bet a bunch it's Colletti, found him gone, but knew where he was going." Katie got back on the radio and talked with the National Guard command.

"The tracks are within a mile of where Highway 1 turns inland to join with 101. Follow them back the other way if you can. Don't know what you'll find, but that's where the Hummer came from. Watch your ass, General, these guys play only for keeps. You are authorized to use as much force as you deem necessary." Of course he already was, but she didn't know it.

Those tracks led to agents following tracks from the fire. There was no doubt now the Hummer was loaded for bear, and was somewhere along this long, wild, beautiful coast line.

And beautiful it was, with the surf coming on shore, not from a bay or inlet, but directly from the Pacific Ocean. Waves that began thousands of miles away were breaking onto intensely white sand. Ranged all along the sand line, where mountains rose tall and fast, grew the mighty Redwood groves, interspersed with stands of oak and other magnificent trees.

Some of the waves had their beginnings in Japan or Korea or even possibly in the Bering Sea. Storms came barreling in from the North Pacific, from the

Alaska Gulf, and there was nothing to stop or slow down the brutal force when they hit the coast. Often the entire coast line, from as far north as one can get to as far south as one would want to be, was covered in a velvet layer of fog, densely flavored with salt. This entire coastal area had been set aside as a "Wild Coast" area, with no conveniences of any kind, no actual roads leading in or out, but with a few trails that snaked down into the dunes.

Coastal kayakers loaded with camping gear and cameras flocked to the area, giant Gray Whales could be seen frolicking off shore, one time of the year heading south to Mexican waters and their birthing and nursery area, and another time, swimming and tail dancing north, herding the young ones on their first and finest adventure.

There were rookeries for numerous shore and sea birds and sea lions by the hundreds used the beaches to haul out and warm themselves in the fabled California sun, or to evade the attacks of Orcas or sharks. Only in a few places does the coastal range dip right to water's edge, and even then, when the tide's out, it's not hard to move up or down the coast.

"I've fished these waters many times, Katie. There's good salmon off shore along with a few kelp forests. Red snapper, cod, halibut, and other fish are thick. We'll be back. At some point in our future, Blondie, we will have to come back here. Come back when we can enjoy what should be a quiet, romantic stretch of Pacific Coastline." To myself, I said, if we live through this awful time.

***

"Here he comes, Blondie," I yelled. She already was putting the brakes on as we popped our seat belts and got ready to jump out. "I'm going out now," I hollered, and rolled out of the seat. She was probably still going twenty-miles an hour, and I would have some good bruises to prove it. I moved as close to the water as I dared, and snuggled down into the wet sand, getting as low as possible. If Katie had been next to me, there would have been a comment or two about Butterball. I snickered thinking about it, tried to keep myself from being overcome with terror. If a wave went over me, that would be fine. Cold though. I just hope Colletti or whoever was in that monster hadn't seen me. "Come on, Katie, jump. Jump, Blondie."

I watched her go out of the Toyota about another fifty yards up the coast and roll out of her side of the car without stopping it. She too moved down to the water line, and we hunkered down for a big fight. God, Katie, live through this. Live, Katie.

Here came that adrenaline again. It seemed ever since I met Katie Dollarhide someone had been shooting at me, and right now, I was facing some big guns. When that fishing boat with the racing engines was coming down on me, I didn't have time to think about the consequences. They had big military type machine guns also. There must be a connection. I wonder if those machine guns and the ones we know were mounted on this Hummer came from the same place?

What the hell, we knew this was an international organization, those guns could have come from anywhere. Why the hell did I automatically think they had to be American and come from an American military base?

That's something we would have to check. Because of all the unrest in Central America, Guatemala, El Salvador, it might not be too difficult to nab some heavy armament. If the Mafia and the Colombian cartels were this well armed, the president was right in thinking the criminal element was a threat to national security.

Right now, I didn't have time to think about the consequences. Damn, he was moving fast.

***

I lost Sami because of these bastards, the first woman I ever really loved. I was in this mess because Sami hadn't told me all about her background. I wondered what would have been my reaction if she had. I wouldn't have known what I knew now. I wondered if I would have been tolerant, or would I have made an ass of myself. I had been known to make an ass of myself. Sometimes, arrogant, egotistical Hollywood producer was an apt description.

Flooding memories of Sami started getting mixed with recent memories of the times Katie and I have had. The two women were so different, and yet, both were special investigative agents in one of the finest national police agencies in the world. Either one could have given any Hollywood actress a run for her money as well.

I liked the idea of spending the rest of my life with Katie Dollarhide, and what I liked also, she didn't mind me grieving the loss of Sami. She loved Sami almost as much as I did. In our own way, this fight was for Sami. Blondie liked the boat, too, and that was so important. Sami loved *D'Anne*, and worked right along side me when we made the changes below decks. I think Katie would too.

The first change would be another fighting seat on the afterdeck. I never had one installed for Sami, but Katie learned the thrill of catching a big fish, and for that she needed her own fighting seat; a good padded seat, strong belt to hold her secure against fish larger than she was, and a deep cup for the end of the fishing rod, right in the middle of the seat. There would be cup holders on each side so she could have something cold during a battle. I would build it for her the same as I built mine.

Sami argued about using hooks to catch a fish, and then always made me put her fish back into the ocean. Not Katie. Hell, I would probably have to put up the long outriggers as well.

Shit, if we were going that far, we would probably end up in the charter business.

Not.

That was, if we lived through this next charge. One big Hummer with a pair of military machine guns mounted on the roll bar, charged down the beach, and all I had was this little fucking 9mm automatic. We should have grabbed some machine guns of our own when we took off.

I should never have left that grenade launcher on board the boat. That would help even the score here. I watched as Katie almost dug herself into the wet sand, became the same level as the rest of the beach, and I did the same thing. This girl must have had some kind of military training somewhere. She wasn't afraid of anything.

What an adversary she would be in a courtroom. The way she stood up to the governor was amazing. Dunbar was known for losing his temper, and I knew he was going to swing on her, even if she was carrying a full automatic weapon. He was not very bright, and she would have creamed him.

She would have creamed him if he was still standing, because, little Blondie, I was cocked and off safety myself. There would have been some pretty good headlines over something like that.

Why was my mind rambling like this? That damned truck was almost on top of us. Did warriors always react this way mentally? My mind should be on that fucking machine gun toting Hummer, and all I could think of was Katie. Sami. Katie.

I whispered John Chandler's words to myself. Good hunting. And added, Good hunting, Blondie.

***

Katie's mind was alive and active as she watched the monster vehicle approach. "That's one fine looking assault vehicle. I've got to talk to Chandler about these." She wiggled down into the sand and watched intently as the vehicle came roaring down the wet sand. "It looks like there's one person driving, and another standing at the guns. If I concentrate on just one shot and make it the best I can, I might disable the gunner. The driver can't drive and shoot, and Butterball can take him out.

"That's one nice thing about the training we get in weapons. Even if the pistol is semi-automatic, doesn't mean you have to fire until the clip is empty. Make your shots clean and accurate. You have one chance, make it good, girl." She could feel her body try to tense up and she worked to stop that from happening. "I have to stay loose, roll with whatever happens here. Make one shot, two at the most. Clean. Accurate. Kill that gunner."

***

The Hummer was screaming down the beach, and I didn't think Colletti had spotted our vehicle yet. When he did, he won't know it was empty, and we would know whether he was alone or not. When the two big guns erupted in fire, we had our answer. The Hummer swung around toward the Toyota and both machine guns opened up. One guy drove, one guy shot the big guns.

The Toyota was destroyed instantly when those fifty-caliber slugs tore through it, and the Hummer went right back onto its previous course. More than one of those hot bullets punctured the fuel tank in the Toyota, and it blew up in a massive explosion, pieces flew high in the air. I think I would have stopped to see if anyone was in the car, but Colletti and friend didn't. As they moved past Katie, I heard two pops, then two more pops. And there was no answer from the twin autos.

The Hummer was swerving now, the driver tried to move into the deeper sand, tried to get closer to the cliffs that seemed to come right straight down to the water's edge. Colletti was close enough for me to hit him, and I took long and careful aim, fired two quick shots from the 9mm. I saw him jerk, but he kept driving. I fired two more quick shots, and again, I saw him jerk. There was no return fire from the big guns. Katie must have taken out the gunner, whoever he might have been. Was it Richardson, or was he gone somewhere else with his motorcycle?

"Katie." I was screaming, running as fast as I could toward her inert body. She wasn't getting up, wasn't moving. "God, no. No Katie. No." Her head was bleeding, and there were several pieces of that Toyota around her. One large piece of steel had fallen on her head, and along with a very deep cut, I could see splinters of skull as well.

I gently lifted her and moved up to dry sand, out of the cold ocean water, told her the whole time I loved her. I was shaking with fear and anger, fear of losing this blonde angel, I could feel the anger and hate for the bastards responsible seething through my whole system..

Her eyes fluttered, and she spoke through what had to be horrible pain. "Go after them, Jason. Go get the bastards. Help will come. Leave me here and get those bastards."

I tried to make her as comfortable as possible, and I knew she was right. The machine gunner was either dead or out of commission, and I could see the driver was hit. I had to follow, but how could I? "Katie," I started to say I couldn't leave her, but she broke me off.

"The National Guard will be here, Jason. Betsy will be here. Go. Don't let them get away. Get them now, Butterball." I could see so much pain, so much damage done to her beautiful head, but I knew she was right. I had to go.

"Don't die, Blondie. Stay alive." I kissed her lightly, and knew she was unconscious again. That was probably a blessing, I thought as I started walking in the tracks of the Hummer. I walked through deep sand that made the going hard and slow. The sand was pure white, deep and fine, and walking through it was more than just tiring, it was almost debilitating. Thousands of years of wave action had broken the sand down to what tourist directors love the most. Deep, white sand, delightful surf that extended for miles. This would be a fine place to come wilderness camping if we lived through this. "Why the hell didn't we bring water, Blondie? Or machine guns of our own? I don't know if we're as smart as we want to think." Machine guns, water, a damned radio. I kept up a complete conversation, as if she was right alongside. She was, you know.

"We should have brought the Coast Guard, the National Guard, Martha Stewart. We need some back up, Blondie." If she was with me right now, she would shush me up and tell me to walk, breath deep, don't talk. I could hear her, probably she would be snickering lightly as my overweight body plowed through those dunes. I continued to talk to myself, as if she was right alongside. It eased the pain.

"If we both hit him a couple of times, he could be wounded, and not really know where he was driving. We need to get a little more alert here."

A couple of miles in the deep sand, and I could feel fire in my lungs, my legs were as limp and worthless as a towel coming out of a washing machine. A couple of miles of tortuous walking, and then I saw it; the oversized assault vehicle stuck in the sand.

I had to catch my breath, calm my nerves, get just a little strength back. That was a mean machine gun, and if anyone was still alive near the Hummer, he had enough firepower to start a war, and all I had was a puny little pistol. "Damn stupid thing to not bring more guns, Blondie." I was alone and faced twin machine guns probably manned by people who knew they had to kill me in order to get away. All the odds were on their side, except for one. They didn't know I was here, and they didn't know I was alone.

***

I met Sami and we had one of the most delightful love affairs anyone could ever ask for. A marriage, and planned for the future. For a man to find that kind of love was sensational, and then to have it ripped from me, torn and shredded was devastating. "Keep that thought Jason. These are the bastards responsible. Kill them, Jason." I was talking to myself, remembering Sami, loving Katie, hating whoever was in that machine just on the other side of that dune.

I knew where that look on Katie's face came from that night at the cabin. She had the bodies of four of her agents, her friends, laid out in front of her. She had just killed a cop responsible for the agents' death. There was hatred in her eyes, and I had that hatred in mine. "I want revenge. I killed those bastards on that boat, I know I can kill again. Let me stay smart, Blondie, let us win this war."

As long as I live, I would have Sami's love. She was the most open, most loving person I had ever known, and I had a chance to avenge her murder. And while I was doing that, was it bringing justice, or was it deep revenge? I didn't care as long as Colletti and all his goons either died or went to prison. "Prison is too good for these bastards.

"Pelligrini is dead. Good. Lopez is in custody and will be doing big time. Good. Now, let's kill this fucker Colletti, and his bastard child Richardson. Hang the bastards from a white oak tree. Katie, don't die, Katie. God, don't die."

I almost hated Katie when we first met. I held her responsible for Sami's death, for taking away the only thing in the world I loved. Now, all this time had passed, all those horrible things had happened, and I was looking forward to marrying her. My mind had always worked better when I was speaking out loud, either talking to myself, or to some imaginary person who never interrupted. I was talking up a storm now, talking to Katie as if she was right next to me. My strength was back, my breathing was natural, I was going to war.

"He stuck that thing, Blondie. He'll try to make it to the cliffs. I'm going way around to the left, because if he even has a suspicion we might be following, he'll be protecting from this direction."

"He could still be with that thing, Butterball so keep that eagle eye of yours open." I could almost hear her saying it. I moved slowly around the dune, keeping it between us, and found a notch I could get close to without giving away my position.

The Hummer was indeed stuck in the sand, and there was one man, in the sand alongside the big military vehicle. It was Colletti, slumped at the side of the Hummer, holding his side, a big automatic pistol was in his blood streaked hand, maybe a forty five. The machine gunner was hanging out the side of the rig, blood poured out of his mouth. Katie was one hell of a shot.

"Give it up, Colletti. You don't have to die here." I wanted to shoot the son- of-a-bitch with hundreds of bullets. Pictures of Sami were swimming in my mind, my life on my beloved *D'Anne* destroyed by this asshole, my entire life upended.

Katie was lying in the sand, bleeding, maybe even dead, and this guy was responsible. Hate was surging as much as adrenaline. I was going to kill this bastard. I was. But all that training from FBI agents, from Katie, told me I was going to do everything possible to take him alive.

"Put the gun down asshole, and you'll live. I'm only going to count to three, and you're one dead fucker."

He tried to stand up, swung the pistol over toward me, but he was very slow. One round, and I could see his head jerk back and slam into the side of the Hummer, splashing blood and brains all over the place. Anthony Colletti was dead.

"Over. This long crusade is over." I stood on the dune, crying gently, rocking to a rhythm I could only feel. "I love you, Blondie."

It took lots of effort to lift Colletti's bloody body into the back of the Hummer, alongside that of the gunner. I wondered who that fucker was? It wasn't Richardson, and I didn't think I'd seen this one before. Someone would know, that was for sure. Colletti had been hit four times, two shots from Katie, and two from me, but only one penetrated his body armor, and apparently did considerable damage. The bullet slipped under his armpit and tore hell out of his internal organs. The gunner was shot twice as well, but the killing round went through his head. "Good shooting, Blondie."

Colletti stuck the big Hummer because of his injuries, and it didn't take too much to get it loose. I followed our tracks back down to the surf. As I came across the top of a dune, I saw two helicopters on the sand, one just about to lift off, and knew that help had arrived for Katie. Among those running to meet me was Betsy Contreras.

"Katie, tell me about Katie."

"She's on that Huey that just left, Jason. She's in critical condition. Come on, we'll ride in the other bird. The nearest major hospital that can give her the treatment she needs for a head injury as serious as hers is in San Francisco."

She looked in the back of the Hummer and drew in a big breath. "Well, I'll be damned. Look who you got. That's Carpenter, the one they call Wiley. He's the number two man in the Pelligrini organization. Jason, he's the biggest fish yet."

"Does anyone have any idea where Chief Richardson might be? We thought he was the gunner, not this guy."

"As near as we can guess at this time, Butterball, Colletti and now we know, Carpenter, killed Richardson and someone else, and tried to hide it in a fire at a secluded ranch."

My stomach churned the whole trip in that helicopter. I saw horrible visions, thought terrible thoughts, felt bile ready to erupt with every breath. "God Katie, don't die." The National Guard crew of the helicopter did everything they could to keep us advised on Katie's condition.

"Sir, the hospital has given us permission to land at their helipad, and has people waiting for us. You and agent Contreras will be escorted directly to the ICU area. Agent Dollarhide is in surgery at this time."

Betsy reached over and took my hand, tried to smile, but tears were splashing across her cheeks. "I've never known a finer agent, a finer friend, Jason. You and she became such a fine team, and you two are responsible for bringing an end to this gruesome conspiracy."

"Irony has always been a part of my life, Betsy, in most of my films, in most of the stories I've written, and now, part of my reality. A piece of the vehicle we were using to capture these ass holes falls on Katie's head. A bullet from that fucking machine gun blew up the Toyota, and a stupid piece of steel falls on Katie's head even after she's killed the gunner.

"That same gun almost wiped us all out at the cabin, and now, Katie is fighting for her life because of it. She can't die, Betsy. She can't. I can't lose Sami and Katie. I can't"

The first person I saw when I stepped from the war bird was Eric Petersen with a look I hope I never have to see again. All I could think is, she's gone, my Katie is gone. He wrapped those huge Viking arms around me, as we stood in the middle of a concrete helipad.

"She's putting up one hell of a fight, Jason, and the doctors haven't given up, but it doesn't look good. I'll take you and Betsy up. She's still unconscious, and the doctors may keep her that way for a while."

"She's alive," is all I could think, all I needed to know. "We got the bastards, Eric, and my Katie is alive."

Chapter Nineteen

For five days there were serious doubts that Katie would pull through and then, in the middle of a tremendous storm, with gale force winds blowing in from the Gulf of Alaska, rattling every window in the hospital, Katie opened her eyes and tried to talk through all the tubes and lines and bandages that bound her head.

Two or three doctors, several nurses, and one egotistical Hollywood producer hovered over the lovely agent and tried to ask questions all at the same time. Finally, the main man shushed us all..

Doc Crummer shooed us all out of the room, I wanted to fight him on that but knew I'd lose, and found my way to a coffee pot and snack machine, had some horrible coffee and three candy bars, paged through ancient magazines, and stared at the ceiling. Half an hour later he came into the waiting room and sat down next to me.

"That's one tough little lady you're going to marry, Agent Caldwell. She has a fractured skull but I don't think there's going to be any permanent damage. She'll need a lot of rest, and no serious physical exertion, for the next several weeks.

"The chances are very good that she'll experience some severe headaches, maybe periods of nausea, and possibly some balance problems, but those will go away in a matter of weeks also.

"Like I said, she's one tough little lady and she's asking for you."

I shook hands with the guy, wanted to hug him, and made a quick walk to Katie's room.

"Hi, Butterball," she said with a grand smile, her eyes, black and blue from the head bashing, were shining.

"They said you got 'em and that Wiley Carpenter was one of them."

We talked for almost ten minutes before the nurses shooed me out. "I'll see you in the morning, Blondie." I hugged her as gently as I dared and slipped out of the room and called Betsy as soon as I was out of the hospital to give her the good news. Erik had an official car and driver waiting for me at the curb.

"Commander Petersen would like you to join him on the *Roosevelt* sir," the driver said, holding the back door of the sedan open. "I believe he's expecting a phone call, too."

"Yes he is," I said, slipping into the back seat for the quick drive to the Alameda Coast Guard Station. "She's going to be fine, Erik, and she said to give you her love and her thanks for getting her out of there."

***

I spent the next several weeks living aboard *D'Anne*, tied up at the Oakland docks, commuting back and forth to the hospital, the federal building and FBI offices, and the Coast Guard station. Katie was recuperating fast and demanding to be released from what she called solitary confinement.

We finally sprung her during the fifth week and got her safely tucked in on *D'Anne*. "I'm home and I'll never leave this boat again," she said, navigating her way below decks to that wide comfortable bed in the bow. "Bring me food, Butterball. I'm home."

"You're home just in time, too. According to John Chandler, our work has been piling up. I've done about as much as I could do, but the paper pushers need a million reports from you. I made the powers that be in Washington understand that we're going to be taking this nice and slow."

"I'm sure they're foaming at the bit, Jason, but I do want to take it nice and slow. Can we take a little cruise, maybe out of the bay, and come back in a day or two? Then, I would be ready for all the reports.

"How's Betsy doing?"

"She and Erik have everything under control, the pressure is starting to build, though. You'll be clobbered with press demands, congressional demands, and the president wants us to come for dinner sometime soon."

"Oh, he does, does he? We might just have to do that," she laughed.

We did pull out of the marina the following morning, and after we cleared the Golden Gate, we turned south, cruised down to the Monterey Bay, and then south to Morro Bay before heading back to San Francisco Bay and the Oakland Marina.

"We will be at the federal building at eight o'clock tomorrow morning, according to this e-mail," she said, after we docked. "Seems as though they are even sending a car and driver for us."

We spent several weeks making sure all the details were in place for the paper pushers who now had charge of the Fort Bragg conspiracy. So many people did so many illegal things, it would take years to sort it all out. Katie and I made hundreds of depositions, and of course, knew we would be called on to testify before hundreds of federal court hearings and trials. I would know the inner workings of the federal judiciary inside out when this ends.

In the middle of all that, Katie and I took a fast drive to Virginia City, Nevada, and got married in an ancient old building that once was the offices of one of the fabled mine owners from the days of the Comstock Lode. There were surprised faces in the FBI offices the following Monday when Katie came in with a plain gold band on her left ring finger.

We hosted Eric, John Chandler, and Betsy to a grilled tuna dinner aboard *D'Anne*, and that was the extent of our wedding celebration. Chandler kept talking about future assignments for us and we kept deflecting the conversation. Katie was still bound and determined to resign as soon as our part in this operation was over.

"It won't end for years, Jason, and the bad part is, all we've done is slow them down temporarily. Drugs will flow, virtually unencumbered by such silly things as laws, and the bad guys will just go around the fence we built. Believe me when I say this, Butterball my friend, the drug lords in Europe, the Near East, and South America have already started making new plans."

***

We spent several months going between Washington and California, and finally were cleared to leave the country. "Where to, Jason?"

"I want to make one more trip to Fort Bragg. I have to say goodbye to Francesca Ripoldi. She has to know that I'm satisfied with the outcome. She was Sami's best friend, was there when Sami was gunned down, and was so adamant in her statements to the cops that it was not a robbery gone bad. I have to say goodbye to that wonderful old lady."

It wasn't easy. "You know, dear lady, we destroyed your little cabin, burned it to the ground by our activities, brought you face to face with some serious danger, and now, I'm here to tell you goodbye. You should probably run me off with a shotgun."

"No, Jason, I won't run you off." That grand Italian smile lit up the lunchroom, and I knew I was doing the right thing. "I was afraid for you when you left last time, but I'm so proud of you right now. You brought justice and an end, a closure, to Sami's death. The nicest person I ever knew, Jason. I cried more for her than I ever did for anyone. I never married, but if I had, Sami would have been the daughter I'd want."

"That would make me son-in-law, Francesca. Are you sure you'd want that?" She cuffed me playfully, we hugged, and I could see layers of love as I looked in her big brown eyes. "I'll be back, dear lady. Fort Bragg will always be a home for me."

***

"Any plans, Jason? Any voyages in the mix?" Katie and I were back on the high sea, blue water and open skies, and no plans that I knew of. Our little cruises were more good therapy for her than anything the docs could have come up with.

"Galapagos, maybe. Pitcairne, maybe. Caribbean, maybe. I don't really know, Blondie. Let's play a game I have heard of. We want to get a hundred miles off shore, spin a wheel, and wherever the pointer lands, is where we'll set our course. The only points on the compass will direct us to warm and tropical. How's that sound?" That thought had been in my mind for months. "Just us on *D'Anne* in blue water, only coming to port for fuel and food."

"I'm ready for that, Butterball. We need to find Erik and let him know. I'll make sure Chandler knows, too."

"So many people have died, and John Chandler says we haven't even slowed the flow of shit coming in. Is there even a reason for us to continue? He's asked us to continue on as an undercover source of information. Why?" I wanted us to be free, not worried that someone would blow us away at any port we stopped at.

"I told him I was retired and he will have to accept that, Jason. Let's send a message to Eric, and push off."

It sounded good, but the work wasn't quite finished. As we got one project taken care of, someone would come up with another and then yet another. Paper pushers were never completely satisfied, and maybe there was just a bit of job protection involved as well.

***

It took another month of trips to Fort Bragg, Sacramento, and Washington before we were finally ready to put to sea. The FBI and Attorney General investigators had followed every lead we gave them, and there were hundreds of indictments handed down, to police officers, county deputies, district attorney prosecutors, local and federal judges, and those we expected to be criminals; drug dealers, killers, and thieves.

The network of distributors spread into every state in the west, and the tentacles were wrapped around some people placed in the highest positions of trust worldwide. Senators and congressmen, politicians and government workers found their names on indictments and in front page articles across the land. "The one good thing was, the president declared all to be traitors. Everyone wants to get out of that charge, and they're doing it by ratting on each other." Katie's eyes blazed when she said that.

There were some that felt the charge of treason was over the top, but the president held to his word and the fear of a charge like that did seem to have an impact, especially on the lower level criminals. Since the big boys in international crime had no use for the concept of law in the first place, there was no impact.

***

Our work was done, and we were finally going to sea. Fuel and food were aboard, there were still some of Katie's tuna steaks in the freezer. Down the estuary, across San Francisco Bay, and through the Golden Gate, our heading had not been determined, but it wouldn't be directed by anyone other than us.

"Are you sure you're physically ready for this? Sometimes it can get pretty nasty out there on those high seas."

"Mentally and physically, skipper," she quipped, giving a full salute. "My balance is fine now, I haven't had a headache in weeks, and I'm one mean machine."

What we hadn't fully discussed was exactly what our place in this wide-wide world would be. "We are not attached to the FBI or any other agency, and we are both young and vibrant," Katie said, watching the boat's bow cleave another incoming wave. "At least I'm fairly young," she joked.

"I need a purpose," she continued, "but I don't want to be an agent, or work for a government."

"I do believe we will always be agents of some kind, Katie. But we will be free-lancers, not employees, not beholden, always available. It wouldn't surprise me in the least to find out that Chandler or Petersen or whoever, is already making plans for us. The key to our new life, we get to say no, if questions are asked."

"I guess we'll always be on a tether to the Bureau, in some way or capacity, but I'm right up to here dealing with criminal slime-balls. Let's chase white collar criminals in their million dollar yachts, wear elegant gowns, drink champagne, and eat oysters. Every day," she laughed, giving me a healthy nudge in the ribs.

We cleared the Farallon Islands, those empty rock rookeries that host millions of birds of so many species, and I brought a game board I made to the wheelhouse. It had all the compass settings for warm waters spread in a circle, and a little pointer attached to a pin that could be spun.

"Two out of three? Or just one? Ah, Mr. Shakespeare, that's the real question isn't it?" Katie and I were in the wheel house, the sea was a little rough, which is something both of us enjoyed. "Okay, here go. One Eight Oh is due south. Two Seven Oh is due west. Anywhere in between will be just fine with me. If it's on the east side of one eight oh, it will mean a trip through the Panama Canal and into the Caribbean."

"I want to spin," she said when I set the board down.

"Wait," I said. I headed below deck, found a bottle of fine Merlot straight from the Napa Valley, California's real golden treasure. I grabbed two glasses, and went back to the wheel house. "One glass for you, my wife. And one glass for me. After I poured, I closed my eyes, and Katie spun the pointer.

The pointer was still spinning when the radio crackled. "Butterball, Butterball. This is the Viking. Put your pants on, hotshot, and come to a heading of Two Four Oh, and rendezvous with my cutter. I'm standing about two hundred fifty nautical miles off shore. Viking out."

We laughed like a couple of idiots, looked at each other with that first big question of our new life. Would we answer the hail? We knew we had to.

"Viking, this is Butterball. You are aware that we are out of business."

"I am only aware that I have lobster on board."

"Turning to two-four-oh, Viking. Light the fire."

-end-

About Johnny Gunn

I'm a member of The Western Fictioneers, the organization for professional authors of Western novels and short stories, and a member of the International Thriller Writers.

My beautiful wife Patty and I live on a small hobby farm about twenty miles north of Reno, Nevada, sharing space with a couple of fine horses, a flock of egg-producing chickens, and some breeding rabbits. You're always welcome to visit. I need help cleaning those corrals.

Social media links:

Facebook: https://www.facebook.com/johnny.gunn.31

Blog: http://johnny-gunn.blogspot.com/

Twitter: https://twitter.com/johnnygunn11 @johnnygunn11

If you enjoyed this book by Johnny Gunn, check out his other Solstice Publishing novels:

Jacob Chance, U.S. Marshal

Banker Preston Miller claims he owns the entire Golden Valley and all the water in the Good Hope River. Jackson cries foul in a letter to the U.S. Attorney in San Francisco, and Jacob Chance, U.S. Marshal rides to Preston, Nevada Territory to "settle this little land dispute."

http://bookgoodies.com/a/B00XWBQ0OO

A Good Life Cut Short

Jacob Chance, U.S. Marshal just made the biggest move of his life. He retired from the Marshal Service and planned to move to a ranch in Nevada Territory, marry a beautiful young woman, and not spend the rest of his life chasing criminals, lunatics, and murderers. Lives are lost, lives are endangered, and a new way of life is threatened. Can Jacob Chance really retire?

http://bookgoodies.com/a/B01F29L6ZQ

Paradise Challenged

Thornton Holiday is a murderer, a bank robber, and a man with a plan, a plan to create an outlaw haven in the New Mexico Territory community of Plainsville. He's mad with power, one might say, 'his ego runneth over.' The village is overrun with the meanest outlaws in the west, ranchers and local businessmen are killed, and election fraud allows a murderer to become sheriff.

http://bookgoodies.com/a/B015QFSMAS

Red Light Raven

The IRS agent was a pit-bull of an investigator and when county officials started turning up dead, he found himself in more of an investigation than just picking off errant taxpayers. There was a definite conspiracy involved in the deaths, but the county officials were also involved in criminal activity surrounding a brothel named The Raven's Nest. A madman was out to clean up the county, and he didn't care how many had to die to accomplish that.

http://bookgoodies.com/a/B01G2B7RUG

So Young ... So Dead

The vicious murder of a young girl leads to the disintegration of the Sandesta County Sheriff's Department. A homophobic district attorney, a misogynist sergeant of detectives, and a serial killer all come together in Johnny Gunn's thriller, So Young, So Dead.

http://bookgoodies.com/a/B0193RHXXW

The Quest

Tom Henry, a writer, amateur archaeologist, and historian, is confronted one hot summer day by what he can only describe as a time and space traveler. He fears for his sanity as he is introduced to what the ancient people of the deserts of Nevada used as areas of intense energy for shamans to travel between realities. His guide is Riba, a

239 • To Serve And Deceive

Quarian, a dominant species in the universe, who introduces him to time and space travel by way of mind power only. Tom fears that Riba is more than a guide.

http://bookgoodies.com/a/B011D3HLUE

www.ingramcontent.com/pod-product-compliance
Lightning Source LLC
Chambersburg PA
CBHW052034020726
47501CB00004B/1401